Electric Castles

(A Book of Urban Legends)

Cliff Burns

Cover Photograph: Gabriele Marras

Cover Design: Chris Kent

Interior Layout and Design: Clark Kenyon

Published by Black Dog Press (blackdogpress@yahoo.ca)

Printed by Lightning Source

ISBN: 978-0-9938721-5-0 (Print)
        978-0-9938721-6-7 (Ebook)

Also by Cliff Burns

BLACK DOG PRESS

"You can only find this place by drifting. It is impossible to walk directly here. You must first surrender yourself to the tides of the city. Takes years to do it. Slowly the tides will take you there."
—John Foxx, "The Grey Suit"

"There is no solitude in the world like that of the big city."
—Kathleen Norris

"When you go looking for what is lost, everything is a sign."
—Eudora Welty

For the Ideal Reader, wherever you may be.

Contents

"There ain't no mansion on the hill
No electric castle for me
I was born to bow and scrape
An orphan of the streets..."

Anonymous

Introduction

"But is not every square inch of our cities the scene of a crime?"
—Walter Benjamin

For millennia, humans have gathered together, *en masse*, in larger and larger communities. At first, we're told, these concentrations of people might have gravitated around sacred places, holy sites that drew pilgrims from near and far, many of whom stayed on as permanent residents.

From villages and hamlets, to early cities with populations in the tens of thousands and on to today with our giant metropolises, so huge and unwieldy any kind of accurate census of their inhabitants is well-nigh impossible. Twenty million people (or more) living at close quarters, with all the advantages and drawbacks that entails.

At some point during the 20th century more people lived in urban settings than in the countryside, a sea change that, barring some massive calamity, will likely be the norm for many years to come.

It's one of the reasons why we're so out of step with Nature, refusing to recognize or mitigate the damage we have inflicted on the environment through rampant consumerism and its counterpart, the "disposable" culture.

But our love affair with cities continues unabated: Paris, Rome, Athens, London, New York, Tokyo…merely uttering their names provokes feelings of nostalgia, romance, magic, possibility.

Each the embodiment of millions of individual storylines criss-crossing, a multi-racial, multi-generational cast interacting every minute of every day. Mostly getting along, but sometimes clashing in ugly ways, manifestations of rage and intolerance duly recorded for posterity by the nearest cell phone or the ubiquitous surveillance systems.

From Toronto to Istanbul, Singapore to Sao Paolo, urban tales and legends emerge or are invented. Narratives that provide some human scale and context to mega-cities that are otherwise oblivious to the teeming millions that fill their streets and maintain the complex infrastructure keeping them viable.

One day rising waters and soaring temperatures might render some of these cities untenable or uninhabitable, but even their flooded, abandoned ruins will possess mystical power and allure, inspiring stories of bygone days, forged or falsified histories and creation myths, cautionary fairy tales of the gods and monsters who once dwelt there.

Their ancient inhabitants will be imbued with special powers, allotted all kinds of strange customs and rituals. It will be implied that once giants walked the earth, making their homes in tall spires wreathed in cloud. Vain, callow creatures who aspired to godhood, only to be brought low by their vaunting hubris.

Our descendants will speak of us in hushed tones, awed by the technologies we developed, super-efficient, sentient machines that might have taken us to the stars, had we not been so narcissistic and prideful.

One day, people will look back on this Golden Age of humanity with admiration and regret, reflecting on what might have been, composing heart-rending elegies for all that was lost.

In the darkest ages, they will remind themselves that we used to live in a world of light and bustle.

Future legends and tall tales will affirm that once upon a time our species possessed real greatness. Until the skies fell, the forests burned and nothing remained but a distant memory of an epoch when misery and want weren't our birthright and human ingenuity was employed as something other than a survival mechanism.

I pray our unfortunate progeny will have the kindness and beneficence to forgive us our myriad crimes, the trespasses we've committed, the dystopic wasteland we knowingly and deliberately bequeathed them.

Cliff Burns
June, 2020

Restitution

At first, I told this Stegal guy, *no way, man, forget it, not gonna happen.*

Acting like I barely remembered her, which, of course, was a lie. A long time ago and plenty of water under that particular bridge. Totally blowing him off—hey, at that point who was he to me? Some West Coast twerp with sun-bronzed vocal cords and a swimming pool in his back yard.

But, give him credit, he wouldn't take "no" for an answer. "I hear what you're saying, now hear *me* out. Emily—she reverted back to her maiden name, by the way, she recently divorced—still regrets what happened. The woman wants to make it right, Dean, and it seems kind of selfish not giving her a chance." Switching gears: "You've seen the show, right?"

"Well, I—"

"But you understand the concept, at least."

"Sure, I guess, but—"

"Then you might want to factor this into the equation: free flight to L.A., limo service, two complimentary nights at a fantastic hotel, meals…" My hesitation was all he needed. "Good, you're thinking about it. Because from where I sit, Dean, ol' buddy, this is a win-win scenario for you. Not many guys get to have their ex grovel for forgiveness in front of God knows how many people."

"She…"

"What?"

"She doesn't have to do that," I finally managed. "I'd just like to find out why, uh, what happened happened."

"And that's what we're offering," he insisted. "Our program is all about closure. Can I fax or e-mail you some things? Just technical, legal mumbo-jumbo…"

"I'm not sure—"

"C'mon," he urged, sounding impatient for the first time, "you've already agreed in your mind. Why not just come out and *say* it?"

"I guess…I'll do it."

"Awesome. I'll get things underway on this end and then I'll be in touch." Pausing. "Hey, Dean, be cool, man, you made the right choice. Sit back and enjoy the ride."

"Yeah, right." I didn't sound very convincing but by then he was beyond caring; he practically had my name on the dotted line.

What did it matter to him that I'd never stopped loving Emily Wheeler?

My friends couldn't believe it. Gerry and Liz, who'd socialized with Em and I, weren't certain I was doing the right thing.

"Emily was a great gal, great gal," Gerry kept repeating.

"But sometimes it's better to leave the past alone," Liz chimed in.

"But we were friends, the four of us. You were as surprised as I was when she left…" They glanced at each other. "Weren't you?"

Neither of them would meet my eye.

And I thought: *what have I gotten myself into?*

The flight seemed to take no time at all and when I arrived in Los Angeles a short, stout fellow holding a sign with my name in black marker was waiting to convey me to the hotel. It was a swanky place, way out of my price range. I felt like a hillbilly in bib overalls as I queued to check in.

Once I made it to my room, a combination of nervous fatigue and just plain nerves soon had me kneeling at the porcelain altar, heaving and groaning. When I finished, I sat back, bracing myself against the bathtub, cursing my stupidity.

I'd finally worked up the courage to watch some episodes of "Restitution" and hadn't liked what I'd seen. The show was much more raw and emotional than I imagined and sometimes there wasn't catharsis and closure, but mayhem and blind, uncontrolled fury. The tears flowed copiously and since this was cable there was no need to censor anything or bleep out bad language.

One episode featured an almost unbearable confrontation between a gay man and the bully who'd made his teen years a living hell. There were no happy endings this time around, no sense of old wounds healed. The grownup victim swore and spat at his tormentor, refusing to be mollified by the show's host, Lyle O'Shea. O'Shea cultivated a soothing, sympathetic persona but his pop psychology and smarmy appeals for reconciliation fell on deaf ears. The embittered guest stormed off the set, leaving the bully, abject and deflated, still waiting for the forgiveness that would never come.

The intriguing part of the show's premise was that it was up to the *malefactor* to contact the program—they had to demonstrate true repentance and accept whatever reaction or vituperation the injured party directed at them. Their humiliation recorded, broadcast, exhibited for the entire world to see.

What made them want to do it?

What made *her* want to do it?

Why did she feel the need to make amends more than five years after she'd left?

And how, exactly, did I feel about that?

A cute little production assistant steered me through the backstage warren to makeup. Not just a little touchup, either, I got the full treatment. I thought I looked ludicrous but they assured me that under the TV lights I'd appear "more natural than natural". Whatever that meant.

Next I was escorted to the "green" room, just a short jaunt away from the main set and studio audience. I could hear people murmuring on the other side of a curtained doorway and my stomach did a little doo-wop as I pictured what awaited me out there.

They stuck to their guns and never let Emily and I lay eyes on each other until the cameras rolled. I waited about forty-five minutes while they wrapped up one show and prepped for my segment (they shot two episodes back-to-back to save money). There was a fridge for cold drinks and snacks, even a small bar. The P.A. fixed me a weak Tom Collins, at my request, and made small talk to help dispel some of my nervousness. At one point she caught my eye:

"I don't want to pressure you or anything but have you given any thought to how you're going to react, y'know, when you see her, like, after all these years?"

I wondered if this chitchat was part of the pre-screening process, trying to anticipate potential ugliness and, if possible, nip it in the bud. Afraid I'd pull a "Jerry Springer" on them.

I informed Tamara, the P.A., I wasn't sure what would be going through my mind, that it had been a long time and much of the pain had dissipated.

"But not all of it?"

"No," I confessed, "not all."

"Because she walked out on you, right? Left everything and—"

"Right, right," I broke in, knowing I'd be describing the whole sorry affair in a few minutes anyway, "didn't even pack a bag."

"*Wow…*" She was thinking about it, running the scenario in her head. "And now you'll find out why."

"I guess so." I took a big bite out of the Tom Collins, nearly finishing it off.

"Let me top you up," reaching for my glass. "One more for the road and that's it. We want you loose but not hammered."

"Right," I agreed, "don't want me going all psycho out there, do we?"

It was meant as a joke but I could tell it didn't go over well…

Lyle O'Shea shook my hand, looking me right in my eye, giving my elbow a reassuring squeeze before guiding me to my seat. Doing his best to make me feel at home in front of a small crew, an audience numbering perhaps seventy-five and, eventually, a couple million cable subscribers watching from the comfort of their living rooms.

The drinks helped but I was definitely spooked. Giving clipped, short answers, relying on Lyle to transmit my tale of woe. I felt wavelets of sympathy from the audience as the story unfolded and by the time he reached its conclusion they seemed genuinely outraged on my behalf.

Then came the moment everyone was waiting for, Lyle and I standing and turning toward the curtained entrance, the heavy material parting and my old flame, Emily Patricia Wheeler, stepping through, momentarily taken aback by the catcalls and boos greeting her appearance.

To be honest, I barely heard them.

Her hair was different and the heels she wore made her seem taller. They'd done their thing with makeup but they were right, under the brilliant lights she shone like Ingrid Bergman in "Casablanca" (a film we both adored).

She was squinting as she walked toward us, holding out her hand, tentative, face an anguished mask. We were close, our fingers nearly brushing. She started to say something, words that would be captured for posterity by a lurking boom microphone. But I surprised everyone and beat her to it.

"I'm sorry," I told her. "You did the right thing. I deserved it."

There were gasps, a few wolf whistles. Emily glanced at Lyle, then came back to me. Confused, flustered…

Looking as beautiful and lost as the day she left.

The Things She Saved
(for Colleen)

Eddie reeks of cigarettes and he's been scrapping again. A purple-black mouse bulges under his left eye and there are fresh scratches on his cheek that likely aren't the result of an accidental faceplant off his beloved Sector 9 longboard.

"Nice," I remark, "has your mother seen it?"

He grunts, having largely abandoned the human vocabulary around his fourteenth birthday. We're both standing, since there are no available chairs, every single flat surface piled high with old magazines and cookbooks, the counters and cupboards overflowing with paper towels, detergent, canned goods, mason jars, used toasters and bread-makers, and a huge assortment of bulk food. We stopped eating in the kitchen months ago. Dry flakes of spilled breakfast cereal and dog kibble crunch underfoot. If we don't have mice, it's a bloody miracle.

Eddie just wandered in, a tall, gawky kid, nearly a six-footer and filling out. He used to be all elbows and knees but now there's meat on his bones, especially his lower body, a byproduct of his passion for skateboarding. I'm constantly amazed at how kids get around on those goddamned things, they look like deathtraps to me, but maybe that's my age showing again.

I told Fay the other night, *he gets any bigger, there won't be room for both of us in this house* and I wasn't kidding. He's already pushing boundaries, asserting his newfound masculinity and confidence. A year ago I caught him crying in the basement because he found a dead puppy in the street. Now it's like he's made of stone and I doubt he'd shed a tear if I dropped a friggin' anvil on his big toe.

Lately, his favorite catchphrase is *Don't know, don't care.* That's Eddie's fallback response to the world around him and sums up his attitude toward his mother, sisters, me, his teachers and pretty much everything else under the sun. I know teenagers are supposed to be narcissistic and self-obsessed but it seems to me this latest crop takes it to a whole other level. I've eavesdropped on those rare occasions when his friends come by and I'm shocked by how utterly stupid they are, dull-witted and casually vicious. Lots of sexual references crop up and about the only thing they seem to have in common is skateboarding and a love of punk metal music. They show no interest in sports, pop culture, movies, the shit most normal kids gobble up.

I creep away thinking *if they're the future, God help us.*

His principal and the school guidance counselor insist that despite his lousy marks and the constant reports of bullying behavior, Eddie's a fairly bright kid, albeit one who can't stay focused on tasks and resents any and all forms of authority.

Ms. Wiggins, the counselor—lovely gal, fantastic legs—has hinted more than once that his "fraught" home life is a major contributing factor to his violent tendencies and lack of maturity. She emphasizes she's not laying blame, nor is she seeking to interfere with our "family dynamics".

If she only knew.

Fay, of course, refuses to have anything to do with either of them, so it's up to me to show up at requested meetings, smiling and nodding my way through them. These days it's just about impossible to get her out of the house; usually she point blank refuses, while offering no valid reason or explanation. Ms. Wiggins has offered to pop by for a home visit but there's no way I'm gonna let *that* happen. I've begged off a couple times already, without going into any details. That's probably raising even more warning flags, but what can I do?

Eddie sticks his head in the fridge but nothing there appeals to him. Probably looking for something freshly killed, still kicking its hind legs.

Not much pleases him or gives him satisfaction and it seems like the smallest things set him off, little annoyances that he blows way out of proportion. His tantrums are fearsome things to behold. Anyone can see that right now his body is growing disproportionally faster than his brain.

Welcome to puberty, kid.

He doesn't really take after his biological father and except for the straight hair and bad temper doesn't much resemble Fay either. Which makes him his own man, I suppose.

"Hey, Malcolm," he says, "can you loan me—"

Usually it's "Malky", not Malcolm, and usually he's *telling*, not asking, so naturally he's after money. And barking up the wrong tree.

I show him my hands. "Sorry, dude, your mother got to me first. I would if I could…"

But having received his answer he's already tuning me out. I have ceased to be an object of interest now that he knows I'm tapped. His eyes glaze over and it's like I've suddenly faded away, like an old picture left in the sun.

Actually, that's another trait he has in common with Fay. She's an absolute master at it.

I exit the kitchen, using one of the narrow paths Fay has considerately left for us to make our way around the house. Her "collection" has completely taken over the place, to the extent that we can't see real walls any more because of the boxes and plastic storage bins she has stacked right to the ceiling. We navigate from room to room *via* thin corridors, hoping and praying a section of it doesn't collapse, pinning us underneath. Not an entirely unrealistic scenario, I assure you.

She used to specialize, believe it or not, but that went by the wayside about five years ago. Shortly before she added me to her menagerie, if I have my timing right. I was a replacement, of sorts: I found out later she had just lost a favorite dog, one of two identically stupid Labs, the brother of which still lives on, to my immense disappointment and disgust. Mangy, near blind, semi-continent, but it continues to draw breath, the filthy beast.

Three of four cats have disappeared since I moved in—either ran off or dead and entombed somewhere behind the teetering walls she's erected.

Mountains of crap, with more being added by the week.

Garage sales, rummage sales, church sales, thrift shops…and then there's the internet. An infinite shopping mall, open day and night, even Christmas. As bottomless as a black hole, an enchanted wishing well you can't help tossing money into. That's what's really killing us. As soon as she got a computer, it was off to the races.

She can't stop and, worse yet, shows no signs of wanting to. The sickness is too deep inside her, part of her being. Even impending bankruptcy doesn't faze her. She's on disability leave from her job in the hospital kitchen but her compensation money doesn't amount to much and I know for a fact she's already spent her way through the little nest egg her folks left her with. She's got a thick deck of credit cards, a mountain of growing debt and no way of getting out from under it.

What would her frugal, practical parents, who never in their lives spent more than they earned, make of their precious daughter, holed up inside the family home, built during the Depression and currently filled to bursting with floor lamps, dressers, quilts, china, rugs, encyclopedias, yarn, end tables, books, records, photo albums, baby clothes…whatever the hell your heart desires and then some?

But don't ever use the word "hoarder" in Fay's presence.

Not if you know what's good for you.

I'd say I'm at wits' end except I probably passed that point at least two years ago. Now I'm merely hanging on for dear life and hoping we'll win the lottery or some other magical solution will present itself, snatching us back from the brink of financial disaster.

Fay might be in denial about many aspects of her life but I do think she realizes things have spiraled out of control and there's a real risk her private universe is about to come crashing down around her ears. It must be gnawing away at her, eating her up inside. Maybe that's why she doesn't go out any more and also explains why she's reduced her interactions with us, her immediate family. Her two older kids, Greta and Sara, escaped as soon as they legally could and have only intermittent contact with their mother. Both point blank refuse to visit or bring their kids by. That really hurts Fay.

Still, if he has any sense Eddie will do the same once he turns sixteen.

Because gradually this collection of hers, this selfish madness, is squeezing us out, leaving no room to live and breathe, forcing us to exist in smaller and smaller spaces until soon we'll be sleeping in tents in the back yard.

I've talked to her and Karen, her sole remaining friend, has tried making her see reason and get some kind of treatment or medication or whatever is required to put an end to this. Fay promised she'd do her best to change her ways and, who knows, maybe she did for awhile, unloading a few items on eBay or restraining herself once or twice as she passed a tempting yard sale. But, really, it was a token effort and she soon slipped back into her old habits. It's reached the extent that we've recently had to stop using the bathtub because it's brimming with an assortment of cleaning products and at least two hundred bars of soap.

It's like she's trying to save at least one of everything in the world, a latter-day Noah, building an ark of survival and hope, stuffing it as full as she possibly can, while anxiously watching the skies and dreading the sound of rain on the roof.

I find her with her dolls, which are kept in the pantry, just off the kitchen. It has built-in shelves, holding dozens of different Barbies and miniature plastic figures of all sizes and ages. A couple hundred sets of shiny, glass eyes gaze at me from every direction; the place gives me the willies and I usually avoid it. Many of the dolls are still in their original boxes, untouched and in pristine shape, worth a king's ransom if she ever decided to sell them (which she won't).

"Honey," I say, and it comes out tired and defeated, like I know I'm beaten even before I begin. How many times will we have the same conversation, with exactly the same result?

Fay turns, cradling a *Thumbelina*, first released back in the 1970s, I vaguely recollect the TV spots.

"I had one of these," she tells me, "but a neighborhood dog chewed her up. It was my fault, I left her outside while I went in and watched 'The Beverly Hillbillies.'" I nod, familiar with the incident, having heard versions of it before. That was the thing: if you tried to pin her down on *why* she had to have a certain knick-knack, she could produce a perfectly plausible explanation regarding its very deep and profound connection to her. Everything came with a history (or *her*story). "Finding her again was amazing. What did I pay? Six or eight dollars? And look at her." Holding out the doll for my examination, smaller than a newborn, cute enough to inspire love and maternal instincts in any six-year old heart. "'Good condition, no visible markings, non-smoking home', exactly as advertised." She carefully replaces the doll in its proper slot. "If six bucks is the price of happiness, count me in."

I'd like to remind her of the price the rest of us have to pay for her nostalgic leanings, but perhaps now isn't the time. She's calm, content, not thinking about her troubles and cares…who am I to deprive her of that?

Maybe tomorrow she'll be more amenable and I'll find the right words to express what must be said.

Space is finite, the money's running out and sooner or later she'll be forced to confront what she's become and, in the best case scenario, determine once and for all what's missing inside her, the desperate need she keeps trying so hard to fill.

And what about me? Thanks to the truck and the occasional long haul to Texas or Oregon, the lights stay on and there's enough food to eat. But I'm getting old and feeling my age, yearning to escape the road. Then I look around here and think: *is* this *how you want to live out the rest of your years, Mal, is this your idea of a retirement plan?*

You never know, one of these days I might wake up and the pathway out will be completely sealed off, nothing there but a wall of boxes and bins, precarious and insurmountable, a barrier preventing escape. No daylight showing, no sound leaking through.

I'd like to think someone would eventually miss me and seek me out. I want to believe they would notice my absence. Hopefully, it would be Fay, anxiously navigating the crazy labyrinth she's constructed in search of her partner and lover. But if I'm being completely honest, it would probably be Eddie, stalking me through those tight, claustrophobic passages, needing money and knowing I'm usually a soft touch.

The Curious Mr. Cavendish

Prologue

They were running out of city.

Fly was adamant, "Keep goin', keep goin'", so that's what they did. But Donny was starting to get that feeling again, the sense of an imminent fuckup. A head on collision with fate or karma or whatever it was that ordered the universe and kept him permanently in the shit.

This was going to end badly and he had no one to blame but himself. *There's something wrong with you*; how often had those words been uttered in his presence? By his parents, teachers, ex-girlfriends, youth workers, parole officers, you name it. A lacking in his moral character, apparently, the wires either crossed or never properly connected in the first place. He had problems with authority figures and impulse control and frequently exhibited poor judgment.

That was *their* side of the story.

Donny knew from an early age he wasn't like other people and nothing he'd learned from the various therapists or shrinks he'd encountered while "in the system" shocked or surprised him in the least. He wasn't stupid or unaware of his shortcomings, he just didn't see the big deal about, for instance, not having what you would call a fully developed conscience. Think about it, in this day and age wasn't lacking empathy for your fellow human beings pretty much universal, an affliction that crossed all boundaries of race, sex and class? Watch the news sometime, if you needed further proof.

He glanced over at his traveling companion. One thing that could use some improvement was his pool of "known associates". Granted, there wasn't a lot to choose from (by and large, the criminal fraternity wasn't distinguished by its superior breeding and soaring intelligence quotient), but, still, Fly came mighty close to scraping the bottom of the proverbial barrel.

Fly. As in, the Human Fly. Real name Kevin-something. Skilnick or Smolinski, and who gave a shit anyway? Not an acrobat or adept at scaling tall buildings, his specialty was information, specifically its collection and dissemination. Experienced villains are, by nature, cautious and reticent, but even they can't resist bragging on occasion, letting their hair down in front of pals and admirers. And under those circumstances, if they weren't really, really careful, they *might* commit an indiscretion and someone *might* be listening, like a fly on the wall. Hardly noticeable, just a speck on the edge of their vision. Constantly buzzing about, noting a name dropped here, a bit of gossip there, storing it away for later use. Divulging what he knew for the right price or, in this instance, a piece of the action.

Fly seemed totally absorbed, leaning forward as far as he could, hands on the dashboard, peering intently through the windshield. "I think we're nearly there."

"Nearly *where*? Fuck's sake, Fly, we're as lost as two babes in the woods."

He turned his head, grinned at Donny, displaying the deplorable state of his teeth. Part of the collateral damage of his meth years. "Don't worry, Professor, I wouldn't steer you wrong. I'll get us there, never you fear."

Donny hated that nickname, had hated it since some mug had hung it on him back during his first stint in remand. A bunch of guys standing around outside, smoking and bullshitting, happy to be away from the range, doors that could only be locked from the outside. "A well-appointed cage," he'd called it and the meatheads gaped at him like he'd suddenly transformed himself into a giant chicken.

"Thank you, *perfessor*," one of them drawled, which led to gales of laughter and a sobriquet that stuck like a brand. From that day, nearly ten years ago, to this moment, sitting at the wheel of a stolen Pontiac *Sunfire* en route to committing his most serious crime yet, in the company of a functional idiot.

If he had the guts or even one scintilla of common sense he'd call it off. But it had gone too far, they were pumped up, expecting action, and there was no way they were going home with nothing to show for it. Not tonight.

Fly was pointing. "It's down that way I think." Donny glared at him. "I'm pretty sure." Donny obeyed instructions, turning left into what looked like a *cul de sac*. A horseshoe of old, dilapidated houses. "Is this still Buchan Street?" Craning his neck, looking for a sign.

"How the fuck should I know?" Donny fumed. "I swear, Fly, if you've screwed this up and led us on a wild goose chase way out here in the boonies—"

"This has to be it," Fly muttered. "I'm pretty sure—"

"'Pretty sure'? Pretty sure isn't good enough, motherfucker. Not for what we have in mind."

"He said—"

Donny snorted. "Is this more of Roger's bullshit? Jailhouse scuttlebutt from a fucking fink?"

"No, man, I told you, this was a different guy," Fly lied. "Dude named Manny. I met him downtown and he told me this old gal keep stacks of money lying around. Going senile, like. Doesn't trust banks, won't let her stash out of sight."

"He knows this for a fact?" They'd gone over it at least a dozen times and he still wasn't buying it.

Fly bobbed his head. "This place was definitely on his radar. But then he got popped on some traffic beef and they violated his ass back inside. He won't see the light of day for another eighteen months, minimum. His loss, our gain." He giggled, thoroughly enjoying himself. He'd been smoking weed earlier in the day, then switched to some shit that had him cranked up *tight*. He was jumpy, spastic, about to burst through his skin. Donny wondered how long it would be before the inevitable crash.

"You think it's that big joint, looks like a barn?"

Fly buzzed down his window, looked it over. "Gotta be. It's the only one without a 'For Sale' sign."

Donny gaped at him. "*That's* your criteria?"

"Huh?" Fly turned back toward him. His pupils were small, whittled to pinpoints, and there was nothing behind his gaze. Twin black holes, leading nowhere.

"The whole neighborhood's abandoned. This isn't Millionaire's Row, it's a fucking run-down, godforsaken—"

Fly shook his head. "No, man, you don't understand. This is what happens when you live in a city that's basically gone broke. This far out they get zip for services: no police protection, not even a local fire hall. These poor fuckers," waving at the houses visible through the windshield, "they're victims. And us," showing those hideous stumps of teeth again, "I guess you could say we're the predators, come to eat our fill."

I. Mr. Cavendish Receives Visitors

For some time, Cyril Cavendish had existed in a state bordering on despair. Frequently he would walk through the three floors of his Depression-era home, sighing like a lovelorn suitor, a man denied his very purpose in life.

Cyril was a collector and a very devoted one at that. While his field of interest was fairly narrow and specialized, he believed it could, given the right set of circumstances, appeal to a wide cross-section of the population. His proposed "Museum of Mystery and Wonder" (only a working title, but he liked it) would eventually become, under his wise stewardship, a popular tourist draw and might even, with sufficient levels of support and publicity, help revitalize the city's prospects and bring about a golden age of investment and development.

Unfortunately, he appeared to be the sole individual who recognized the potential his collection represented.

Every so often, Cyril would wander over to the antique, roll top desk where he kept his correspondence and flip through the thin file containing his letters to the city. Right from their very first response, it was evident the powers that be down at city hall put little credence in his concept. In several short, terse paragraphs they dismissed the "commercial practicality and viability" of his museum and gave every indication that they found his entire presentation rather pie-in-the-sky, if not downright kooky.

Further attempts at clarifying his position appeared to only make matters worse. The most recent communication he'd received from them bore the return address of the municipality's legal department.

Cyril Cavendish was normally a very retiring, genial man, but as he re-read his missives to the administration, he experienced a surge of asperity directed toward the bean-counters and functionaries who were denying him his dream. Some of it could be detected in his last few letters.

For instance, this excerpt, sent after two previous messages had been ignored:

"Am I to understand that you have no interest in even viewing my 'cabinet of curiosities', as you put it? That you are dismissing its special qualities and appeal out of hand? Surely, that is the very definition of short-sightedness..."

And this, from his final dispatch, again unacknowledged:

"It's clear that I erred in assuming that this city, even in its present, moribund state, has the slightest inclination in pursuing a venture that promises great benefits and returns for one and all. Your skeptical, arrogant natures prevent you from exploring this incredible opportunity and your bureaucratic, hidebound minds only reveal your inane etc. etc."

It was all very well for them to plead financial hardship as a reason for rejecting his ideas, but the fact that the city was currently under bankruptcy protection and had a court-appointed trustee minding its affairs was hardly Cyril's fault. Good on the chap for keeping the taps flowing and the lights on but, for heaven's sake, couldn't he recognize a golden goose when it was staring him in the face?

Sadly, Cyril fared little better with local media. The *Post-Express*, the city's daily "newspaper", existed in name only, a few token print copies, most of its content only available on-line, stuck behind a paywall. The majority of its articles and columns cribbed from other sources; the *PE* seemed to employ very few actual working journalists and none who were inclined to make the drive out to Grant Park—not the choicest neighborhood in the city—and have nothing to show their superiors at the end of the day.

One lone, intrepid gal, a lowly production assistant for a popular morning radio show, made an appointment to take the tour and actually showed up.

It should have been a red-letter day, his coming out party (as it were). He made tea and began to lead her around, apprising her of the history and provenance of the various pieces, but at one point she interrupted him:

"So the house itself isn't haunted, right? It's these things you've collected, they're what create the—the phenomena or whatever."

He nodded, encouraging her. "Exactly. Think of the famous *djinn*, or genie, if you will, associated with Aladdin's lamp. The lamp contains the very essence of the *djinn*, it would be powerless without it. It has long been known that certain items, keepsakes of a personal nature, can, in rare instances, retain an impression of their former owners, especially if the object in question had strong associations with that person."

She appeared dubious, but willing to cut him some slack if

it made for an entertaining segment. "What kind of stuff can I expect? Will there be things moving around on their own or—"

"Oh, yes," he assured her, "I absolutely guarantee you will experience noises, cold spots, the occasional visual manifestation—"

"You mean *ghost*?"

He stiffened, cleared his throat. "I've never cared for that word. It has too many supernatural connotations. I prefer the term 'incorporeal entity'. What I hope to demonstrate to patrons is that while what the visitor experiences here may *seem* uncanny and inexplicable, it is, in fact, in keeping with basic principles of science and metaphysics, states of being that only appear to defy our limited—" He was boring her, he could tell she was anxious to get on with it, see for herself, so he cut his spiel short.

"If we may continue," he indicated, with a little bow.

He showed her just about everything: the infamous "devil doll" of Lemb, a coat rack from the Bates Motel (discovered on eBay, believe it or not), and a bloody bed sheet belonging to Mary Jane Kelly, Jack the Ripper's last known victim; or how about the notorious Woodruff mirror (don't stare too long into its depths!)… and have a look at this painting of an 18th century courtesan by an unknown artist, it inspired at least a dozen murders. "Notice the eyes moving independently of the rest of her face and how her lips occasionally curl into a slight smile…"

The P.A. hadn't seen it. All in all, it was a very quiet, tame afternoon. Honestly, it was like the entire menagerie was deliberately acting coy, refusing to perform any tricks for her. Other than a few slamming doors and the occasional chilly draft, her visit was a bust.

At one point, in a second floor storeroom, they encountered

a terrible stench, definitely an emanation of some kind, and she gave him a reproving look. Only afterward did he realize that she believed the pungent smell originated from *him*.

He never heard from her again.

It was a devastating experience.

Cyril was not, let it be abundantly clear, a man who cultivated isolation for its own sake. While not especially outgoing or garrulous, he did not shun human society, he merely wished to engage with it on *his* terms. Opening his home to outsiders did not reflect the mentality of a recluse or misanthrope—he was anxious to share his enthusiasms with all and sundry, as long as they came with an open mind (and a willingness to pay a modest admission fee).

And though he hadn't any close relatives or intimate friends, he *was* active in the small circle of experts and aficionados specializing in studying and assaying haunted relics and esoterica, recognized as something of an expert. Thanks to an inheritance from his parents, he was financially independent, able to devote the remainder of his life to his passion. In the past decade, in particular, his modest hoard had expanded appreciably, to the extent that it was arguably the best, most diverse of its kind in the Midwest...and perhaps even farther afield.

Unfortunately, despite the best efforts of mice and men (as it were), his collection remained largely a secret to the outside world and he was not so much a curator and administrator, more like a housemaid or perhaps even janitor. Keeping the place clean and relatively tidy in the hope that one day, in the not so distant future (he was seventy-four, after all), it would be the smashing success he envisioned and he, Cyril Ramsay Cavendish, would be vindicated at long last.

Part of the problem was geographical in nature. His house was nowhere near other points of interest or shopping complexes, and the closest interstate, well, wasn't close at all. The roads were in terrible shape, signage next to nonexistent. As a result, visitors to his abode were quite rare; the only people he'd seen in the last few weeks were a pair of Jehovah's Witnesses and that encounter ended abruptly when they spotted something shimmering on the stairs behind him and fled screaming.

Perhaps that explained why the gal who used to read his meter had stopped coming by as well...

Possibly the worst, most unfair aspect of this situation was that Cyril had recently taken possession of what had to be the crown jewel of his meticulously inventoried trove, an absolutely peerless artifact, still potent, buzzing with all sorts of weird energies. That little beauty would eventually be a showpiece of the museum, with its own display case (hardened against all eventualities, of course, mustn't take any chances). For now, it was tucked away in his upstairs safe, along with several other items deemed too fragile or dangerous to be safely exhibited.

Imagine, a relic from the actual chapel of the infamous Belasco house. What a treasure.

When the doorbell rang, Cyril, for reasons just related, was under no illusions that he would be opening his home to a troupe of parapsychologists or a delegation of researchers from the local university. More likely it would be someone else who'd gotten turned around and required directions. He kept a map on a table in the front entranceway for just that purpose.

The first thing Cyril noticed about the two individuals on his doorstep was that both were wearing gloves, the kind paramedics or dental hygienists used, thin and bluish. That seemed odd, but then he noticed one of them held a satchel, which made him seem reassuringly professional.

The taller fellow turned to his counterpart. "I thought you said it was an old lady."

His associate appeared flummoxed. "Mebbe I heard wrong."

Cyril was about to interject a thought when, without warning, they pushed through the door, crowding him back into the vestibule. He was so startled and nonplussed by their behavior, he found himself behaving compliantly, not objecting even when the small chap closed and locked the door behind them.

"You alone, pops?" The larger one again.

"Yes, I…" And then the full import of his circumstances finally became clear. "Good gracious. You two lads aren't…well, you're not *burglars* or anything like that, are you? Surely, you don't intend to—"

The big man, clearly in charge, silenced him merely by raising a finger to his lips.

"You're laboring under a misapprehension. Burglars come at night. We're here and it's still light out. Burglars wait 'til you're asleep, then grab what they can and run. We're going to be staying awhile." He patted the satchel. "And if we get bored, I brought along some toys to keep us entertained."

Oh, dear, Cyril thought, *this is not good at all.*

II. Mr. Cavendish Shows His Mettle

They called each other "Fly" and "Professor".

They were clearly up to no good and following the rough outlines of some pre-arranged plan. Unfortunately, they also seemed to be operating under the impression that he had a large amount of cash on the premises, an opinion they were loathe to abandon, even when he insisted on its inaccuracy.

"Don't try bullshitting us, man," the little fellow, Fly, remonstrated, "otherwise me and my buddy will tear this fuckin' place apart."

Immediately following that worrying exchange, Cyril adopted a more conciliatory and docile mien. He had no wish to antagonize such amoral and desperate characters. One heard about these "home invasions" on the news and more often than not there was some level of violence involved. He would have to exercise extreme caution if he wished to escape similar treatment.

Fly escorted him into the parlor, while his partner conducted a speedy reconnaissance of all three floors, ensuring the house contained no other living inhabitants.

On that count, he needn't have concerned himself.

The Professor chap returned, satisfied, but obviously put out by something. He buttonholed Fly, started ticking off fingers: "You said it was an old lady, you said she'd be loaded, that there would be, quote, 'bales of money lying around', unquote." He glared at the diminutive figure. "This place is full of old junk, Fly. *Junk*. Nothing valuable or antique or vintage, just fucking garbage." Cyril cleared his throat, deeply offended by the effrontery of the man, but no one paid him the slightest attention. "You see this?" He pointed to a nearby funeral amphora (7th century B.C.), four feet tall, grey and stately, but sporting a patchwork of cracks and repairs. "It's *crap*." He pushed it over but, luckily, it didn't break. Something stirred inside it, a rustle and creak of wings, then resettled itself. The two housebreakers took no notice. "Listen, you," the ringleader directing his ire at Cyril now, approaching him, wearing a look of menace. "You'd better start making this worth our while. I'm seriously running out of patience and that doesn't bode well for you, if you get my drift."

Cyril spoke up, his voice sounding shaky, reflecting his growing unease: "But, I'm telling you, you've been misinformed. I'm not, I assure you, a wealthy man. This—" opening is arms to encompass the entire house, "—worthless though it might seem to your, er, untrained eyes, is a selection of the finest antiquities and rarities, each piece retaining its own—"

"*Junk!*" The brute grabbed him by his lapels, giving him a bone-rattling shake, then thrust him away with a stiff-armed shove. Cyril, not a sprightly man, backpedaled, catching a heel on a bulge of rug, going down hard. He gasped, his spine and hip badly jarred, the impact bringing tears to his eyes. His assailant was bending over him, his face huge and furious. "We want money, understand? Jewelry, something we can hock. You got that, you old fuck? You want to fucking die? Right here and now?"

Cyril shook his head, wiping at his eyes. "B-but you've got the wrong house, I'm not—"

The piano started playing, a small, upright Mason and Hamlin wedged into a corner of the parlor. Space was at a premium, even with three stories and several thousand square feet to work with.

"Turn that fucking thing off," the so-called Professor snarled at Fly, who scurried over to see to it. Cyril recognized the melody: Chopin. Which meant is was probably Charlotte at the keyboard, she tended to favor the Romantics.

"There isn't anything to turn off," Fly reported.

His partner grimaced. "Then unplug it. Jesus, do I have to tell you everything?"

"There's nothing—"At that moment, the piano stopped playing.

The Professor straightened, still looming over Cyril but wearing a crafty expression. "You don't want to tell us where you're keeping the good shit? You gonna keep making with the dumb act?"

"No, really, I—"

He was seized by the arms, hauled to his feet. His back and tailbone felt bruised, sore, he could barely stand.

"Then I guess you're gonna suffer," the vile man informed him, "and I'm gonna enjoy every minute of it."

He was a man of his word.

Within a matter of minutes, Cyril was secured with duct tape to a sturdy chair that had once belonged to a bloodthirsty Arab *emir*, notorious for his affinity for certain cruel practices involving—well, another time perhaps. They hadn't been too gentle completing their assignment and immediately upon finishing, the chief villain administered a short, brutal, backhand slap that snapped Cyril's head back. "Stay awake, old man. Don't want you zoning out on me."

Cyril could conceive of no happy conclusion to this episode. These individuals would stop at nothing to steal what little he had worth taking and once they were satisfied he'd given them all he could, they had no intention of sparing his life, of that, he was now all but certain.

He was frightened, unnerved…and yet part of his mind remained calm and deliberate. He was not, by nature, an excitable individual, prone to overwrought emotional states. A septuagenarian, he was only too aware of the fragility and impermanence of any creature that draws breath and inhabits the living realm.

Seventy-four years. That was a fairly good run, even if too much of that interval had been spent here, alone, in this decrepit, drafty house, on the edge of a disintegrating city. Totally obsessed with making his collection the best it could possibly be, spending long, irreplaceable hours tracking down some obscure trinket that had once allegedly belonged to the great John Dee…

Suddenly, Cyril knew exactly what he had to do.

It wasn't going to be easy and his scheme required sacrifice, a willingness to endure a great deal of discomfort before it reached fruition. He wasn't a fan of pain—not squeamish, exactly, merely in the habit of avoiding unpleasantness, whatever guise it might choose.

Never mind. His primary purpose was saving the contents of the museum. All other considerations were secondary, including his pitiful life.

The Professor ceremoniously flourished his mysterious satchel. Fly was looking distinctly ill at ease, not as vicious or heartless as his friend. Definitely the weak link. Sweating and shivering, no doubt under the thrall of drugs, which led so many young people astray these days. His presence here a testament to the level of his addiction. Anything to feed the screaming in his veins, the profound emptiness in the center of his being nothing could fill. Not evil, merely stupid.

"Please, guy," he begged Cyril, "ain't you got *any* dough stashed away? Just tell us and we'll leave, cross our hearts and hope to die."

Cyril didn't believe him. His eyes were drawn back to his main nemesis as he began laying out an assortment of implements on a nearby glass-topped coffee table. The captive felt his courage falter as the grim display grew to include a flat screwdriver, ice pick, needle-nosed pliers, a portable drill (plus assorted bits), not to mention a small hammer, several knives and cutting blades, as well as a hacksaw.

Oh, Lord, Lord…

"Why are you doing this?" he appealed to Fly, who averted his eyes.

"Well, since you're asking, I'll tell you," the Professor offered. "It was my old daddy who said it best. 'Son,' he told me once, 'there's them that got and them that don't'. And that about sums it up."

"You don't have to—"

"The trouble with living alone like you do," the Professor broke in, "is there aren't many people around to hear any noise you might make." Under the present circumstances his logic seemed unassailable, so Cyril remained silent.

He was aware his relative isolation had its drawbacks but, frankly, crime and safety had never been serious considerations. Even after the last of his neighbors pulled up stakes, he held on to the property, convinced that one day there would be a change in administration and people would be beating a path to his door. The Museum of Mystery and Wonder would become a *mecca* for those drawn to the otherworldly and bizarre. Open to the public five days a week, everyone welcome to wander its spacious interior, sometimes encountering only stale air and barely heard whispers, on other occasions, coming into direct contact with a manifestation as clear and sharply detailed as the objects of torture currently being arranged a few feet from him.

"How's your state of health, old man?" The Professor inquired, his manner solicitous. "Any pre-existing medical conditions or—"

"My name is Cyril—"

The Professor pressed his face close, close enough to bite him. "*I don't give a fuck*," he hissed. "I don't want to know your name, or anything about you. Got it? You could be a war hero or a pedophile for all I care. You're just a *thing* to me. A means to an end. And that's me leaving here with everything worth taking."

"Please—"

But he had already snatched up the ice pick and in one swift, savage motion, plunged it into Cyril's leg, just above the kneecap. Cyril was consumed, *immolated* in an explosion of white-hot agony that tore screams from his throat, his back arching, hands clenching into purple knots of flesh. Fly covered his ears, retreating to a spot by the piano, which was now performing a Beethoven "Nocturne". Probably Captain Albert, then; the keys would be damp with seawater.

The pain and the shock broke something inside him; Cyril could feel a wrongness in his chest and was having trouble catching his breath. The pick was still embedded in his leg. He observed it as through as mist. There was very little blood, there rarely was with puncture wounds.

The world got dimmer—no, it was only his tormentor, kneeling in front of him, blocking the light. Scrutinizing Cyril with great interest. "No one has ever hurt you like that before, have they? I can tell. That experience was entirely new to you." Fly moved away from the piano, which had now commenced playing…was it Schubert? The Professor glanced over his shoulder at his craven confederate. "Fucker wasn't expecting that. Thought we were gonna sit here and have a nice, little chat. But I soon disabused him of that notion, didn't I? Huh? You still with us?"

"Hey, man, that piano—"

"Shut up. Can't you see he's trying to talk?"

"...*tell you...I'll tell you...*"

The Professor gripped Cyril's shoulder, a friendly, almost collegial gesture. Giving it a squeeze to further reassure him. "Sure, you will," he concurred, "hell, there was never any question of *that.*"

Cyril suspected he was dying. His vision kept going in and out of focus and it seemed like the flow of blood to his extremities had either stopped or slowed to a trickle. He was experiencing a spreading coldness, a chill moving through his bones. His heart felt sluggish and there was a sense of an insurmountable weight growing inside him, swelling to the point of bursting.

He knew he must hurry and so it came out in a convincing rush of words, a verbosity they undoubtedly attributed to self-preservation. He told them about the safe in the master bedroom containing his most valuable items, locked away behind a framed print of Doré's 1889 masterpiece "The Fall of the Rebel Angels".

He gave them the combination, begging them to handle the contents with as much care and delicacy as possible.

What he *didn't* divulge was the counterspell. That he would take with him to the grave.

"Priceless," he whispered, barely able to draw breath at that point, his heart now but a distant murmur, the room getting darker and darker, closing in around him.

His interrogator finally nodded, satisfied, and Fly was dispatched to check on the veracity of the information. Meanwhile, the Professor went over to the coffee table, selecting a long, thin knife from the implements arrayed before him.

"You did well, old man," the thug congratulated him, "held out longer than I thought. I give you credit. But you also knew when to cut your losses. I respect that. And that's why we'll make this quick and easy, no pain or fuss, okay?" He paused, testing the sharpness of the blade. "We'll just wait until my colleague—"

"Cyr-il…" He sighed.

"What?" His eyes narrowed, the knife poised in his hand. "What did you say?"

"My…name…is…Cyril."

The Professor scowled, stepping closer, intending something nasty, then saw how the old guy had slumped down in the chair. "Well, shoot…"

He checked and, sure enough, Elvis had definitely left the building.

Good of him to save them the trouble and mess.

Cyril knew all along he couldn't rely on his exhibits to save him. As he explained to the lady from the radio station, they were attached to a very specific time or place and retained zero interest in earthbound affairs. Many ran on a continuous loop, materializing for a few, scant moments, then flickering out. An endless cycle, never altered or varied.

The vast majority of curios he'd acquired over the years were relatively benign and well-behaved. Harmless, unless grossly mishandled. They might rattle the occasional door handle, levitate a table or knock a few photographs askew, but that was about it. After all, he was a responsible proprietor and hoped to attract families to his establishment.

Still, even the most benevolent entities had their limits. While alive, Cyril might have had little opportunity or cause to provoke them; however, in death, by the very nature of his death, he could rightfully adopt the role of avenging angel. Now that he was one of their number, he could organize them, serve as a guiding spirit (so to speak).

Freed from the bonds of his body, unencumbered by the weight of life and experience, Cyril felt renewed, powerful.

Moving through the rooms of his longtime home, lighter than air, invisible and ineffable. Greeting his charges by name, seeing them as they really were, in all their glory and spectral splendor, drawing them to him, rallying them to his cause.

III. Mr. Cavendish in the Afterlife

Donny found Fly in the master bedroom, standing a short distance away from a compact wall safe. He checked: nothing inside but a few old cobwebs. Even the spiders had left the scene.

"The old fuck *lied* to us?" Incredulous, turning on Fly in a fury. "Are you telling me you came up here and—"

Fly was drooling, a thin ribbon of spittle dripping from his chin. "Did you see it?" He groaned, swaying on his feet. "I opened it and—" Shuddering. "It ain't empty. It *looks* empty, it *seems* empty, but—"

"It's empty!" Donny showed him, swinging the hinged door, demonstrating for his benefit. "See? *Emp-ty.*"

"There were things," Fly insisted, "I felt them…" His face crumpled. "We gotta get outta here, man."

"I ain't leaving with nothing for my pot."

Fly looked at him, his expression imploring. "He had them

locked up. Locked away." Bringing his hands to his face. "It rushed out at me, I could feel it, *taste* it. Like old blood..." Choking: "It got out, don't you understand? It could be anywhere—"

"That's *it*? That's what you're telling me? We torture buddy downstairs until he coughs up the combination for the family jewels and you're saying—" Donny advanced on him and Fly saw that one of his hands gripped a knife he probably intended using on their hapless victim in the parlor. "—you're saying, what, that when you cracked the safe, nothing came out but a big fucking gust of air? Huh? Is that it?"

"Please, Donny..." Fly desperate enough to call him by his real name, hoping to dissuade him from rash action. "I wouldn't lie to you, man." He was backed against a wall, hemmed in by a chest of drawers. "Please, don't do this..."

"Sorry, *Kevin*," Donny said, raising the knife, "gotta wipe the slate clean—"

But all at once it got cold, like, *polar*, and they could see their breath, cloudy exhalations in the chill air.

"*What the fuck—*"

"Oh, man, you gotta be kidding me," Fly babbled. "This is like a nightmare."

The bedroom door banged shut and now they were on high alert, trying to accommodate something that made no sense...and it was right around then that things started going wrong with the perspective, walls receding from them, the room stretching into a long, thin extension of itself, flexing and bending around the edges.

Fly emitted a panicked bleat and lunged for the door, howling when his bare skin made contact with the frozen, metal knob. Scalded, screaming, he pounded on the only exit until his fists were sore and slick with blood, unable to find purchase, weeping in frustration. Yet somehow he managed to spring the door open, slipping through, even as it began rapidly shrinking, sliding backward, into the far distance.

Donny was bigger, slower to act, not a born survivor like Fly. He was about to follow his erstwhile partner when, at that instant, a woman emerged from a nearby wall, paused, eyed him up and down, queried "Philippe?", then dissolved before his eyes.

The carpet came to life, writhing and bucking beneath his feet. He cast caution to the wind, dove toward the door, tumbling and rolling the last few feet, bruised and breathless when he reached it.

He was scared and pissed off. A dangerous combination. "Fly!" He roared, stomping down the hallway. "Where are you, asshole?" No answer. The fucker would pay dearly for his cowardice.

Donny stopped, looked around. Originally, this short corridor had branched into a series of cluttered compartments, including the master bedroom and a bathroom, a flight of stairs leading back to the ground floor. That's the way he remembered it.

The stairs were gone.

"Fly! Get your ass up here!" He could hear it in his voice, he was definitely losing it. Creeped out by the place, seeing things on the periphery of his vision, scuttling movement, leering faces—

Whirling about, checking behind him, but there was nothing there, his instincts disagreeing, every single one of them shrieking *watch out, they're coming, they're all around you, closing in…*

There was a hatchway, leading up into the ceiling. An attic access or crawl space. He hadn't seen it before because it hadn't been there until now. And he was relieved to discover he was tall enough to reach it without assistance. The handle turned, the hatch fell open. No ladder, just a square hole. Jump up, snag a grip, pull himself into that dark space. Had to be better than here.

And then, as if he needed it, further motivation. It started as a sound, a wet, sucking noise, its source at first indeterminate. At last, he saw what appeared to be a face, pressing outward from a nearby wall. The fundamental structure of the wood and plaster warping, altering, as more of the figure—two arms and then a leg—emerged from the surrounding material.

Donny prepared to spring for the opening but discovered to his dismay it was contracting, visibly smaller. He leapt, grabbed hold of the edge, began hoisting himself up. He could hear the creature below struggling to extricate itself, so he redoubled his efforts, gasping and straining, desperate to gain the attic and swing the heavy gate shut behind him.

He was only halfway through when he realized he'd miscalculated, the aperture was closing faster than he thought. It squeezed against his midriff and he soon discovered further progress was impossible, he was wedged in tight.

That's when he began screaming.

Kicking his feet and howling until he was weak and hoarse. "Fly," he whimpered, "where are you?"

Something seized his legs and began pulling, the pressure growing by the second. Muscles and sinew stretched past their limit, ripping and tearing unevenly, a protracted and excruciating vivisection. He wailed, his struggles futile, growing weaker; a helpless plaything clutched in mighty, gripping hands.

The force being exerted from below was enormous but the power holding him in place was equal to the task. It became a battle of wills, with only one possible solution, devised long ago by the wise and just King Solomon but, of course, never meant to be taken literally.

Donny stayed conscious almost to the end. His two halves slowly separating, *bisected* cell by cell, his unseen adversaries well-versed at the art of prolonging the inevitable. Like seasoned inquisitors, their capacity for cruelty seemingly limitless. To him, the ordeal was interminable, each succeeding moment establishing new thresholds of agony. Suffering all the torments of Purgatory, without the faintest promise of redemption.

Once it was over, the various entities involved squabbled over the scraps of Donny's malformed soul.

There wasn't much to choose from…

Kevin cut the old man loose from his bindings, lugged him over to the sofa. His blistered, fucked up hands complained bitterly, but he managed. Once the body was properly positioned, he thought about it, crossed the thin, spotted arms over its chest. More dignified that way. Had he some coins, he would've put them on the dead man's eyes. The occasion seemed to call for it.

Cyril, he remembered, he said his name was *Cyril*. One tough dude, no question, standing up to Donny like that. Talk about guts and dedication to duty. How long had he been living here, protecting this place, securing its treasures from harm?

Maybe now that he was gone the denizens of the house would require someone else to take over, another human agent acting on their behalf: opening the door to occasional visitors, keeping up appearances, dealing with representatives from the outside world.

He was still a young man, after all, plenty of years ahead of him. With luck, he could gain acceptance and stick it out here, secure a permanent position and, meanwhile, have a roof over his head and a warm bed to sleep in. Why not? Sure beat the hell out of his former life.

Kevin seated himself in a tall-backed, lumpy armchair, feeling hopeful, expectant.

Happy to be of service, eagerly awaiting instructions.

Higher Physics

My father was Adam Cullen and just to give you an idea of the sort of man we're talking about, his nickname, bestowed by family and what few friends he had, was "the *adam* bomb".

Dad's temper was legendary. He'd be listening to someone—or pretending to—and suddenly erupt with a caustic remark like: "And what exactly makes you think I give a fuck?"

It was a guaranteed conversation-stopper.

Rude, direct, easily offended, that was dad. He could also be charming and witty, depending on his mood or how much he'd had to drink.

Though he died relatively young, his demise was hardly premature. Frankly, it was amazing he lasted as long as he did. Over the years I've heard more and more about his antics, the bar brawls and brushes with the law. He wasn't an *evil* man, but he wasn't a very good one either. The accident which claimed his life only the latest in a long series of mishaps and near misses dating back to a wild, carefree youth. On the positive side, at least he wasn't behind a wheel when it happened and didn't take anyone with him.

But I'm getting ahead of myself.

The third time my mother left my father was preceded by yet another row over money, the confrontation nearly ending in violence. He stormed out, slamming the door behind him, off on another one of his benders. No way of predicting when he'd be back.

We snuck out of the house at 4:30 the following morning. He'd taken the Gran Torino, our only vehicle, so Mr. Forbes agreed to come and collect us, spirit us away. Dad had once worked for Mr. Forbes' farm machinery dealership but the two of them had fallen out. Sooner or later that was bound to happen; with dad you got, at most, a six-month grace period before you were unceremoniously consigned to the category of "irredeemable asshole". Mr. Forbes, Wally, felt sorry for us and possibly had a soft spot for mom. Karen, my sister, thought so, though I detected no hint of impropriety between them and was, after all, nearly a year senior to her and that much wiser.

We were only allowed a single suitcase each, allotted a garbage bag for "essentials". I had a hard time choosing which books to take. I consoled myself with the knowledge that this wasn't the first time we'd bailed on dad and, if history held true, sooner or later I'd be reunited with my abandoned property.

I have to say, however, with attempt #3 my mother had definitely done her homework, more so than on previous occasions. First of all, she enlisted the aid of Wally Forbes, plus she'd scouted out possible locations, finding us a cheap place to live and even securing a position at a local hardware store. The community, Cranmer, was two hours away from Davin, far enough, she hoped, to thwart my father's efforts at finding us.

At first blush, it seemed like a good plan. However, neither Karen nor I was convinced mom had the strength of character and willpower to make it on her own.

The previous escape bids hadn't gone well, for various reasons, and we had no reason to believe this one would be any different. Sooner or later we'd hear a knock on the door or dad's voice on the phone and know the jig was up. The last time, she had broken down and called *him*. Tried to explain her convoluted reasoning to us afterward but couldn't.

I'm sure she could feel the negative vibrations emanating from the backseat. During the drive, Wally hardly spoke, but she chattered away, trying to lighten the atmosphere. Constantly twisting around to look at us, smiling encouragingly, craving the support and comfort we were so determined to deny her.

I found out later from Tim Hofstadter, who lived down the street, that when my father returned and discovered we'd flown the coop, he went berserk. Hung over, broke, unemployed (yet again), sporting a fresh shiner (courtesy some half-remembered fracas), he seized on a crude method of exacting vengeance on his absent family. He went inside and began hauling everything he could carry or drag out of the house, piling it on the front lawn. Working with furious energy, in full view of our neighbors, some of whom stood on their front steps and watched, he succeeded in removing a substantial proportion of our possessions—including the sofa bed and practically new, twenty-six inch, color TV—creating an impressive mound of goods. Then they saw him march into the garage, returning with a gas can.

"Ah, no, Adam," someone called, "you go too far." Other voices chimed in, a Greek chorus of disapproval, imploring him not to take the next fateful step.

"Fuck off, the lot o' you," dad barked, meanwhile liberally sloshing gasoline on our heaped belongings, the neighbors' dismay growing. Someone had undoubtedly phoned the cops by then, but they had to come all the way from Whitewood, the nearest detachment. No one had the guts to confront him or frustrate his plans and he knew it. "Fuck you all!" he yelled. "Gonna have me a wienie roast."

And that's what he was doing when the Mounties and the town volunteer fire department finally showed up. A partly frozen smokie stuck to the end of an unbent wire coat hanger, perched as close as he dared, eyebrows and forearms singed from proximity to the careless flames. Tim said it was great, all the lights and sirens and commotion, and my father sitting there, his clothes steaming, puffing on a ciggy, trying to barbeque that damn smokie.

The firefighters didn't know what to do. Constable Salt lumbered over and stood behind dad's aluminum lawn chair, the frame of which was almost too hot to touch. "Come along, Adam. Let's have no more trouble today."

My father looked back over his shoulder, incredulous. "Fuck's the problem, man? Can't you see I'm fixin' dinner?"

Of course, they arrested him.

But Tim said dad handled it well, flipping off the neighbors as Salt escorted him to his patrol car. Even on his way to the hoosegow he couldn't resist one last demonstration of defiance and contempt.

Then the firemen went to work, tapping the nearest hydrant and running their hoses, though it was plain the blaze was burning down, any danger already passed.

I was well-acquainted with the routine: as new kids at school, we were the lowest of the low, on the receiving end of every malicious cruelty and slight imaginable, *with absolutely no right to complain or protest.* It was part of a tradition dating back to the beginning of time. A hazing ritual that would make a West Point plebe quail.

Arriving mid-term, inserted into a class of in-bred, close-knit primates, most of whom had known each other since kindergarten. I was an "outsider" in a sense that even someone like Albert Camus would have a hard time grasping.

It was November, chilly, a light dusting of snow on the ground. Soon it would be slush. I walked with my head down, going so slow Karen had to keep doubling back in impatience.

"We're gonna be *late*, Joe..."

Which, who knows, might stand me in good stead with my fellow pris—er, students. Strolling in, all cool and collected, ten minutes after the final bell had rung.

"Joe? Do you hear me? What time is it, do you know?"

"Who cares."

But I wasn't that kind of kid. A physical coward, my fears and anxieties too numerous to name. On top of that, I was on the smallish side, shy, uncoordinated, lousy at sports and, to complete the picture, fitted with wire-framed glasses. My nickname back in Davin was "Professor Kitzel" (an eccentric cartoon character who taught children about Canadian history). You might as well paint a target on my ass and hand out bows and arrows. I was definitely in for it. They'd probably line up to see who could sock me first. Drawing lots, maybe, or holding a raffle. *God.* The worst ones would be the bib-overalled, backwoods bumpkins, bused in from hamlets and farms in nearby districts, still reeking of the fields and sties, eager to erase social distinctions with fists and feet.

Remember Rodney Wiebe? Size eleven feet and still in Grade Five. A freak of nature, with a disposition to match.

Hey, Cullen, see ya at recess…

One of the least fond memories of our brief stint in Percival (and there was plenty of competition, trust me).

I hadn't been *un*popular at Davin School, more like imperceptible, anonymous. And I'd worked hard to achieve that status, refusing to volunteer answers or speak up in class, avoiding every opportunity to distinguish myself, appear *too* smart, stand out. Never challenging anyone, never excelling, never competing. The last one chosen for floor hockey, baseball or, well, just about anything else.

You take Cullen.

Aw, I had him last time, he sucks like a toothless granny.

An oft-repeated refrain, versions of which I heard throughout my childhood years.

I was that kid you came across in a yearbook a decade later and you'd pause, finger tapping the thumbnail-sized headshot: "This guy…Joey Cullen…" And then pretty much draw a blank. Which, in all honesty, is what I tried to be, a tactic I'd adopted as part of my survival routine. Become blank, absolute zero. An absence, a mere outline or shadow on the wall, Xs for eyes. Nothing anyone need concern themselves with, easy to ignore.

We arrived at Miriam M. Dumont School just in the nick of time. Most of the other kids were already inside, except for a few stragglers.

Mr. Derdall, the vice-principal, met us at the front entrance. Chubby, balding, harried; a typical middle manager. Waiting while we shucked off our damp shoes, placing them on hinged metal shelves to dry. Now in our stocking feet, he led us down the main hallway, calling out to students, urging them to get to class before the second and final bell rang. Obviously, he intended to escort us to our designated homerooms, the two of us scurrying along in his wake like a pair of lost ducklings.

Thanks a lot, pal. You just handed another quiver of arrows to my tormentors, these ones likely dipped in poisonous curare.

Karen's was closest, so her ordeal was soon over. Once we'd divested ourselves of my sister, Mr. Derdall had me all to himself. He kept shooting me these concerned looks, trying to coax me out of my shell.

"…hope you'll be happy here at Dumont School, Joe. Is it Joe or Joey? Hey, did you know 'joey' is what they call a baby kangaroo…"

Even at the time I thought he was trying too hard. A nice man, full to brimming with the best possible intentions.

The road to Hell had its paving stones laid by his sort. Thoughtful, conscientious, utterly sincere. They were the bane of my existence. Against them, my cloak of invisibility was useless. No matter how hard I tried to hide, the tricks I employed, they always detected me. It was uncanny. And they were forever trying to *help…*

We'd finally arrived. The cell block door loomed before me, Perdition waiting on the other side.

Abandon hope, all ye who enter here.

"What was that, Joe?" Mr. Derdall was staring at me.

I forgot to mention: I talked to myself. Well, it was more like *muttered*. It had started a number of years earlier and I thought it might be getting worse. Yup, yet another weird quirk to add to the checklist, one more black mark against me. At least the bed-wetting was over and done with.

He was expecting a response so I gave him a sickly smile, but he still seemed a bit unsettled. Rapping on the door, then ushering me inside, as if suddenly eager to be shed of me.

Three times. Three times in the past five years our mother had avoided reconciliation with her troubled, wayward husband long enough for it to become necessary to register us in a new school.

Hateful, that was the only way to describe it. And it never got any better.

Percival: Grade 3. Miserable experience and Rodney Wiebe was only part of it. Lasted barely two months but seemed like an eternity. No friends, strict teachers, still young enough to miss dad, willfully blind to his faults. Blaming mom for running away. Hating her, perhaps for the first time.

Regina: Grade 5. Welcome to the big city, boys and girls. Somerwell Elementary School.

Make that Somer*hell*. A three-month long nightmare of anxiety and violence. Seeing the building for the first time, cruddy neighborhood, that institutional red brick, small windows, gloomy interior, I knew I was in trouble. Sure enough, I soon became everyone's whipping boy, including teachers. Bullied and threatened right from day one, I also had to put up with a pushy guidance counselor, who tried to make a project out of me (not sure which was worse). And mom on little, blue pills that rendered her aloof, disconnected from worldly cares. Dad enticed her back with long, heartfelt letters, saying how much he missed us, swearing he was changing his ways, playing the role of reformed man to the hilt.

But what sealed the deal was that he'd somehow landed a position with the town of Davin. His duties included operating the snowplow during winter months, a grader in the summer, maintaining the gravel roads, filling in potholes. Full-time work, not seasonal, and with his employment record and reputation it was a miracle he'd managed such an achievement…and all but inevitable he'd blow it within a short period of time (which he did).

And now *Cranmer*: Grade Seven. The kids older, the stakes higher. This was when society's pecking order really asserted itself, the Alphas separating themselves from the rest of the pack and plotting how to make everyone else do their bidding. A microcosm of life.

I stood between two adults, looking small, frail and vulnerable. Found myself facing a classroom of perhaps twenty-five students, most of them a blur of round, undifferentiated balloon heads. No detail, just a smear of features. I kept swallowing even though my mouth and throat were bone dry, every drop of moisture in my body concentrated in my bladder, which I had conscientiously emptied *twice* before venturing out of the house that morning.

My homeroom teacher was Miss Maas. "Miss", not "Ms." Pretty, soft spoken, trying and failing to make eye contact with me, getting a preliminary read from my posture, the sharp, animal tang of fear I exuded, pulse beating rapidly in my throat. The room had gone all echo-y, white noise hissing in my head. The lights were too bright and I *really* needed to pee.

Finally, they decided I'd suffered enough and could take my seat. I can't remember any of what was said. At least they didn't ask me, *a la* Somerhell, to "tell us a few things about yourself, Joseph". That was the beginning of the end. Within two hours, I had been gifted with my first bloody nose.

If tradition held true, I would either be stationed at the front, an extra desk wedged into a row or, worst-case scenario, forced to share a table with what we now call a "special needs student" but back then went by a different, uglier name.

I had to share a table all right, but it was with a girl named Theresa Provencher. It took a few minutes for Theresa's remarkable, unprecedented beauty to work its way through my defensive fog, penetrating the Fortress of Solitude I'd carefully constructed around myself as part of my morning preparations. To put it bluntly, she was *stunning*. Dark eyes and a Mediterranean complexion; she seemed irresistibly exotic to me and I couldn't help sneaking looks at her, ogling her profile.

Helen of Troy, Jaclyn Smith, even the Dallas Cowboy Cheerleaders had nothing on that gal. Not as far as I was concerned.

Normal sound was starting to fade in and I could make out individual words, a few phrases. I had yet to open a book or pick up my pencil. Gathered from the numbers Miss Maas was jotting on the chalkboard we were getting a lesson in arithmetic.

More bad luck. I hated math. Hated, hated, *hated* it. I could write out the word "hate" in big block letters for the rest of my life and that *still* wouldn't cover it. My abhorrence of mathematics took on phobia-like proportions and I'm not exactly sure why. Maybe its much-touted logic, the cut and dried answers it purported to provide, scared me off. Could life really be like that? Did two and two *always* equal four, couldn't there be exceptions or special circumstances?

Nothing in my personal experience led me to believe there was any such state as "normal", and yet great minds down through history stipulated that the cosmos was perfectly ordered, empirical, adhering to certain commonly accepted principles, formulas and theories, as predictable as night following day.

And didn't that kind of symmetry imply a Creator, a central, guiding consciousness?

Someone to blame when things went from bad to worse, when reality became so unbearable you wondered what you could have possibly done to incur the displeasure of your Maker.

Especially when you were only thirteen years old.

I squinted at the equation Ms. Maas had just finished writing out.

Gobbledegook.

Then I got to wondering how long I'd have to maintain a pretense this time. Doing the minimum amount of work, switching to academic autopilot until mom threw in the towel once again. A few weeks? A month? Surely no more than that. Sooner or later, dad would find us or else she'd run out of money or get lonely and the jig was up. Usually it was the latter that put paid to her schemes.

In Regina, she even had her parents to fall back on. They owned several properties in the city, including a small house on Athol Street, situated in the in north-central region of the city. It was a bit of a "hood", even back then, but the rent was free, the place furnished, and Somerwell, the nearest school, only a few blocks away.

Both Karen and I found life in the provincial capital eye-opening and scary. I remember the first time we walked to a 7-11, some creep dumped a cold drink on me as they drove past.

Sploosh. Drenched in sticky cola, shrieks of laughter receding as the car accelerated away, tires smoking. No rhyme or reason to it, an unprovoked act of spite and callousness I still have a hard time accommodating.

It never got any better. It came as a relief when dad finally showed up to collect us, loading all that new furniture (*thanks very much, Kate and Angus, and toodle-oo*), into a borrowed truck, while my grandparents watched, helpless and resigned. Grandma Kate looked mad enough to chuck rocks. Those big, strong hands of hers.

I was just glad to get the heck out of there. A few more weeks at Somerhell and they would have needed dental records to identify my remains.

Hey, Cullen, see ya at recess…

Recess.

I shuddered to think about it. That's when they could get at you. The teachers couldn't be everywhere and sometimes they'd look the other way when a kid was being roughed up or razzed. I'll bet they sat around the staff room, laying odds on which student was in for it that day. A misery pool.

But I had a few tricks up my sleeve. After the bell rang and while the rest of my classmates filed out, I dawdled, stacking my books, carefully lining up pencil, eraser, ruler, etc. on the tabletop before sliding out of my chair. Collected my coat, double and triple-checked to make sure I had both toque and gloves, laced and re-laced my shoes a total of three times before I was satisfied with the result.

Once outside, I stuck close to the building, avoiding blind spots, remaining in sight of a teacher at all times. Theresa

Provencher and a few of her friends wandered by, checking me out, but I displayed proper newcomer etiquette, refusing to acknowledge them, gazing off at some point in the middle distance. I'm sure they thought I was mental.

There was only ten minutes or so left and I tried to blend in with the wall, mumbling "Think chameleon, think chameleon", resisting the urge to taste the air with a quick, darting, bifurcated tongue.

If my thousand-yard stare didn't scare them off, the muttering should do the trick.

Then I made a critical error.

There was a spirited soccer game in progress in the schoolyard on the north side of the building. I heard yells and whoops, I was bored and curious, so I edged closer to watch. I recognized two or three boys from my homeroom, right in the thick of the action.

I thought my camouflage was perfect but somehow one of them spotted me.

"C'mon!" The kid (*Doug?*) was beckoning with his arm. "We need one more guy."

I was petrified. Frozen solid. A human popsicle.

No, God, please…

"C'mon!"

Who did he think he was dealing with? I wasn't some newbie with shit for brains. The moment I strayed from the view of a teacher/monitor—who usually combined their supervision time with a smoke break—I'd be easy pickings. He and his buddies would reduce me to my component atoms and then collectively claim I was the one who started the whole thing.

"What's that kid's name? Joe? Hey, Joe! You wanna play? We're a guy short."

Now someone had called time and picked up the ball. The game was delayed, everything on hold while I deliberated, hardly able to breathe, my heart thumping in my ears. I made a mental note that the chameleon trick was a bust and next time it might be preferable to "think mole" or some other furtive, burrowing creature.

And then I was pushing off the wall, starting toward them. But it was like I was moving in slow motion or had suddenly been teleported to a high-gravity planet. It seemed to take a *loooonnnng* time to get there. All at once everything exploded into noise and activity and boys were tearing around on that muddy, snowy patch of turf. I was caught up in the midst of it, trying to figure out whose team I was on and which net, its goalposts demarcated either by stones or discarded mittens, was mine.

Soccer was among the many games I was lousy at so I don't think I distinguished myself in any way. When the bell rang, we started back toward the entrance of the school and I felt someone give me playful shove, knocking me off stride. I flinched from the contact but then another kid clapped me on the back.

"Good game, Joe."

"Yeah, way to go, Jo-Jo!"

"Wait 'til it *really* snows and we can start hockey—"

"We play here at noon too," Doug informed me.

The invitation all but explicit.

I followed them inside, hardly believing my ears.

It wasn't Somerhell, it wasn't Davin, it was *paradise* (without the snakes and smothering, over-protective parenting).

Within a week I was invited to my first sleepover. I don't know if they were *friends*, but there were three or four guys whose company I enjoyed and who shared similar cultural touchstones ("Star Trek", "The Flintstones", hockey, *The Hardy Boys*). They seemed to like me and often included me in their plans. For the first time ever I had a decent social life and wasn't spending most of my waking hours alone, wondering what everybody else was up to.

Karen was doing okay too but that wasn't surprising, she never seemed to have trouble attracting friends. In terms of genetics, she got the looks and personality (mom), whereas I tended to be solitary and anti-social (dad).

But during the nine blissful weeks we resided in Cranmer, I was, for the most part, cheerful, positive and seemingly on the verge of finally getting my shit together. I wouldn't say I was "happy", that would be out of character for me; too optimistic, or maybe *presumptuous* is a better word. Besides, happiness was fragile, impermanent, and could be snatched away in a heartbeat. All it took was a phone call or the sound of an engine idling in the driveway. I knew this from bitter experience.

While Karen and I were adjusting to our new environment, our mother was struggling. In truth, she wasn't much suited for life in the outside world. She was a good homemaker, she could cook and clean and enjoyed wielding complete control over her personal domain. But in a workplace, under someone else's thumb, she lost confidence, made mistakes, lost even more confidence…

Her job at the hardware store was pretty demanding, especially for a woman whose frequently unemployed husband was usually around to handle repairs and maintenance. She had to learn the retail side of things, including running a cash register, as well as knowing tons of stuff about tools and appliances so she could chat knowledgably with her customers and not sound like a dumb woman.

I recall one night she came home in tears because a friend of Keith's (her boss) had recklessly demonstrated his new Zippo lighter by flicking it in her face, setting fire to her bangs. Mom said she could hear hair crackling and burned her hand patting it out. And afterward the guy hadn't even apologized. That bothered her more than anything else.

Keith Anderson had inherited the store from his father and felt entitled to having things done *his* way, no questions asked. A real tyrant. The first time I visited mom at work, he strolled past and made a point of telling me: "Remember, kid, you break, you pay". Total asshole. I pocketed two screwdrivers and a ten-dollar pack of drill bits on the way out the door.

At some point my mother started having trouble sleeping. Obviously, she was under a tremendous amount of pressure and feeling very much out of her depth. She developed dark circles under her eyes even makeup couldn't conceal, her mood alternating between lethargy and fretfulness.

Once I got up in the middle of the night to pee, noticed a light on and found her sitting at the kitchen table, smoking. She looked at me and couldn't even muster the strength for a smile.

My heart dropped into my stomach with an audible *splash*.

I knew it was only a matter of time.

I didn't share my fears with Karen and tried not to alter my behavior around my new companions. They were urging me to sign up for baseball in the spring, try out for the town little league team. I didn't have the heart to tell them that, if anything, I was even worse at baseball than soccer.

In English class we were reading John Steinbeck's *The Red Pony*, maybe the saddest story ever written. "Old Yeller", times a thousand. I found myself relating to Jody's sense of betrayal once he realized that even those closest to you are destined to let you down.

We finished the book two days before I came home and found a vehicle parked in front of our house. It was a big, red, Buick Riviera. Plenty of power under the hood. He'd traded up from the Gran Torino. It was a steal of a deal and, oh, yeah, his new job with Saskatchewan Highways provided the down payment and financing. Arnie Wessel's dad owned the Chevrolet dealership in Davin that sold it to him. Arnie was a spoiled, rich kid who lorded it over the rest of us, always behaving like he knew something we didn't. And maybe because he *was* rich, it was generally accepted that this view had some validity.

I walked in and there was dad, seated at the kitchen table, ashtray in front of him. My mother was leaning against the sink, acting skittish and wary. Which meant he hadn't been there long. The first thing he did after shaking my hand was offer me the keys to his new used car.

"You know how to start it. Play the radio, check it out. I'll take you for a spin later on. It's a bomb."

"An *adam* bomb," I muttered.

He either didn't hear me or chose to ignore it. Used to my little tics by now. "Go on," he urged, "fire it up. Your mom and I have things to talk about."

They talked, and a week later we were on our way back to Davin.

Saying good-bye to my Cranmer classmates was hard. Saying good-bye to the lovely Theresa Provencher hardest of all. I had a difficult time looking anyone in the eye. Miss Maas reserved the last period of the day for a farewell party, with games and music. If anything, her thoughtful gesture made me feel even *worse*. Not only was I leaving them, I also knew perfectly well what I was returning to. Consigned, once more, to the bottom of the heap…

As soon as we pulled up in front of our house in Davin, I saw the big scorch mark on the lawn, like some kind of alien rocket ship had landed there.

No one offered an explanation.

Five months later, around dusk, my father, who had recently been demoted to flag man (lowest position on the road crew), was struck by a vehicle when, the driver claimed, he suddenly lurched out into oncoming traffic, behaving like he was drunk.

What came next was as inevitable and unsurprising as everything else that had ever happened to me.

After the funeral, our widowed mother, medicated to the gills and glassy-eyed as a toy doll, called Karen and me into the kitchen and tearfully informed us of her desire to live closer to her parents, especially under the present circumstances.

We would be moving to Regina in time to start the fall semester. Same house, same neighborhood, same school.

Somerhell, here we come.

She knew we'd understand.

I didn't react, kept my composure. Nodding in apparent acquiescence.

All too aware of the larger forces at work, the same immutable laws and processes that created and powered the stars and spun planets in their intricate orbits. Incomprehensible mathematics blithely indifferent to my puny prayers and dreams. For some reason I started thinking about Jody, the kid in *The Red Pony*, and how by the end of the book the pain and disillusionment he experienced had revealed both the relentless cruelty of the universe and the extent of its vast, terrible reach.

The Kuleshov Effect*

Perspective is a funny thing.

From your point of view, my wife's disappearance might seem puzzling, inexplicable, suspicious. Seen in another light, however, coming at it from a totally different angle, it conforms to a pattern of abandonment and loss dating back to my childhood, and therefore any implication of wrongdoing or skullduggery is not only unwarranted and irresponsible, but also demonstrably cruel. Do you see what I mean?

No?

To give you some context: my father walked out on us when I was eight years old. Like he was heading off to buy a newspaper. Telling me to watch my little sister until he got back. I never saw him again. He moved away, grew another family. No birthday cards, nothing at Christmas. A complete severance. I suppose in his mind he was being kind.

My sister didn't understand. "Where's daddy?" she kept asking.

---

* The *Kuleshov Effect*: a film editing (montage) effect demonstrated by pioneer Soviet filmmaker Lev Kuleshov. It is a mental phenomenon by which viewers derive more meaning from the interaction of two sequential shots than from a single shot in isolation. (Source: *Wikipedia*)

"Gone."

But she persisted. "Gone where? Where gone?"

No answer.

Gone. Like *dead*, only without the closure.

People around us are constantly absenting themselves from our lives, losing significance, gradually fading away. Do you remember the faces of your neighborhood mail carrier or the pharmacist who filled your last prescription? Is it *our* fault they are so completely unmemorable? Are we somehow complicit in their effortless anonymity?

I can tell Inspector Haas doesn't believe me.

"I'm a pessimist by nature," he says, somewhat defensively. "Part of the job description."

I pass two different lie detector tests but he remains dissatisfied.

"You're hiding something," he insists.

"Aren't we all?" I shrug.

He stares at me, but I give no indication of sarcasm or flippancy. He's itching to charge me but there's nothing he can do about it.

There's no body, no evidence.

The case remains open, pending.

Pending *what*?

"—you're both angry, yelling at each other, and your wife, she storms out of the room."

"Yes. Correct."

"And you say there's a pause, no more than a few seconds—"

"I told you—"

"And when you did go after her…"

"I walked in there and it was empty. No sign of her. Maybe a hint of her scent, her perfume, that's about it."

"A locked door mystery."

"It was the bathroom and the door wasn't locked."

"Still."

The press seizes hold of the story, play up its unusual aspects. Soon I am besieged by every manner of kook. Religious nuts and amateur sleuths. A team of parapsychologists want to camp out in my living room. A semi-famous psychic with her own syndicated radio show tells her listeners my wife is in hiding somewhere in Michigan and there's more to this story than meets the eye.

I get on with my life. Cope as best I can. I genuinely *loved* my wife, that's what they don't understand. Whatever happened to her, I feel remorse, a sense of responsibility.

But that's ridiculous. How can I bear any blame? It's not like you can *wish* someone out of existence in a fit of pique.

If that was possible, the good Inspector's job would suddenly become a lot more difficult and challenging.

Did my father ever regret his actions? The irreparable harm he inflicted on my sister? She never got over what he did. It was as if he'd given up on us. That was the worst part. How *easy* it was for him to let us go.

My mother calls, leaves a message. A few mealy-mouthed

words of support and then she comes to the point: reporters are harassing her, ambushing her every time she steps outside her building. Whining about the embarrassment and inconvenience. On and on it goes.

Press "7" to erase?

Yes.

You can't rely on people. Not even those closest to you. Every time you put any faith in them, they let you down.

My sister, April 10, 2014.

At least they can't blame me for that.

From her last note: *I just see myself getting sadder and sadder. But mostly because I'm so bloody bored…*

In the end, we are subservient to that most basic animal instinct, self-preservation. The world may come to an end, the stars going out one by one, but the struggle for survival continues unabated. And so we endure all manner of pain and horror, lose those closest us, persevere in the face of insurmountable odds.

The optimists call this "courage", but I am not convinced.

My wife's family refuses to let their daughter slip from the headlines. They never liked me and this is a golden opportunity to exact some revenge. Seeking their pound of flesh and sizing me up for the choicest cuts. They call numerous press conferences, air outrageous accusations. My lawyer refuses to sue, saying it will only make matters worse.

"Bring me my daughter's body!" my mother-in-law shrieks, weeping histrionically. "Let us at least bury her with the respect she deserves." Her husband, meanwhile, maintaining a cowed silence, grimacing and blinking at her side.

I wish I could make *them* disappear.

Their blatant appeal for attention leads to a renewed onslaught from the gutter press. Soon I am virtually a prisoner in my own home. My neighbors resent the noise and traffic, circulate a petition demanding my eviction. Left to wander the streets in rags, a pariah and a penitent.

I barricade the doors, disconnect the phone. Sever contact with the outside world. Determined to wait them out…

After three days, I'm going stir crazy. But if I so much as stick my head outside to check the weather or fetch the mail, I hear shouts, running feet, a small army of protesters erupting into chants and waving placards, insisting I must face her grieving parents, somehow assuage their bereavement and rage. A woman gets within a few yards of the front step, screaming I ought to be ashamed and—

I catch her eye and she stammers, her tongue tying itself into a loose, slippery knot. Gagging, clutching her throat.

Gotcha.

I am hauled in for questioning, yet again. Haas and his superiors feeling the heat. But I stick to my story, which is absolutely consistent with the forensic evidence. Not the slightest hint of violence or foul play. Nothing that directly contradicts me.

But no one speaks of exoneration.

I am still the prime suspect in their eyes, in the eyes of the world.

Now *I* want to disappear.

New crises, new headlines, *real* dead bodies.
I move to a different small city, grow a beard, change my name.
Try to make the past go away.

This is me today. You'd hardly recognize me. And perhaps you'd be surprised to discover I've become something of a community activist. I donate time and money to the right causes. Some would say I'm trying to make amends. So be it.

The thing is, people no longer see that other guy when they look at me. They see the volunteer work, the model citizen and good neighbor and *that's it*.

I keep the old face in a box, under my bed.

Labeled "Keepsakes", tightly sealed with packing tape.

Except they find me. The vengeful valkyrie and her timid, tight-lipped spouse.

They slip fliers under every windshield on my block.

"This man killed our daughter..."

With my picture, from our wedding photo, looking so young and hopeful.

My lawyer won't take my calls.

So much for the presumption of innocence and due process.

Time for more desperate measures.

Flee in the middle of the night. A hastily improvised plan. Using cash and a fake ID to cover my tracks.

Disappearing.

Just like my poor wife.

For the diehards, it will be one more unsolved mystery. Like unmasking Jack the Ripper or discovering the true fate of Judge Crater and Amelia Earhart. Some will seek supernatural solutions, a case of karma circling back and biting me on the ass. Others suggesting less fanciful scenarios…but they'll *all* be wrong.

These days you can change your face, your eyes, even the color of your skin. The trick isn't finding some bolthole, locking yourself away. No, better to blend in with the crowd, hiding in plain sight.

I might be standing next to you on a subway platform in Tokyo or queuing up behind you at a busy terminal in Frankfurt Airport. Barely perceived, hardly more than a shape, not worthy of a glance.

A notorious character, never indicted or absolved, still at large and quite possibly dangerous.

…or a polite, dapper, middle-aged gentleman, considerately hoisting your heavy suitcase, escorting you to the counter, waving off thanks. *Très debonair*. Leaving you with a warm afterglow and a renewed faith in the essential decency of your fellow human beings.

I guess it depends on how you look at it, doesn't it?

The Lure of Ancient Places

Athens (I)

The temperature was over a hundred the day they climbed up to the Parthenon. Had to be. Mid-July in Greece, are you kidding? Hotter than the devil's favorite frying pan, as Mrs. Strickland, Gina's Sunday school teacher, used to say.

They spent most of the morning at the Acropolis Museum, situated near the foot of the stony hill where, long ago, grateful citizens had erected a temple dedicated to the city's patron deity (and namesake) Athena.

The guidebook made a big deal out of the museum but, to Gina, everything seemed to be in pieces. Fragments, rather than a complete statue or frieze or what have you. Many of the best artifacts and relics had been carted off as loot to Britain (those famous "Elgin Marbles"), Russia, Italy and points elsewhere. What they were viewing were the leftovers. To be honest, she found the whole thing underwhelming.

Not Anthony though, he was in his glory. Flitting from gallery to gallery, taking everything in, frequently bugging dozing docents for more information, disturbing their much-needed rest. Oblivious to their grumpiness and babbling away at them, unaware that they were probably only getting about ten per cent of what he was saying. The guy was clueless. Which was, at once, kind of endearing and utterly maddening.

It was his bright idea to tackle the Parthenon during the hottest part of the day. Why not? It was so close and, anyway, it would be a good, bracing climb, and at the top, a world-famous landmark, as recognizable and iconic as the Great Pyramid of Giza. Looming over the city, centrally located to emphasize its paramount importance in the lives of ancient Athenians. Spend a couple of hours at the museum and then up they go.

But when he related the plan to Alex, their host and owner of the little bed and breakfast where they were staying, he seemed polite but dubious.

"The forecast says it will be very hot." He didn't attempt to discourage them but she could tell he thought the notion of a couple of overweight, out of shape forty-somethings hauling themselves up that steep grade on a day that promised to be a scorcher wasn't too smart.

And he was right.

The forecast didn't lie and the ascent was unbelievably grueling, that big, yellow Mediterranean sun glowering down at them every step of the way. The limestone and bare, exposed rock reflecting its glare, making the ascent twice as difficult and tiring. She and Anthony kept pausing, finding whatever cover they could, gulping bottled water and giving the evil eye to other, heartier climbers who were practically bounding their way up the slope. Hope a few of them ended up turning an ankle. *Bastards*.

"Having fun yet?"

Anthony's idea of humor. The joke nearly as lousy as his timing. There were long tracks of sweat descending into her butt crack. Her thighs were chafing, even with the decidedly un-sexy half-tights she'd donned to avoid such an eventuality (Anthony referred to them as "bloomers"). By the time they got to the top, she'd have abrasions, if not open sores. He saw the expression on her face and quickly glanced away.

He knew what was riding on this trip, the investment they'd made, *she'd* made, to ensure it was the vacation of a lifetime. Things had not started well and hadn't improved much since. They weren't bonding, weren't working together to overcome obstacles and annoyances; instead, the two of them took turns getting on each other's nerves.

Gina tried but nothing she said or did seemed to please him. She couldn't fake it, couldn't disguise the fact that she wasn't enjoying herself and regretted leaving home. She wished she could be a tougher, more resilient traveler, but the heat was killing her and, to be perfectly candid, history was never really her thing. At *all*. Running around from ruin to ruin seemed, well, foolish to her—she didn't give a damn about ancient citadels, ancient statues, ancient *anything*. It was old, meticulously preserved, but it was also *dead*, the brittle, dried out remains of a once glorious past.

For God's sake, there were something like six million people living in Athens at the present moment, surely some of them had to be up to something new, original, contemporary and, well, *fun*. Anthony might have been gung-ho to dive headfirst into this classical shit, sifting through the detritus of yesterday, getting his jollies from that, but that didn't mean *she* had to play along.

So far, they'd hardly spent any time doing things Gina enjoyed—and contrary to what Anthony might think, that didn't necessarily mean shopping and eating. Here they were, in this modern, over-flowing city, and their days consisted of gawping at headless sculptures and busted pottery, while paying dearly for the privilege. The Acropolis Museum. The Archaeological Museum. The Cyclades Museum. The Museum of Byzantine and Christian Art. She would've given an eye tooth for a few more hours on the *Plaka*, browsing, letting her mind roam, stopping at an outdoor café for an espresso, perhaps an ouzo on the side. Flirting with a friendly waiter, getting a bit tipsy. Where was the harm in that?

To Anthony, down time was wasted time. He was always in a rush to get somewhere, refusing to chill out, take a few minutes and process the experience. It was like he had some sort of personal checklist he was working his way through.

As soon as they found out about Grandma Clara's bequest, he set to work planning how to spend it. All the places *he* wanted to see. She would've settled for ten days in Cozumel or Hawaii but not Anthony, nossir, he would have none of that.

"Greece is where it all started, sweetheart. The dawn of western civilization. Democracy, philosophy, architecture, you name it." They couldn't do everything, he explained, time and funds were too limited (Clara's gift modest, a kind and unexpected last gesture from a notoriously frugal woman). In other words, there was no possibility of doing cool stuff like visit one of the resort islands—Naxos or Corfu or Santorini. From what she'd read in travel brochures, life on the islands was one non-stop social event, an opportunity to meet people from around the world.

According to Anthony, the islands were expensive and more for tourists than serious travelers (*oh, please*). Anthony wasn't interested in leisure, not when they had only ten days to see as much of the country as logistics allowed. He showed her pictures of some of the places he had in mind and, she had to admit, the scenery looked pretty spectacular. And they'd be part of a guided coach tour once they left Athens, which meant there would be other people to talk to or bitch at, depending on her mood.

To her eternal shame, she'd bought into his pitch, gradually allowing herself to be worn down until he just about dictated the entire itinerary. He bought her off with two days in Paris on the way home but he'd probably find a way of controlling that too.

Which was why she was presently standing on top of the Acropolis, gazing at the big-deal-who-cares Parthenon, wishing she had the nerve to run over and shove Anthony off the sheer face of the bluff to his certain doom.

Head pounding from the sun despite her wide-brimmed hat, sweating like a pig, surrounded by a debris field stretching over a couple of acres. Her face damp, filmy, sunscreen leaking into her eyes, making them sting like a bugger.

Anthony, meanwhile, had attached himself to a tour, people from a Middle Eastern country by the look of them. *They* didn't seem to be suffering from the heat as they made their way around, taking pictures, trailing after their guide like obedient geese. Knowing Anthony, he was waiting for the first opportunity to interrupt and correct the harried, underpaid woman on some trivial point, while displaying his obvious erudition and brilliance.

That was mean.

Mean, but true.

Christ, the sun was unbelievable, inescapable. A physical force, an insistent, pressing hand. There were occasional patches of shade but they barely mitigated its effects. It was pervasive and nothing short of industrial strength air conditioning offered any kind of relief.

Why was she putting herself through this? *I mean, look around*: pillars, worn down by a combination of time and air pollution. A row of statues with their faces eaten off (*ditto*). Much of the Parthenon covered by scaffolding, the umpteenth restoration in its long history, and despite the best efforts of mice and men, the structure was slowly, inexorably, returning to dust.

Anthony was waving for her to join him near a bald promontory, above which dangled, limply, the blue and white flag of Greece. She supposed she'd better go over and make like a dutiful wife, putting on a false show of enthusiasm. Mustn't give him anything to use against her later on.

Except it took such an enormous act of will power to compel herself toward him, energy almost beyond her remaining reserves just to take that first step in his direction…

Athens (II)

Watching her approach, face flushed, red as a boiled beet. Unhappy and not making the slightest attempt to hide it.

Gina, Anthony realized, was not the sort of person who coped well. Life's sudden left turns and unpleasant surprises totally discombobulated her, made her feel like the universe had it in for her personally. Rather than rise to a challenge, she retreated, waving her hands in abject surrender, while uttering a non-stop series of complaints about the unfairness of it all and how none of it was her fault.

Okay, it was hot. There was nothing anybody could do about that. They worked in a school, which meant their holidays came mid-summer. Positively the *worst* time of year to be sightseeing anywhere near the Mediterranean. Sorry, but that's the way the cookie crumbles.

The same thing went for that long layover in Heathrow. Their plane from Toronto was late so they missed their connecting flight, lost half a day of their vacation but, hey, you deal with it and move on. Eight hours of hanging around a huge, modern airport wasn't his idea of nirvana either but even that couldn't spoil the great times awaiting them once their plane finally touched down in Athens.

Gina could've made the experience a lot more enjoyable—at least tolerable—if she had gotten into the spirit of the thing, laughing off their misfortune, going with the flow. But, no, she had to go into her act, giving him the silent treatment, shutting down and shutting *him* out. What the fuck? How was any of it his fault? But that was how she behaved. Hardly spoke five words to him while they cooled their heels, waiting for the next plane.

Who knows what was going through her mind? To him, it was a breath-taking act of petulance and self-absorption. Tuning him out, staring into the middle distance, making like a zombie. He nearly throttled her.

Once they landed in Athens her disposition improved but, truth be told, most of the time he found her more of an anchor than anything, dragging him down, restricting his movements.

For instance, it took *forever* for her to get going in the morning. He'd be up around eight, at the latest, but she'd laze about in bed, then fix herself an intricate breakfast, periodically checking her phone for messages or Facebook posts before sauntering into the bathroom for a shower. Meanwhile, he'd be practically dancing a jig of impatience, thinking about all the places they had on the schedule that day. Alex wasn't any help, popping by every so often with a bowl of fresh fruit or bottle of sweet *retsina*, urging them to live life "the Greek way", which seemed to be a combination of lassitude and hedonism. No wonder the country was in such dire economic straits. The ancient Spartans must be spinning in their graves.

So he'd start the day off fuming and, really, things didn't get much better after that. Gina would usually manage the first museum all right and perk up during lunch, but, then, as he outlined their afternoon schedule, he could sense her fading on him. Jesus, there was so much to see, why was she so stubbornly resisting the opportunity to immerse herself in a culture and society with roots dating back millennia?

"Can't we do something *interesting*?" It was a jibe that always nettled him. It really meant, *can't we do something for* me? She was so childish that way. Refusing to be elevated by her surroundings, the sublime wonder that Greece presented to visitors young and old—how could she be so immune to its manifest charms?

She held out her hand and he helped her up to where he stood on a jutting ledge of stone. "Best view in the city," he told her, waving his arms expansively. "I give it to you, m'lady. An early anniversary present."

Athens spread out around them, a metropolis containing more than a third of the country's population. It was the seat of governance, center of commerce, history, tourism. One of the Eternal Cities of the world. And he was there, in person. It still made him giddy. He turned toward her, smiling, saw her face and blanched.

"If I don't get out of this heat soon, I'm going to kill someone." Meaning him, her bumbling, well-meaning husband of eight years. The two of them marrying, *ahem*, later in life (and feeling the pressure maybe?). So different in many ways but until now they'd sort of muddled their way along, putting up with their partner's idiosyncrasies, trying to stay out of each other's hair, live and let live.

If this trip did turn out to be a disaster—and at present it was touch and go—it would be perceived as *his* fault; of that, he was under no illusions.

He knew for a fact she resented the Greek portion of their excursion. If she was going to spend her dear dead granny's money on a dream vacation, she had other places in mind. Resorts. Sun and fun. Endless food and drink and idiotic exchanges with other *tourista* fuckheads. Jesus, he would've gone out of his mind. Cozumel? Puerto Vallarta? He'd rather be staked to an anthill with his eyelids glued open.

For awhile she had her heart set on a little sports car and when that turned out to be impractical (her favorite model cost three or four times what Clara left her), she was sullen, feeling cheated by circumstance. That's when she decided it might be better to sink the money into a down payment on a house.

The Dufferin Street place had problems, sure, but they'd put a lot of work into upgrades and renos. Not only that, the neighborhood was showing signs of taking off, some gentrification definitely happening, which, naturally, raised the value of their property.

But Gina wanted a *new* house, everything shiny and state of the art. Old character homes were out. He appealed to her reason and, when that failed, showed her the going prices on the kind of places she had in mind. Once again, Clara's small bequest would not make the nut.

He kept pushing the trip, would not take his foot off the gas. This was important, maybe their one chance to expand their horizons, visit locales featuring place names they'd only read about in books.

"How much more time do you need?" Covering a yawn. "I think I've just about had it."

He turned away, pretending to take in the view but, meanwhile, struggling to control his irritation. "We just got here, Em," he said, his voice odd, even to his own ears, "can't you just take it all in, see what's right in front of your eyes?"

"This place hurts my eyes." It sounded like she was climbing down, leaving him. "It's also giving me a headache the size of Ethiopia."

"But…don't you understand…" He sounded doleful, hopeless.

She snorted. "This is nothing more than a glorified rockpile, sweetheart. Now get me out of here before we both die of heat stroke."

Mycenae (I)
(Two days later)

More rubble and wreckage.

Whoopie.

She was looking at a bald plateau of unearthed structures, foundations and partial walls. Unrecognizable as a place where people once lived and loved and served a series of clannish kings including, most famously, Agamemnon, the leader of the Greek forces at Troy. That was as far as her history went. She hadn't read either *The Odyssey* or *The Iliad*; that stuff had always seemed like "guy lit". Books about wars and battles and manly heroes and dates you were supposed to remember.

No, thanks.

Anthony had given her a lecture on Agamemnon during the bus ride down but she barely paid attention. He reminded her of the thin, golden mask of Agamemnon Heinrich Schliemann had discovered—they'd seen it displayed in Athens and she supposed it was his way of tying things together for her. He did love his little connections and historical footnotes.

God, his students must hate him.

The one thing that did stick in her mind was what happened to Agamemnon when he got back from Troy. During his long absence, his wife, Clytemnestra, had taken a lover, Aegisthus, cousin of the king, and upon his return the two of them conspired to murder the tyrant and rule in his stead.

Frankly, Gina's sympathies were with the wife. Agamemnon, the way Anthony described him, sounded like an egotistical, cold-blooded asshole, who got his comeuppance at the hands of a sharp-witted, ambitious woman and her young stud. Good riddance to bad trash. She imagined there wasn't such a thing as divorce court in those days, so you were forced to take other, more extreme methods.

Besides, the creep brought poor Cassandra back with him, spoils of war, his personal concubine and plaything. You don't pull that kind of shit on a queen.

Not only that, *look* at this place. She turned in a complete circle, taking in a panoramic view of the site and surrounding range of low mountains. If some hairy-assed, half-civilized oaf had dragged her away from home and loved ones to this tabletop of land in the middle of fucking nowhere, she would have served him his own balls in a white sauce garnished with locally grown mushrooms and herbs.

"My God," Anthony kept saying, "we're here, honey, we're actually here. Aeschylus's *Oresteia* is set on this spot, right where we're standing."

It took all of Gina's self-control not to explode and start yelling that *here,* hot and bored on this elevated, wind-swept plain, was the last freakin' place she wanted to be. That this had been *his* trip, right from the get go, that she'd had no input on how *her* money was spent, she was basically just along for the ride. She fled from him before she really did lose it and they had another row like they did after they got back from the Parthenon.

That was a brutal one. The combination of the heat and the tension that had been building since the layover in Heathrow caused a meltdown. In some of their exchanges no quarter was given and things were said that couldn't easily be retracted or forgiven. The last straw was when Anthony referred to her as a "cold fish" and she hurled a *Frommer's* guidebook at him, storming out, half-blinded by tears of frustration and fury.

Any intimacy that had existed between them bled out like an arterial wound. They'd barely touched each other since, incidental contact, two bodies brushing past each other in a narrow corridor or sharing space in the small kitchen. There was no kiss-and-make-up-session in the offing, nothing to burst the bubbles of self-protection they'd erected around themselves.

And there was Corinne.

Corinne McBride, part of their Argos Tours group, the bus ride to Mycenae lengthy enough for everyone to chat up the driver and guide and get acquainted with each other. Corinne was the only one in their company traveling alone, the rest were couples. But if she was self-conscious of her status, she never let on, appearing confident, sociable, occasionally prevailing on one of the others to take her picture. "A person gets tired of selfies," she explained, "a little variety is nice."

Corinne was older, early to mid-fifties, but she took care of herself and it showed. Petite and well-toned, with nice, tanned legs, short, stylish hair. Her and Anthony hit it off right away. For most of the trip to Mycenae she sat in the seat opposite them, the pair of them nattering away about Greek drama and all sorts of historical mumbo-jumbo, making little in-jokes and asides. Older women tended to be drawn to Anthony, some sort of mothering complex.

And he was lapping it up, the pompous prick, hardly bothering to include Gina in the conversation, focusing completely on Corinne, both of them talking too much and too loud. It was probably bugging the hell out of everyone else.

She had to admit, Corinne was easy on the eyes. Nice crow's feet and small, white, perfect teeth. She looked like an aging television news anchor, past her prime, but still radiating beauty and allure. She didn't perspire or break wind and once she exited a bathroom stall, it probably smelled like roses.

Gina wondered what it said about her that she half-hoped they'd have some sort of fling, something that would bring this Greek idyll to a speedy and definitive resolution.

Anything to get me out of here.

Anthony posed for a picture inside Agamemnon's tomb,

an immense, circular chamber, cavernous, smoke-stained and empty except for the graffiti left on the walls by generations of visitors. The feeling inside was sepulchral, a secular space that somehow still contained the essence of something unknowable and momentous. The place had incredible acoustics; two German women harmonized an old hymn together, their voices combining to create a melody that was simultaneously uplifting and hair-raising. When they finished, the others present applauded vigorously.

She and Anthony exited the tomb, coming across Corinne, who appeared to have been waiting for them. She held out her smartphone, the latest model, very expensive and compact. She was a curator at a private gallery in Berlin. Apparently, it was a lucrative job. Either that or she had a rich boyfriend with money to burn. Women who looked like she did were never short of paramours and seldom reluctant to refuse whatever gifts were lavished on them.

"Can I get a picture?"

Gina kept right on walking, leaving them to it. Calling over her shoulder that she'd see them back at the bus.

Yanis wanted to know where the others were and how long she thought they'd be. He was their driver and once they reached their destination, his job was finished and it was a matter of either hanging around the bus, killing time, or dozing inside. He pulled a couple of chilled water bottles from a cooler, offering her one.

The central government in Athens actually legislated the price of bottled water so retailers couldn't gouge poor people in such a hot, pitiless climate. Gina thought it was a great idea, especially with the economy over here in such terrible shape. *Everyone* was suffering. Yanis, for instance, was an architect, a man with a university degree, expert training, and yet here he was, conveying foreigners about, eking out a living.

They squeezed in next to each other on the stairs. This side of the bus was shielded from the mid-afternoon sun, a welcome respite. Yanis's English was passable so they made small talk. He wasn't the slightest bit interested in her but she appreciated that he made an effort to appear polite and attentive. He could've taught Anthony a thing or two about simple human civility.

Gradually, the other passengers started trickling back, some appearing winded, the site spread out over rocky terrain, open to the elements. The Jewetts, an Australian couple on their second honeymoon, looked completely fagged out. They were in their seventies and you had to admire how they never shied away from exertion, even in this killing heat.

Forty-five years together and they still appeared madly in love.

How did they manage it?

Anthony and Corinne were among the last to arrive. Their clothes didn't look rumpled and they weren't avoiding eye contact or behaving strangely so Gina assumed they hadn't gotten up to anything. Anthony came and sat with her, but Corinne moved further back into the bus.

A failure of nerve or biding their time?

Gina decided she honestly didn't care.

Mycenae (II)

He'd been doing a slow burn since their huge dust up in Athens. It had dealt a major blow to the atmosphere surrounding the trip, producing a poisonous pall that had yet to dissipate. God knows, he'd tried steering them back on the right path, doing his best to keep the conversational ball rolling, filling in the silence, chipping away at her resentment.

Gina wasn't helping at all. Giving nothing back, either ignoring his comments and gambits or regarding him with a cool, dispassionate gaze. The "mannequin look", he called it.

And, needless to say, she'd turned the sex tap right off. *Tight.* Just to add insult to injury. Not that that had ever been a key component of their relationship but, still, it showed her determination to play the bitch queen to the bitter end.

Why couldn't she let things go? Yeah, they'd had a spat, every couple did, married or unmarried, straight or gay. It was part of the price you paid for sharing up close and personal space with someone for prolonged periods of time. Sooner or later you grated on each other, it was only natural. So you scrapped, had torrid sex and put the sorry episode behind you. That was tradition.

But what Gina was doing went beyond all convention. It showed real malice on her part, amounting to cruel and unusual punishment.

Okay, the "cold fish" comment was a low blow and Anthony had even admitted as much at the time. Once he'd had a chance to cool down.

And she hadn't held back either—calling him a "pretentious twat" wasn't exactly playing by Marquess of Queensberry rules, was it? Hmm?

If theirs had been a healthy, robust relationship, they would have quickly recovered from the imbroglio, treating the incident like the tempest in a teapot it was. Instead, Anthony found himself baffled as to how to proceed. They ate together, shared the same bed, lived side by side, yet for all intents and purposes they might as well have been distant cousins.

How long could this nonsense last?

Until Paris and she finally got her wish, unleashed on its shops and restaurants, practicing her high school French, hanging out with Linda and Wendy, two old friends with similarly insipid tastes?

Christ, he'd go out of his mind.

Mycenae hadn't improved the situation. In retrospect, it was the *last* place he should've taken her. But the tour had been booked months ago, the money paid (transportation, lodging, food). A fairly hefty investment and most of it non-refundable. Were they supposed to just walk away from it?

He could tell from the moment they arrived, the look on her face said it all.

More...fucking...ruins.

And, sure, it was that but so much more, things she either ignored or refused to acknowledge.

For instance, look where it was placed, strategically you couldn't do better. Agamemnon's people knew the importance of a commanding view and from the battlements you would've been able to see for miles in every direction. The passes through the nearby mountains well-guarded, so there was little or no chance of a surprise attack. The castle was even built over a natural spring, which meant its water supply could be guaranteed even in times of drought or when enduring a prolonged siege.

It was rugged, spiny country and no doubt spawned a tough, tribal people. A topography suitable for brigands and rebels, the perfect terrain to seek refuge after raiding and pillaging surrounding domains.

He had tried transmitting or—or infecting Gina with some of his enthusiasm but she shrugged it off. No interest. He couldn't get through to her. He wanted to grab her by the shoulders, shake her, scream at her:

We're in Greece, for fuck's sake! A true cradle of civilization. You're walking the same hallowed ground that once kissed the feet of Aristotle, Euripides, Ptolemy, Homer. The very first versions of the Bible were written in ancient Greek, did you know that? It was the lingua franca *of scholars and kings. If you were of noble blood, it was almost a given that you were fluent at both reading and writing Greek. You're at the heart of the world, honey, and you're acting like you've got a great, big stick up your ass and aren't sure what to do about it.*

This thing with Corinne was also getting to be a bit of a distraction. Okay, make that more than a bit. She was giving off all sorts of vibes and not being too discreet about it either. He was certain Gina's radar, acute and well-maintained, had already picked up on it.

A dalliance of any sort was the last thing he had in mind. It was flattering that she was paying attention to him but, on the other hand, look at everyone else on the tour. They were either geriatric or, in the case of the two Toms (as everyone called them), clearly gay.

Still, there was a moment, at Agamemnon's tomb, when something almost happened between them, slow-burning embers flaring to life.

She *was* good-looking, no question, but she was also single and at her age that was suspicious. How many marriages and how many times around the block? And why no permanent takers?

On the other hand, there were those legs, that ass. She kept herself in good shape and wasn't shy about showing it off. It was difficult not to sneak looks at her thighs, her cleavage, hard to stay focused on her face and what she was saying.

C'mon, Anthony, he kept telling himself, *you're not some stupid fucking schoolboy with a crush. Get over it…*

Gina said Corinne reminded her of a news anchor and he could see that. It was her poise and elegance. She was intelligent and well-spoken too. And she knew how to listen.

Okay, yeah, *definitely* a distraction.

How was he supposed to concentrate on patching up his relationship with his wife when he was also fantasizing about carrying on an affair right under her nose?

This trip was going to take years off the end of his life.

What about the way she looked at me at the tomb? Was I supposed to do something? Did she expect me to sling her over my shoulder, bear her off behind the bushes and screw her senseless? Is that the European way of doing things? If so, then I guess I failed the test. Part of it is that I've never been a ladies' man. Dumpy, tending to baldness from a relatively young age. But I'm a good conversationalist and I know how to fake sincerity with the best of them. At one time Gina was attracted to me—

Gina.

Were they only now finding out they had even less in common than they suspected? Were they discovering that when all was said and done they didn't much like each other? Had they made it past the "seven-year itch" only to rack up on the rocks of year number eight?

Sitting beside her on the sixteen-seat, Mercedes mini-bus as it departed Mycenae, Anthony turned toward her, hoping to draw her attention. Gina was staring straight ahead, ignoring the scenery outside the window. She wasn't aware of his scrutiny and appeared, to his eyes, detached, adrift. Was she puzzling over how to make things right between them? Was she, too, feeling the pain of separation?

What would happen if at that moment he reached over and took her hand…

Epidaurus (I)
(Two days later)

Magnificent.

The amphitheater was well-preserved, to the extent that it was still used as a venue for live performances, attended by thousands of spectators from around the world. Apparently, Tom Hanks and his wife secured front row seats for "Oedipus Rex", presented in its original, ancient Greek dialect.

Unfortunately, their schedule didn't permit he and Gina to enjoy that truly once-in-a-lifetime experience. That would have meant lingering in the vicinity several more days, which wasn't possible, sadly.

Gina certainly wouldn't share that sentiment. As far as she was concerned, Epidaurus was only a slight improvement over the usual fare of "stones and bones". That said, he had to admit she had been unusually attentive as George, their affable guide for this portion of the trip, talked about how the place had initially been a temple of healing, the theater an essential component of the convalescent experience.

Drama therapy.

Much of it was familiar to Anthony, of course, so he moved off, climbing up into the concentric rows of stone seating for a good vantage point. Should he bother with a picture? It would end up resembling a million others but no matter. Sometimes one must bend to tradition.

He could hear George telling the others about the unique acoustics of the place and mentally added, yes, and don't forget to mention Alec Guinness called Epidaurus "the greatest theater in the world". It was certainly true that the sound in this nearly twenty-five hundred year old performing space was nothing less than phenomenal. He was halfway up and George's voice carried clear as a bell. And he could hear people speaking three or four other languages as groups and individuals from various parts of the globe prowled about, exploring the hillside bowl and, yes, taking *a lot* of pictures.

He and Gina were flying out of Athens tomorrow afternoon, off to gay Paree. The situation between them hadn't improved and sex remained off the table, not subject to discussion or persuasion. He couldn't recall the last time they'd embraced or displayed more than a token amount of affection toward one another. This thing was showing definite signs of going completely off the rails.

Who would've imagined that Gina would find Greece so tiresome and dull? It had never once crossed his mind that their dream vacation would turn into a debacle and they would return home, marriage in tatters.

He seated himself on a stone bench—not the most comfortable accommodations, especially if you were watching a three-hour production and not comprehending a single word (even modern

Greeks were stumped, George assured him). He pulled the brim of his Outback hat lower, shielding himself from the sun. They always seemed to be seeing these sites in the white heat of day, why was that?

Since he was taking stock, he had to admit his own culpability in this mess. He'd let his enthusiasm get the better of him. All his life he'd wanted to see Greece, from childhood had fallen in love with the idea of the place. The rivalry between Athens and Sparta, eventually leading to the bitter, ruinous Peloponnesian Wars and the decline of both powers. The love of Paris for Helen and the insidious meddling of various partisan gods. Conflict and heroism and betrayal...he couldn't get enough. One of the first books he could remember enjoying as a child was *The Great Adventurer*, a young adult retelling of the perilous adventures of Odysseus, from the beaches of Troy to his extended voyage back home to his island kingdom of Ithaca.

He reread the book a few years ago and it was pretty terrible. Nonetheless, it was the tome that kindled his love of history, which led to university, a degree, and twenty-one years at Aden Bowman Collegiate, doing his utmost to explain the relevance of the past to roomfuls of brain dead teenagers. Who evinced shock and disbelief when he and Gina revealed their intention to wed. Him and *Ms. Weaver*? The *secretary*?

He had a feeling many of his students—and some of his colleagues—had always assumed he was gay.

Anthony rubbed his forehead, his fingers coming away slick with perspiration and coconut-scented suntan oil.

Fucking heat.

Below, at stage center, various individuals were taking turns standing on a specific spot, marked by a metal disk embedded in the ground, and either clapping or dropping coins, the sound carrying with perfect clarity. But it wasn't enough for one of them to do it, they *all* had to—typical moron tourists. George looking on benignly, waiting for them to have their fun. Sometimes Anthony found it hard to believe he shared the same species with such cretins.

Okay, just for the sake of argument, what would happen if worst came to worst and it really was over and they returned to Canada, called it quits, went their separate ways? Would they continue working at the same school? How reasonable would she be about the division of property and assets? Could they manage the process without turning on each other like a couple of rabid badgers?

He sincerely and honestly believed Gina would be spellbound by Greece, believed it right up to the moment they boarded their plane in Saskatoon. She might have expressed a few mild reservations here and there when he first detailed his plans for the trip, but Anthony couldn't recall her even *once* balking or demurring.

So what the hell happened?

Heathrow was the beginning…or was it? Now he wasn't so sure. Had she been dragging her heels all along, pulling her passive-aggressive shit on him? The ground had shifted beneath his feet, his position seemed precarious, a balancing act he couldn't maintain much longer. A week of being completely estranged from each other, barely communicating. It was getting to him. She was so cold, man, cold as a Saskatchewan winter.

How much longer could it conceivably last?

The members of the Argos group had dispersed, allotted time to wander and ogle their exotic surroundings. There wasn't anything like this back home, was there, folks?

He couldn't see Gina, wondered if she'd left the amphitheater altogether. Which would be par for the course. The last time she posted anything on Facebook, it had been a selfie taken at an Orthodox monastery dating back to the Medieval era. The photo, with an ornate, intricately wrought altar framed behind her, bore the caption: "More old stuff".

He made his way down the wide, carved steps, the *orchestra* area all but empty now, the Attic sun taking its toll on wimpy tourists. He stood a few feet from its center, holding up his phone, trying to compose a shot that would encapsulate the experience for him.

Sensing someone in the vicinity, he turned, and there was Corinne. She looked fresh as a daisy, not so much as a drop of sweat apparent, even on her upper lip. Gina said it was because she was a cyborg. It was one of the few remarks of any note his wife had made in the past three days. Mostly, she communicated through sighs or grunts. It didn't make for scintillating dialogue.

And in the meantime, there was Corinne, their little moment at Agamemnon's tomb not forgotten, still floating in the air between them.

My God, she was attractive and never mind her age. Wearing a thin, sheer blouse, only a camisole underneath. The woman knew how to dress to accentuate her best qualities. His maleness rose to the occasion, responding to her proximity by standing straighter, sucking in his gut, greeting her with what he hoped was a rakish grin. There might have been a murmur of complaint from his conscience but Anthony chose to ignore it.

"Hey there." She paused two steps away, cocked her head playfully.

"Hey there, yourself." He'd lowered the phone, was facing

directly toward her. Not really cognizant of where he was, vaguely irritated by the omnipresent sun but also bewitched by the beauty of the woman in front of him.

No one was nearby, nobody hovering about, eavesdropping, and so for the briefest possible interval he—he *slipped*, lost control, some of that frustration and hunger and thwarted desire leaking out. It was an unforgivable breach of decorum, yet when his mutinous gaze finally made it back to her face, her expression was mocking, amused.

"Do you like what you see?" It was little more than a murmur but the invitation was plainly expressed, like a handwritten card, awaiting an RSVP.

Anthony opened his mouth, not sure what he was going to say, not sure of *anything* any more. He was five thousand miles from home and his entire fucking world was falling apart before his eyes…

Epidaurus (II)

Greece.

If anyone ever mentioned the country in Gina's presence again, she'd scream and froth at the mouth. Let that name become an epithet, a curse word never to be uttered in front of children or delicate company. The ultimate expletive, referring to anything that was *old, past its prime, dull, pointless, obsolete.*

When a friend or acquaintance asked her, and they invariably would, what the best part of her trip to Greece was, she'd tell them: "Leaving!"

She couldn't wait to get to Athens airport, catch that flight to Paris tomorrow night. It was all that was keeping her from tearing out her hair in big hanks; every single minute in this place was torture.

But, she had to concede, even once she got Paris her problems were hardly over. There was still the small matter of her disintegrating marriage.

Basically, they'd hit rock bottom, her and Anthony avoiding each other, refusing to expose themselves to further harm. This trip had been the ultimate test of their union and it had failed, miserably. Instead of bringing them together...well, you never really knew someone until you existed alongside them, 24/7, shared space with them, fought with them and endured all their little foibles and peccadilloes.

Eight years of marriage? But a trifle compared to eight *days* in Europe, living at close quarters. This so-called "vacation" had turned out to be a real education and eye-opener. And an object lesson to mature women everywhere *never* to get hooked up out of loneliness or desperation or because that old biological alarm clock is ringing and there's no one there to switch it off.

Ladies, she would advise them, *if it looks too good to be true, it probably is.*

Gina would never have suspected Anthony as the type of guy with a wandering eye. Matter of fact, he was one of the least sensual men she'd ever met. Not sexually adventurous or kinky, more workmanlike in bed than anything else. Which was all right as far as that kind of thing went—she'd never been that much into it anyway. Sticky, messy and usually unsatisfying, that pretty much summed up the act of intercourse as far as she was concerned.

So his flirtation with Corinne McBride came as a complete

shock to her. She couldn't believe he had it in him. The two of them were getting more and more brazen about it, chatting and interacting whenever they could—on the bus, at meal times, sharing their observations and insights. She was certain at least some of the others in the tour group had taken notice. The Jewetts, the sweet Australian couple, often shared a dining table with them. Vonda Jewett, a saucy septuagenarian who loved her bourbon and Cokes and made some of the others uncomfortable with her raunchy remarks, had pulled her aside last night, all sweetness and concern:

"Keep an eye on that Irish lassie, honey. She's got ants in her pants."

She almost told Vonda the "lassie" was welcome to him.

Besides, wouldn't that simplify things?

Because as it now stood, her marriage to Anthony was toast, unless there was some kind of divine intervention that somehow made things right. Which Gina wasn't banking on, at least at the moment.

It wasn't *just* Greece or Anthony's insufferable personality or this thing he had going with Corinne, it was an accumulation of a thousand small, niggling details that were driving her batty. If they didn't divorce when they returned home she'd probably end up killing him.

Did he *constantly* have to be lecturing her, showing off his knowledge? She supposed it was a teacher thing but that didn't make it go down any easier. This was the first time she'd experienced it full force and it was really wearing on her.

Didn't he ever shut up?

The thing was, in a way she was complicit in her own misery. She could have put her foot down, vetoed this Grecian holiday, but she hadn't. Why? What was it about her that was so accepting, so weak and malleable, that it encouraged others to walk all over her, only pausing to wipe their feet?

Anthony wasn't the first, nor was he, by any standard of measurement, the worst. People, mainly men, were always taking liberties with her. Assuming she was stupid because she was *only* a school secretary, someone who answered phones and took messages, a glorified receptionist. Or she was frigid or nutty or a lesbian because she was unmarried at her age. She probably lived with a bunch of cats and kept a vibrator in her bedside table. Etc. Etc. Etc.

Did she really think Anthony was "the one", her perfect match, the man of her dreams? We're talking about *Anthony Dewar*, longtime social studies teacher, well known stick in the mud, humorless prude, an educator noted for teaching the same courses, using the same test papers, year after year. Hadn't he once confessed to her that his greatest teaching tool was a photocopier?

That Anthony?

But at least he showed an interest. Took the time to joke with her and once or twice remembered her birthday. And then one year, at the annual Freshie Dance, both of them chaperoning, pitching in to help clean up afterward, followed by a drink back at his place…

Six months later, she was walking down the aisle of her Alliance Church, shell-shocked, wondering what the hell was she doing. Her mother chalked it up to nerves but it was more than that. It was her inner Cassandra, warning her of grim times ahead.

Give them both credit, they'd made a go of it for eight years. You couldn't say they didn't try. Sometimes gritting their teeth, pouring an extra glass of wine to rid themselves of a bitter taste that lingered, like old cheese. Biting their tongues until they nearly bled.

There would be good memories, for sure, occasions in his company she really treasured. Not so much this trip and certainly not here, once again exposed to that angry fucking sun, which seemed determined to pursue her around the dry, scorched countryside like one of the Furies.

As soon as she could, she drifted away from the rest of the tour group, feeling bad about missing George's spiel but also anxious to find shade. Another ninety-degree day; she'd be lucky if she didn't come down with malignant melanoma. Divorced and dead within a year and the universe had the last laugh once again.

Christ, talk about taking a turn for the morbid.

It had to be the heat. It short-circuited higher brain functions and turned her into the ditz everyone thought she was. If she could escape the glare, find a cool place to rest, collect her wits, she'd be all right.

After all, this joint was consecrated (or whatever) to the great healer, Asklepios: physician, do thy stuff!

Gina found a spot about two thirds of the way up the bowl. There was some sort of repair or restoration work going on and workers had erected a blue tarp, in the form of a lean-to, so they could complete their tasks out of the skull-melting heat. There were no laborers about and no yellow tape sealing off the area, so presently she was nestling in a slant of shade thrown by the tarp and, she realized later, virtually invisible to most of the other people in the amphitheater.

Not a big crowd, the early afternoon sun undoubtedly part of it. She couldn't understand how the locals endured it, day in and day out. It was *unrelenting*. There were hot days back home but the sun closer to the equator was different, more intense;

now she knew what ants felt like when a magnifying glass was trained on them.

Gina tugged a water bottle out of a mesh sleeve on her backpack. Earlier, she'd dropped in a couple of sodium tablets, to aid hydration. God bless Sophie for recommending them to her. The tablets sweetened the water. It was warm but tasted good. She had a long drink, then resleeved the container.

She spotted Anthony's green Australian hat from where she was sitting. He *loved* that hat. Sent away for it, paid by VISA. The purchase showed up on their credit card bill: nearly a hundred and fifty bucks. Distinctive and ridiculous on his melon-like head. There was no such thing as a hat that looked good on him. He somehow defeated them all.

And looky-looky, observe who else was present and closing in for the kill. Ms. Corinne McBride. Slutty McSlutface. Dressed as provocatively as ever. Bitch ought to sell advertising space on her ass. Probably used a trowel to apply her makeup and a sandblaster to remove it.

Gina was perched forty or fifty yards above them, a prime viewing position. All that was missing was a Chorus, to provide commentary. Maybe a laugh track might be appropriate, as well.

Anthony wasn't aware of Corinne yet. He was trying to take a picture, which was inevitably a long, drawn out process because, for Anthony, it had to be the absolutely *perfect* snapshot to meet his exacting standards. Corinne was preening, arranging her body into a pleasing configuration, waiting for Anthony to notice her.

Finally, he did, executing a kind of double take, the hand with his phone dropping to his side, perfect picture suddenly forgotten.

"Hey there."

The acoustics were as good as advertised. She could hear every syllable, like they were standing a few feet from her. In the old days, Anthony told her, actors used to have to speak through masks, so the sound quality had to be amazing in order for the audience in the upper decks to follow what was happening.

"Hey there, yourself."

Their body language said it all. They looked like they couldn't wait to get their hands on each other.

Gina sat, immobile, still as the dead stone beneath her. Waiting for what happened next, knowing she was powerless, a prisoner of fate, which, after all, the Greeks had practically invented.

"Do you like what you see?"

There was a pause, the slightest hesitation, while his resolve and sacred vows put up a token resistance.

Then he fell, all the way.

"Yes," he replied, his voice husky, "and I think I'd like to see more."

The Grey Men

*F*iat lux!
Easier said than done. A hangover, lethal as the sword of Damocles, dangled over his head, suspended by a single hair. His stomach gurgled and *blooped*, making its displeasure felt. If he so much as twitched there might be dire consequences. Best to lie here awhile, totally immobile, allowing his system to continue processing the toxins he had spent most of the previous evening pouring down his throat.

C'mon, Reaper Man, up and at 'em...

His eyes snapped open, the hangover briefly receding from awareness. *What? Where the hell did* that *come from?* No one had called him that since...well, a long time.

There was a water glass on the nightstand. Empty. Not even a drop in the bottom.

If there were any poison left in his kit, he would have taken it. Anything to negate his pounding head and rising nausea.

But now, at least, he was upright and ambulatory, moving toward the bathroom, putting one foot ahead of the other, letting gravity and momentum do the rest. If he could only manage to disgorge the corrosive contents of his stomach, somehow rid himself of the giant water buffalo rampaging around his skull, he *might* be able to pull himself together in time to make his flight.

It wasn't going to be easy...

It was Henry Anthony Thorburn who emerged from #451 less than an hour later. Good ol' Hank Thorburn who plucked the "Do Not Disturb" sign off the door handle, flipping it back inside. His stay over, the room barely marked by his passing. Ready for the next anonymous traveler in search of a warm, clean place to lay their head.

Paid with cash, making sure he got a printed receipt. The bean counters very particular, almost obsessive. It wasn't advisable to get on their wrong side. A short cab ride to the airport and never mind quizzing anyone about his appearance. The cabbie, the gal back at the hotel, even the effeminate security guy checking his boarding pass would never come to a consensus about it. Ditto his seatmate, who spent nearly *two hours* next to Henry Thorburn and, if queried, could provide only a brief, unhelpful description of his fellow traveler.

It was no trick. Some people have that kind of face. A gift, of sorts. They move through the rest of us, stealthy, noiseless, practically invisible. Conducting their business, pursuing their mysterious agendas and no one the wiser.

The ultimate camouflage.

Often the best disguise is no disguise at all.

Now his name was Paul David Unger. Same face. Same man. Keeping up?

He had a lovely wife, Denise, and an adult daughter, Wendy, who, due to a run of bad luck with men, harbored more than her fair share of resentment toward anyone of the male persuasion. Including, it seemed, her father. *Especially* him. Apparently one of her therapists had informed her that the emotional remoteness and lack of affection she'd experienced as a young, impressionable girl was to blame for her romantic woes.

If only he'd hugged her more, her life would be completely different. She'd be a better, more confident and centered person. Happily married, with 2.5 children, a hefty mortgage and a family dog.

Currently she was living on the west coast, over fifteen hundred miles away.

"You're too far away to hug," he joked the last time they'd spoken.

"Sometimes, dad, I wonder if it's far enough…"

She could be cruel like that.

He was a teacher, but due to health problems, could only work part time.

It was hypertension or, at least, that was the cover story. He had letters from several doctors, including a well-known cardiologist, detailing the condition, sounding very authoritative and convincing, but it was all bogus. Sometimes he even went to the extent of holding his breath for lengthy periods of time so his wife or friends would see him red-faced, florid, and he'd confess to feeling dizzy and would have to sit down while everyone present crowded around, expressing concern. It made him feel somewhat guilty because his "spells" worried Denise sick, but they were necessary for maintaining the subterfuge. It meant a drastically curtailed work schedule, basically showing up a couple of mornings a week at an elementary school library. His duties mainly consisting of helping kids find resources for class projects and keeping the noise down to a reasonable level.

The head librarian appreciated his calm, gentle demeanor, the soothing effect he had on students, especially the little ones.

It was unfortunate his illness limited his capacity to teach and influence children.

The man was a natural and a credit to the profession.

Denise, his wife of more than twenty years, was an ambitious, intelligent woman, with a Ph.D in Structural Engineering (McGill University, Class of '89). She jetted about the country—and sometimes beyond—taking care of the problems architects created with their grandiose visions and blissful lack of concern for practical considerations. Like allowing for proper drainage or creating sightlines at sporting venues or factoring in a human component to interlocking blocks of luxury condos. She was well-respected in her profession and had helped identify and correct many design flaws and technical oversights, saving developers and contractors millions.

The long intervals away from home suited his clandestine activities but it definitely put strains on their marriage. The emotional remoteness his daughter alluded to could also be extended to Denise. They were a devoted couple but hardly demonstrative. Hugs definitely *not* the order of the day.

But they persevered and had promised each other a Christmas vacation on Maui this year, the perfect opportunity to re-kindle the flame.

Except that was still over eight months away...

No family in the city and only a few close friends, mostly hers. Was that deliberate too?

The so-called "surveillance state" made things more complicated but his employers were powerful and resourceful people. He never had any security hassles at airports or train stations, treated as just another bland, white businessman doing the bidding of his corporate masters.

Safe.

No existing footage of him anywhere.

But he always left his mark.

The Bureau Noir.

One of a myriad of Special Access programs.

Black ops.

Off the books.

Unlimited funding, inconceivably powerful, no oversight.

Officially, it didn't exist.

Which meant, of course, neither did he.

There was goofy stuff too. Myths that had developed, little codes and signals. Like how, among themselves, they were "VIs".

Vee eyes?

Yeah. You know: *vindices injurarian.*

Come again?

Avengers of wrongs. Get it?

Each of them granted a territory or jurisdiction over which he or she had complete autonomy. There were no overlaps or disputed ground. There had been misunderstandings in the past, near catastrophes. These days, conflicts were settled with a phone call or text.

The Director rarely involved.
Plausible deniability.

Methods might vary but VIs were expected to be prompt, professional and mercilessly efficient. They invariably lived up to their billing.

The man sometimes known as Paul Unger favored a technique perfected by the Bulgarian secret police. Poison secreted in the tip of a cane or umbrella. A quick, seemingly inadvertent jab, followed by a muttered apology from a distracted businessman, nose buried in the financial pages. Rubbing the area of your calf or thigh affected, a tingling sensation where, undoubtedly, a bruise was already forming, cursing the stupid accountant or flack, then almost immediately forgetting about it, an act of willful amnesia that would eventually cost you your life.

So what were the criteria? What sort of crime or wrongdoing made you eligible for "special treatment"? Who made the assessment, the call? Who took Paul Unger away from his ordinary, strait-laced existence and turned him into an avenging angel?

No comment?

Sometimes he suspected it was PTSD. All at once he'd start shaking. And he'd get terrible chills too, as if his core, the very center of his being, had turned to ice. Nightmares of waking up and finding people standing over the bed, two men, one in the process of subduing or throttling Denise.

He knew he should report it, was required to report it.

He didn't.

Instead, he drank.

No one had ever explained the Bureau's retirement plan.

He took that as a hint.

Sunday. Somewhere on the outskirts of Detroit.

Nagging head cold, chest congestion. Unproductive cough. Another ugly hangover.

It was getting to be a habit.

Finish the job, then back home to Denise. Oh, wait, she was on her way to Dubai—

"*Ow*! Watch that thing, will you? *Shit*, man, you really clipped me…"

"Sorry about that, wasn't paying attention..."

Was the affair inevitable or was that merely hindsight?

She was unhappy and certainly made no attempt to hide it from him. They kept separate lives and certainly there was ample opportunity for her to stray. Had there been hints, clues? The prolonged silences, lack of intimacy, icy civility. He hadn't been very attentive, that was one of her chief complaints against him.

She chose to break the news with an old-fashioned card, leaving it on the dining room table, his name printed on the envelope. So quaint.

"*One of us has to start telling the truth…*"

The truth being the last thing he could confide to her.

The NDAs he'd signed were adamant on that point.

The card didn't say where she was staying but he found out

anyway. Had a pal at the Bureau hack her phone records (one of the perqs of working for a super-secret, ultra-powerful agency with its hooks in everything).

He soon had all he needed, including a street address. Hell, within a matter of hours he was strolling up the sidewalk and knocking on the front door of their cozy, little love nest.

And of course they let him in. What was there to be afraid of? Such a small, rumpled, sad-looking man.

Shifting his umbrella from hand to hand. Containing a special, fast-acting dose he'd whipped up for the occasion.

Her lover hoped everything could be settled in a calm, civilized manner.

It was.

He called it in himself. Explained what he'd done to the remote operator, rang off once he'd provided the salient details.

He considered making a break for it, using his training and know-how to escape their net. Obviously, he wouldn't be the first to fly the coop. Instead, he walked out of the duplex and into the nearest bar, ordering an expensive, single malt scotch, starting a tab.

The place was practically empty, mid-afternoon on a weekday. The regular crowd not due for several hours, at least.

He figured he had some time to kill, but was only on his third drink when someone pushed through the door behind him. Without turning around, he raised a glass of Scotland's finest in mock salute.

"Welcome, O Reaper Man. So glad you could join me..."

The barman watched the two of them exchange a few words, then the scotch drinker settled his bill, adding a generous tip.

They left together and later, even when pressed on the point, the bartender was insistent: the smaller guy went along willingly. There was no sign of force or coercion.

Matter of fact, they acted like they knew each other, and he recalled thinking at the time they seemed like a couple of old college pals, meeting up again after a long estrangement, happy to be reunited and planning a night on the town.

Coping

"—and so, to make a long story short, in the space of six months I went from drinking *Laphroaig* out of solid crystal tumblers, to sharing a jug of cheap wine with some bums behind Kentucky Fried Chicken." Fred delivers the line with the faultless timing and stage presence of a second-rate comedian. And why not? He's probably performed this routine dozens of times over the years, hopefully to larger and more appreciative audiences than this.

Bernie glances right and left. From his position near the back he can make out the entire company, at present numbering nine people, including Fred. There are a couple of obvious juicers, a shaky-looking meth-head, as well as three or four others who, bless them, appear to be solid, upstanding citizens. Well, addiction plays no favorites.

He's thankful the room is well-ventilated. Lately he's become overly sensitive to smells and keeps forgetting to ask someone if it's yet another manifestation of drying out. No doubt a few of these folks would be able to give him the lowdown. What to expect next, now that the good ol' shakes and midnight sweats seem to be done with him (knock wood).

Not for the first time Bernie wonders if he's doing himself any favors attending these meetings. At least this one's located midtown, the Third Avenue United Church only a ten-minute walk from his workplace. But regardless of the setting and a rotating cast of characters, there are always certain commonalities: the same lousy coffee and stale doughnuts, the same stories endlessly recycled and repeated. He'd caught Fred's act a couple times previously and recognizes his standard set list; Bernie knows it pretty much word for word. You'd think the guy would have the decency to come up with some fresh material now and then.

He catches Joanne's eye, pulls a face but she gives him nothing back, the vixen. Still nursing a grudge. They'd hooked up when he first joined the program, two shipwrecked passengers temporarily sharing a life raft, clinging to one another for warmth and comfort. Those scenarios hardly ever play out well and this was no exception.

Wow, if looks could kill. Clearly she isn't willing to let bygones be bygones. Painting him as the bad guy when she was equally in the wrong. What's that saying: it takes two to tango. So deal with it, sweetheart. Don't play the innocent with me. I know every weird kink and convolution of that junkie mind of yours…

Fred finally finishes, acknowledging the tepid applause with raised hands. He'll be three years sober next month, but God knows how many people he's driven back to the bottle with his inane rap. Completely oblivious of his status as world-class bore and blowhard. Beaming at them as he shares one last nugget of wisdom: "I lost everything I had to drinking, but I also found peace through the grace and forgiveness of my Lord and redeemer, Jesus Christ, which means I still came out ahead in the end. I am washed and cleansed by the blood of the Lamb. Amen to that and may God bless you and deliver you from the temptations of evil."

What a doofus. His wife walked out on him, leaving him flat broke, kids are estranged, his entire world in ruins but, hey, he's got his faith to keep him warm at night. Talk about pathetic.

Dorothy, who drew the short straw after Kurt was a no-show today, looks set to wrap things up a few minutes early. Unlike Kurt, who's a real stickler for routine. It's a noon hour meeting so maybe somebody else has booked the space after them. She casts a cursory eye about the room, seeking any takers, and is about to dismiss them when one of the "normals" rises and asks permission to speak.

Bernie nearly groans, picturing the rest of his lunch hour going up in a puff of smoke.

Serves you right, he thinks, you made the choice to come, now you're going to sit here like a good boy and take your medicine.

Sobriety comes with a price tag, asshole.

Time to ante up...

Bernie is genuinely surprised when Joanne approaches him outside the church. She appears shaken; he suspects they all do.

"That was...unexpected." She gazes at him, foxy brown eyes that never fail to provoke libidinous thoughts.

Easy, boy, he tells himself. Don't want to open that can of worms again.

Or do I?

At that moment, they come out: Dave, who's just gotten over *shattering* everyone present, and Clio, who hadn't spoken, not a word, merely clutched his hand throughout his testimonial. The two of them blinking owlishly in the sunlight, then making their way down the steps and crossing the street, heading for the parking lot. Bernie and Joanne follow their progress. The couple seem unaware of their immediate surroundings, leaning on each other for mutual support. Sharing the weight of the world.

"They stuck it out," he murmurs.

"*What*?" Joanne nudges him. "What did you say?"

"They stayed together." Bernie motions toward them. "Even afterward. That's amazing, don't you think? How they managed…"

"How she forgave him, you mean."

He shakes his head. "Not just her. He had to forgive himself too. Had to come to terms with it, in his own mind. Otherwise how could he go on?"

"Telling yourself you were drunk doesn't cut it." Taking a breath, releasing it. "You and I both know that."

"It's no excuse," he agrees. "I'll bet it's the first thing he thinks about when he wakes up every day, the poor fucker. Killing your own daughter. Getting in that car, backing up, hardly knowing what he was doing—"

"That awful *bump*, the way he described it…" Joanne shivers.

"You wouldn't be the same again. How could you? It would be too fucking horrible."

"Or maybe you would. You saw them, they seemed—"

"No," Bernie insists, "they've learned to live with it, like we all do. This counsellor I was seeing told me we never really get over anything, we just find ways of carrying it, bearing the load. I think there's some truth to that."

She's staring at the sidewalk, her straight, dark hair loose, concealing most of her face. Pondering her own lapses, toting up the cost of her weaknesses. The steep price she's paid for wonky brain chemistry.

At that moment she's vulnerable and Bernie knows he could initiate something if he wanted. Invite her out for coffee, pretending it's nothing more than a bit of harmless chit-chat. That's how they got involved in the first place. She's mostly a good person, reasonably intelligent and thoughtful. Except she has huge personal issues to deal with, stuff dating back to childhood. Therapy and abstinence help, although every so often she still has a tendency to throw caution to the wind, just going for it and fuck the consequences. Which makes her rowdy and high-spirited, but also kind of scary too. Once she gets going, there's no "Off" switch to Joanne. Just wind her up, stand back and watch the fun.

She hasn't looked up. Waiting for him to say something, wondering if he's feeling as lonely and fragile as she is. Willing to forget about the fucking Twelve Steps and higher powers and green coins and sobriety pledges, and instead give in to weakness and despair, breaking all the rules for a few exhilarating hours.

And, at the same time, probably hoping he'll be strong enough for both of them and with one noble, selfless act of denial, save them from the worst of each other.

More Real Than TV

My agent, the venerable Ignatius Guilders Farben, was not a man who minced words, so when he called and gave me the old good-news-bad-news routine, I did my best to steel myself for whatever was coming.

Iggy was pushing a hundred but still a force to be reckoned with. His sole concession to age was that he mostly worked from home, texting and video messaging his clients, stroking their egos or kicking ass, as the situation required. His turtle-like visage blinked at me from my laptop which, in computer years, was practically as old as he was.

"Well, dear boy, I'm afraid the network has decided to pass on the pilot. Nothing to do with you this time, the show didn't test well. The demographics were wrong or some such thing. Although what the demographics of a program about competing panhandlers might be is rather moot, in my opinion."

I was gritting my teeth, bearing down hard. If I wasn't careful I'd crack another crown. "Shit, Iggy, I really busted my hump for that show. I'm not saying 'Battling Bums' was fucking Ibsen but, seriously, I totally created my character. I came up with a backstory as long as *Crime and Punishment.* I had this arc I was gonna develop and—"

"Totally out of our hands, I'm afraid." He sipped from a strategically placed martini glass. It was ten o'clock in the morning on the coast but when you're approaching the century mark who's going to begrudge you your little affectations.

"And I stuck to our deal, kept my mouth shut, no fucking around—"

He raised a skinny, spotted hand. "I know, I heard the reports. By all accounts your behavior and attitude were exemplary and that, of course, bodes well for our relationship as well as future job prospects."

He almost dumped me after the "Ship of Fools" debacle. We were only two days out of Long Beach when I slugged the sound guy because I was seasick, not to mention lethally hung over, and thought he dissed me. It turned out I was mistaken but that, as they say, was that.

Had I deliberately sabotaged myself? From the beginning, I hated the concept of the show, hated the notion of being stuck at sea for weeks at a time with a horde of hormonally unbalanced airheads who were supposed to somehow band together and sail an ocean liner halfway around the world with little or no outside assistance. Once the captain and skeleton crew got us to international waters, they climbed aboard an Airbus passenger helicopter, waved "Cheerio, bye" and were speedily transported back to shore.

So there I was, stranded with a bunch of Brads and Emmas and Noahs, average age nineteen years old, about a thousand working brain cells between them, no one with the slightest idea of how to pilot or navigate a vessel the size of three fucking football fields. After the first day the novelty wore thin and most of us got bored, paired off and snuck away to fuck and/or consume whatever illicit substances we'd managed to smuggle aboard.

The producer harangued us, pleaded with us, cursed us, while his young, beautiful P.A. and the lighting guy basically eloped, joining the revelers, the project collapsing within a span of about seventy-two hours.

Looking on the bright side, at least we didn't sink the boat.

"You said there was good news," I prodded him.

"A new gig," he confirmed, rubbing his hands together like the true capitalist he was. "Still a bit rough around the edges but already in the pipeline. It's cheap to shoot and topical as hell. You're just about guaranteed a slot since I happen to know some of the parties involved."

"And you're saying these are quality people, not fly-by-nighters?"

"I get the feeling they're desperate. They've been knocking on doors, pitching like crazy, trying to make something stick, and somehow they got the right word in the right ear and this one looks like it's going to be green-lighted. They'll shoot it quick and dirty, limited series, fast turnaround time. What's not to like?"

I leaned forward, my face likely overflowing his screen. "Tell me more…"

At first, I wasn't impressed.

"The People Next Door" seemed like tepid fare, pretty standard as far as these things go.

Three separate families embedded in a racially homogenous neighborhood right in the heart of some small, midwestern city, hidden cameras, discreet microphones and stealth drones capturing what happened next.

One family, the Meyers, were Jewish, the Dennisons were African-American and my bunch, the Castles, were whitebread but hiding dire secrets, most of them centered around their troubled son, Dexter (played by you know who).

I flew out to meet the producers, a pair of go-getters belonging to an outfit aptly named Small Fry Productions.

"We're hoping for fireworks," Karen Singleton told me. "We want to see what happens when we introduce a little diversity into an ordinary, middle class environment. All of a sudden there are colored faces walking their streets or people who worship a different god. And then there's you, I mean *Dexter*, representing randomness and chaos, stirring things up. You're our ace in the hole; when things seem a little boring or stale, you up the ante, so to speak."

Not to blow my own horn but I had really fleshed Dexter out, drawing up a detailed biography, suggesting ways my character could add excitement by indulging in the occasional bit of nefarious fun, mayhem and disorder. I got Iggy to pass my ideas on to the production team and they loved them, incorporating much of my material into the series "bible". Not sure what the rest of the cast thought about my input but, then again, fuck them.

"The way I understand it," her co-producer Albert Griswald ventured, "your guy is your classic sociopathic narcissist with, like, zero conscience or sense of right and wrong. A complete fucking whack job." Tapping his pen on the blank notepad in front of him.

"Right, right." Grinning at them, totally in Dexter mode, my eyes sparkling with malign glee. I could tell they were impressed. "I'm one of those dudes who downloads recipes for pipe bombs and toys with rightwing extremism. I fantasize about taking a semi-automatic rifle to a playground or synagogue and *brrrrrup!* mowing motherfuckers down for my fifteen minutes of fame."

They were nodding right along, totally in tune with me. Karen looked like she was about to dry hump me, swear to God. "In a way, we see our show as a microcosm of contemporary America, the good, the bad and the ugly."

"The melting pot, bubbling over, leaving this huge mess." Griswald, trying to be clever. "In terms of casting, we already have your parents and the Jewish family signed. But…the others…" He cleared his throat, glancing at Karen.

"We're having trouble finding the right combination. We're looking for average, fairly well off, assimilated Black people. Quite passive, amiable, non-threatening. We don't want them too confident or cocky or else the audience will have a harder time sympathizing with them."

"Fresh Prince, rather than Malcolm X," I chimed in helpfully and they practically hugged me.

"Yes! Yes! Exactly!" Karen crowed. "We want them to react but we don't want militants. They can't be scary or aggressive. The people playing the Meyers are so sweet, they wouldn't raise a hand to anyone, even to defend themselves. The girl we cast as their daughter is gentle as a butterfly. She writes *poetry*, for God's sake. A little wisp of a thing."

"The viewers will love her," Griswold agreed.

"And they'll hate any creep who tries to hurt or sully her," I said, slipping them another feral grin.

They liked that, laughing, high-fiving me.

"Once we get set up and the cameras start rolling, we'll rely on you to keep us on pins and needles. Within reason, of course," Griswald added, "we don't want things getting *too*, ah, excessive or out of control, do we?"

"Of course not," I concurred, brushing off his concerns with a casual wave. "Only, there's a fine line sometimes, isn't there?"

There wasn't much time or money for rehearsals so I only met my fellow cast members on two occasions, basically just get-acquainted sessions. Everything was improvised so there were no scripts to learn and because of the hidden cameras, very little blocking. Real seat-of-the-pants stuff.

The people playing my "parents", Stuart and Irene Castle, were a couple of non-entities whose only previous experience in front of a camera was in infomercials. They had some stage training but, y'know, BFD. No presence or charisma so I hoped that meant more screen time for Dexter. Daddy was supposed to be a deeply closeted homosexual, while wifey was a lonely, forgotten woman who took various medications which rendered her complacent and addle-brained. Yawn-worthy stuff, nothing new or newsworthy. Bit players, and rightfully so.

Our target neighborhood was called Fairview, for absolutely no reason I could ascertain. Dull and sedate, everyone conforming to norms, at least while in public. What happened behind closed doors was another thing.

My folks were supposedly recently retired, looking for a fresh start. Unfortunately, they had to cope with their ne'er do well son and "troubles" they were reluctant to talk about. Dexter was allegedly preparing to start university in the fall, staying at home to save money.

The Dennisons and Meyers lived a few streets from us, easy walking distance. They moved in the same day so I made a point of wandering by for a quick reconnoiter.

The casting people had done a better job with them: the Meyers, Harold and Lillian, chattered incessantly and fussed over their belongings as the movers trudged back and forth from the truck to their small bungalow. The deal with them was he'd had a long career in academia which ended in scandal when he impregnated one of his graduate students. Lillian tried to forgive his indiscretion but the wound went deep, testing her faith to its limit.

Nancy, their sixteen-year-old daughter, was a real cutie and our producers were right to draw attention to her fragility; she appeared as vulnerable as a wounded sparrow and I knew I could really play with that. She seemed so insubstantial and ethereal I was surprised she had the strength to grip a pen.

The Dennisons looked like a family of nerds and had already gained a certain amount of familiarity with each other, enough to seem believable, though none of them were, in fact, related. There were two children, Charlie, thirteen, and Tamara, eleven, veteran thespians with credits from a variety of cable shows and low-budget movies. They bickered convincingly while I looked on in approval. I wasn't the only bystander, there were neighbors stationed in their yards or on the sidewalk, peering through parted curtains; the Dennisons' arrival drawing extra scrutiny. Theirs' the only dark faces for miles around and we all knew it.

I sauntered back to my house, pausing occasionally to break some fence boards with a few well-aimed kicks. Setting the tone for things to come. I banged open the front door, slouched through the living room without sparing a glance at my parents. Sullen and uncouth, not giving one shit for anybody or any*thing*.

Dexter had arrived.

They deliberately didn't tell us where the cameras had been secreted, which was all right with me. It would help us focus on staying in character—you never knew when you were "on". Keeping it real, keeping it *raw*. That was the pitch and that was what we were shooting for.

I constantly found excuses to clash with my parents, creating angry scenes out of the smallest, most trivial incidents. It wasn't long before an atmosphere of hostility and recrimination set in. I exasperated and annoyed them, at least some of their frustration unfeigned and authentic.

I hoped Albert and Karen were getting good stuff.

It became a regular occurrence for me to stomp into my bedroom, shouting and swearing, slamming the door behind me. Later, once it was dark enough, I'd slip out the window to flit through the neighborhood, seeing what trouble I could cause. I egged houses, turned outside water taps on, sprayed graffiti on fences and garages, all the while debating the best way of engaging with my co-stars.

Gayle Dennison rarely left their house, whether naturally reclusive or spooked by her monochromatic surroundings, I couldn't say. Earl, her husband, was more gregarious, shepherding the kids around town, taking them to the park and swimming pool, doing most of the shopping. He seemed very attentive, very credible, playing the role of father to the hilt. Sometimes I'd spy on them through their side windows, certain that, somewhere, a camera was watching *me* watching *them*.

Clearly, I was one spooky bastard, up to no good.

The Meyers were working hard to fit in, just another all-American family, right down to the flag that flew a few feet from their front door. Cheerful, friendly, greeting their neighbors warmly, inviting them over for drinks and barbecues, laying it on thick. Nancy's bedroom was on the second floor so there was no easy way to shinny up and peep in on her. I had to settle for occasional glimpses of her in the back yard, slumped in a lawn chair, writing in a small journal or notebook. I'd walk down the back alley behind their house while she, for her part, pretended not to see me. No doubt intrigued by the attentions of an older boy but too insecure and timid to do anything about it.

She was going to be a cinch.

I just had to find the right way in.

I "happened" to come across her in the library, though of course I'd trailed her there. I could tell she felt at home surrounded by books and although I wasn't much of a reader tried not to hold that against her.

I paused by her table, waited until she looked up and acknowledged me.

"You do anything except read?"

She blushed, which made her appear even *more* sweet and innocent. Either she was a better actress than I was or she was easily twigged. She shrugged, that was it for a response. The weak, silent type.

"We're practically neighbors, y'know." She kept her eyes on the page in front of her. "You hear what I'm saying?"

"I've seen you. Around." She glanced up, met my eyes without flinching.

"Hey, it's not like I'm stalking you or anything…" She blushed again. Jesus, she was good. "What you reading?"

She showed me the book. "Poetry. Mary Oliver. I *love* her."

"You some kinda lesbian?" Nancy Meyer gaped at me. "Well, you just said you *loved* her."

She frowned. "You know what I mean."

"You shouldn't mumble," I informed her, "it's really annoying to other people." Pulling out a chair, I straddled it, getting comfortable. "I've got perfect hearing and it's still hard for me to catch what you're saying."

"What are you doing here?" Her eyes were brown, maybe hazel is the right word. Clear skin, nice hair, a beauty if she'd only try harder.

"Talking to you."

She almost smiled. "That's not what I meant." Indicating our surroundings. "Here. In the library."

"You saying I'm illiterate?" Pretending to bristle.

"No, of course not, I—"

"'O, that this too too solid flesh would melt, Thaw and resolve itself into a dew! Or that the Everlasting had not fix'd His canon 'gainst self-slaughter! O God! God! How weary, stale, flat and unprofitable, Seem to me all the uses of this world! Fie on't! ah fie! 'tis an unweeded garden, That grows to seed; things rank and gross in nature Possess it merely. That it should come to this! But two months dead: nay, not so much, not two: So excellent a king; that was, to this, Hyperion to a satyr; so loving to my mother That he might not beteem the winds of heaven Visit her face too roughly. Heaven and earth! Must I remember?'" And I kept going, right to the end of the soliloquy, verbatim and note perfect. I'd memorized the speech a few years ago, when I still dreamed of a serious acting career. Before reality set in and blew those dreams away like dry chaff.

She seemed genuinely astonished. "How—where—"

"That's enough for today." I levered myself to my feet, replaced the chair. Fixed her with a hard glare. "Maybe that'll teach you not to label people before you really know them."

I bounced back and forth between the Dennisons and Meyers, lurking, eavesdropping, trying to keep tabs on them, their habits and routines. I was also getting acquainted with the neighborhood, poking around, seeking opportunities. I continued committing acts of vandalism and once stole a couple of expensive bicycles from a few blocks away and left them carelessly lying on the grass in the Dennisons' front yard.

Everyone knows that crime inevitably follows once the wrong types start moving in. It was a bit of a hard sell since the family were such a decent bunch, neat and courteous and friendly.

Still, you can't top race when it comes to sowing division and, sure enough, the bikes were soon discovered, accusations leveled, hard feelings exposed. Later that night, I broke two windows of the house where the bike owners lived. Payback is a bitch.

The next morning there was a police car parked in front of the Dennison's abode.

Perfect.

My parents pretended to wise up, confronting me about my midnight rambles, demanding a full accounting of my activities. I was unapologetic, rebellious. Soon, we were screaming at each other, the two of them practically frothing at the mouth.

Great TV.

You're welcome, Small Fry Productions.

"Hi, Mr. Dennison. I'm Dexter Castle, I live a few blocks from here. Having trouble with that?"

Earl Dennison straightened, taking a break from cranking the lawnmower I'd tampered with during one of my nocturnal excursions. He looked hot and grouchy. "What can I do for you, Dexter?"

"I was wondering if you needed any help with yard work. I'm home for the summer and hoping to make a little money. Like they say, no job's too small so, y'know, if anything comes to mind..."

He thrust his jaw toward the recalcitrant machine. "Think you can do something to get this brute going? I'm just about to give up on it."

"Maybe…" I sounded doubtful. "I could give it a try. D'you have any tools?"

Ten minutes later I was puttering around the yard, cutting long swathes through the grass while he observed, hands on his hips. Then I went with him to pick up some potting soil and fertilizer, toting it to their backyard garden.

Afterward, he toasted me with a Heineken. "You were great today, kid, a real godsend. Any time you want to come by and help out, I'd appreciate it."

"Will do, sir. I start university in late August but I'll be around 'til then." Taking a few sips of his sour, European beer. I was a Coors guy but I put up with it for the sake of staying in his good graces.

"What will you be taking?" I stared at him. "At university."

"Oh, political science, maybe. Or psychology." I raised my shoulders. "I haven't settled on which one."

"Those are smart courses, important to know that stuff."

"Yes, sir."

He scratched his head. "I…don't suppose you happen to know anyone locally who babysits, do you?" Glancing toward the house. "I think it would be good for my wife and I to get out more but we're worried about leaving the kids alone. I don't know if you've heard…" Eyeing me.

"Heard what, sir?"

"Ah, leave it for now. Just ask around, will you?"

"As a matter of fact, I happen have my Red Cross child care certificate. First aid and everything. I've seen your kids playing in the yard, I don't think they'd be any bother."

He nodded, trying not to smile. Knowing what I was up to. "Thanks. Maybe we'll take you up on that…"

While the Meyers were at a movie, I broke into their house. It was a quick reconnaissance, a snooping mission. I went into Nancy's room, found her journal, paged through it. Most of it soppy girl stuff but there were a couple of steamy episodes where she recorded some erotic dreams, one involving me. I found her mother's vibrator and scrolled through her father's emails.

Playing to the hidden cameras.

God, people were gonna hate me.

The Meyers were being pestered by someone who left unsigned notes in their mailbox, anti-Semitic slurs, veiled threats, poorly spelled but clear in intent. Then the packages started arriving, Nazi paraphernalia, even a copy of *Mein Kampf*. I noticed they didn't seem to be interacting as much with their neighbors. Eventually they had proximity lights installed over their garage and in their backyard. Then a private security truck showed up and wired the place from top to bottom. They weren't taking any chances.

The people on the Dennison's block were being driven to distraction by a series of thefts and break-ins. Home security companies were doing good business on their street, as well. Whenever I saw Gayle and Earl, they looked harried, nervous; the kids stuck close to the house, never going anywhere without at least one adult accompanying them.

One day as I was trimming bushes at the back Earl admitted that they'd found a disturbing letter wedged in their door. It was composed of words and letters cut from newspapers and magazines and basically said unless they vacated their house and moved elsewhere, bad things would happen.

"These people are cowards, Dexter. Crackers who smile on the outside but secretly hate our guts."

"I'm sorry this happened to you," I said. "I wish we could find out who left that message."

One thing I know for sure, I thought, walking home that same afternoon, *it definitely wasn't me.*

I had to be more cautious. Everyone in the area was on high alert, vigilant for any occurrence out of the ordinary. There were more dogs, lights, CCTV, and the police had stepped up their patrols. I did what I could, maiming a few cats with a slingshot, stealing, general mischief-making and high jinks. I don't know how much of it was caught on camera but, one way or another, my efforts would have the desired effect of ratcheting up tensions, while pointing a giant spotlight at the new arrivals.

I kept running into Nancy, usually on purpose. The library

was always a safe bet and I got the feeling she was spending more time there because she knew it was the logical place to find her. Making it easy for me, clever girl.

We talked about books and movies, our families, keeping our voices low, which meant we had to sit in close proximity to each other. Soon we were so chummy our knees frequently brushed under the table.

"I should probably tell you something," I said, during one of those intimate *tete a tetes*. She cocked her head: puzzled, intrigued. "I'm not a good person. What I mean to say is, I do really rotten stuff for no reason. It's not safe to be around me. For you. For anyone." She stared at me, trying to gauge my seriousness. "You definitely shouldn't ever be alone with me."

"Are you mad, bad and dangerous to know?" She was teasing me, paying no heed to the warning. Seeing my confusion, she clarified: "You know, like Lord Byron?"

She was too cute.

I kissed her. She gave as good as she got.

"Just promise you won't hurt me," she breathed.

I said nothing. Tired of lying, already pondering where I'd take it from there.

"These people," Earl Dennison growled. "These goddamn people…" He shook his head, his irritation evident. We were standing in his driveway, looking at the damage to his car. Long scratches from the front fender to the trunk, on both sides. The defacement even worse in the bright light of day. "Why would someone do that? Where does it get them?" He gave the nearest tire a desultory kick.

Stay in character, I thought, *let more of your anger show, really play it up.*

He told how the neighbors were giving his family the cold shoulder, even the kids shunned when they went out anywhere. "And there was another fucking letter, can you believe it? Assholes misspelled every single word except 'nigger'. At least they got that one right."

We moved to his back yard, where we spent long moments examining a low, white fence with a number of boards either missing or broken. More of my doing, I'm afraid. "Can you believe this shit, Dexter?" Pointing. "What did that fence do to anybody? Whoever does something like that is a fucking savage, plain and simple."

"I'm really sorry about all this, sir. It makes me sick thinking about it. Your family—"

"I practically have to drag my wife out of the house these days, and we don't let our kids wander around unsupervised. How can we when it's pretty obvious people have it in for us."

"Sir, I—"

"I told you, Dexter, call me Earl." I nodded sheepishly. "You're about the closest thing to a friend we've got in this shithole." He spat for emphasis. "Only one with a lick of decency."

"Thanks, uh, Earl."

"Gayle claims she heard someone in our yard last night. She got up to look but didn't see anything. Should've hauled my lazy ass out of bed and seen for myself. Maybe I could've caught whoever keyed our car."

"Might have been dangerous to confront them."

"Fuck that. I'm not afraid of any peckerwood with a

screwdriver. Fuck 'em. I'd hand them their ass they tried to pull anything." Lowering his voice. "She thinks someone's been in the house. I told her she's crazy, nothing's missing or moved around, but now I'm not so sure. Somebody's trying to mess with our heads, that much is clear."

"D'you think this is, y'know, a race thing?" He stared at me. "I guess what I'm trying to say—"

"We're just like everybody else, Dexter. We don't try to stand out or ask for special treatment. But some people can't get over their prejudice and there's nothing anybody can do about it."

"Maybe in time, once they get used to you—"

Shaking his head again. "As far as that argument goes, I'd say history isn't on your side. This country was built on slavery and genocide. That isn't gonna change, now or two hundred years from now. The only animal I know that's color blind is a goddamn dog." He put his hand on my shoulder. "Sorry to be so blunt but that's the reality we have to deal with, day in and day out. There's still good people out there, people like you." He dropped his hand. "I just wish they'd make themselves heard more often."

It was a good speech, just the right amount of anger and disillusionment.

I could tell he'd been working on it for awhile.

I set fire to a backyard storage shed and left one of Charlie Dennison's *Nike* sneakers on the scene (Gayle was right, I *had* been inside their house). Planted some gas-soaked rags next to their garage, which was maybe a case of overkill but I'd leave that up to our viewers to decide.

Intercepted Nancy on the way back from the library and tried to arrange a midnight rendezvous. Promised booze and weed but she wasn't as enthusiastic as I hoped. I slipped an arm around her, urging her to join me for an erotic assignation, letting my hand slide down until it cupped her shapely bottom. She brushed it away, glancing around to make sure no one had seen, walking faster now, trying to put some distance between us.

"I won't beg you," I called after her. "You want to hook up, I'll be waiting."

Once she got to her front door she paused, looked back at me. I stood at the gate, not smiling or frowning, keeping my face blank so she could read into it whatever she liked.

The police were back at the Dennisons. Two cars, four cops.

Their neighbors made excuses to be outside, pretending to weed or trim and not doing a very convincing job of it. But if they expected drama and fireworks, they were disappointed. The policemen came out, but no one was in handcuffs, being quick marched to the car for arrest and processing. There were murmurs of anger and dismay. Someone shouted at the cops as they drove away. Something about getting their own brand of justice.

The front door to the Dennisons was closed, triple-locked.

Thanks to me, they were under siege, pariahs, a family of troublemakers.

Exactly where I wanted them.

Right around then I got a phone call from Karen Singleton, our producer. It had been decided ahead of time that contact between cast and crew would be kept to an absolute minimum. No interference, the various scenarios playing out organically, very little structure or planning, trying to be as naturalistic as possible.

But Karen expressed reservations regarding some of my unorthodox tactics. Like hurting animals and burning down garden sheds.

"We're worried that matters could get...out of hand," she explained, "We can't determine if the Dennisons are in actual danger or if it's all just, pardon the pun, white noise. We don't want anyone getting injured, as I'm sure you understand."

I curtly informed her that as far as I was concerned, the suspense was building nicely and if her camera people were on the ball, they should be getting some dynamite footage.

"Oh, we're pleased with what we're seeing. We already started showing people some of the footage and the feedback has been great." Whispering confidentially. "I've heard the Grunge Network has expressed an interest. And they're affiliated with Crave... or maybe it's Amazon Prime." But then she started acting all squeamish again, fretting that I was "preying" on Nancy and possibly traumatizing the Dennison brats.

"Nothing to be done about it," I snapped. "To find the edge you gotta get right up close to it. Close as you dare."

"Are you still in character?" she marveled.

"Maybe," I barked, vibrating with anger at the nosy cow. "Now fuck off so I can get back to making this show a hit."

I switched off, then slammed the cell phone down on the countertop over and over, shattering its case, exposing its innards. A gesture of frustration and defiance.

"The People Next Door" was going to break new ground and gain a wide audience, no matter how hard they tried to neuter it, water it down.

Things were coming to a head, like a great, big, angry boil.

All I had to do was apply a bit more pressure.

Nancy snuck out to meet me. Impetuous girl, ignoring all my warnings.

We walked to the nearest park, climbed onto the swings, dragging our toes in the dirt, flirting with each other.

I got her stoned, a little drunk on a flask of gin I'd brought along for the occasion.

"I don't know why you bother with me," she confessed.

I grabbed one of her chains, pulled her closer, stuck my tongue in her mouth. Things got pretty hot and heavy after that. I had my hand inside her blouse and likely could've gotten further.

I wondered what viewers would make of our shenanigans. By now, they'd expect the worst from me but what about Nancy? Would something like that make them turn on her or would they be more forgiving, seeing her as a mere pawn in my sick game?

She told me she was falling in love with me and I pretended not to hear.

The plot was convoluted enough without throwing that particular spice into the mix.

The neighbors circulated a petition and a quartet of the braver ones paraded up to the Dennisons' front door to hand it to them in person. Numerous harsh words were exchanged and someone shoved Earl. He didn't like that. He ducked back inside, returned brandishing a bat. They dispersed, hurling insults at him, nasty slurs and epithets. Luckily, no one produced a gun.

Intense stuff. Better than anything I could've expected.

Nancy sightings became rare. She even stopped going to the library.

Was it something I'd done? I had to know and, anyway, home security systems were mostly shit; even if I tripped some alarm I'd likely have plenty of time to make my getaway.

Her diary entries were confused. I read them out loud for the benefit of the microphones. Like all of us, she was contractually obligated to waive any notion of privacy. She liked me but wondered at my motives. She thought things were moving too fast but also speculated what losing her virginity would feel like.

I masturbated between the pages, left the soiled journal under her pillow.

Too much?

My parents grounded me, can you believe it? Fed up with my attitude, wishing to impose some kind of control over my aberrant behavior and reckless disregard for others.

I pretended to absolutely lose it, telling them to fuck off and threatening to burn the house down around them as they slept. Dear old, queer dad looked shaken and mother junkie locked herself in the bathroom with her pills, wailing that I was a demon from hell and she was ashamed to have given me life.

A great performance, though a bit on the hammy side.

I was furious at being upstaged and stormed out of the house, vowing to make them pay for their treachery.

Someone fired a shot through the Dennisons' living room window, narrowly missing young Charlie as he struggled to wrap the last stage of *Fallout 4*. Within minutes, their street was swarming with cop cars and emergency vehicles. The incident made the news, the first serious act of violence in the neighborhood in living memory.

I finally caught Nancy in her back yard, luring her into the gap between her house and the one adjoining. There, I roughly fondled her and when she protested, covered her mouth with mine, aggressively tongueing her until she gagged. Then I seized a fistful of her hair and whispered filthy propositions into her ear, telling her in graphic detail what I was going to do and promising it would happen soon.

An ambulance took her away the following morning. She'd ingested half the medicine cabinet, or so they claimed. A cry for help that was bound to resonate with viewers. Provoked by my dastardly assault, the psychological equivalent of Munch's "Scream".

I recognized a true master at work.

Nancy was going to be star some day, I was certain of it.

I kept myself apart from the rabble watching the guys reloading the Dennisons' moving van.

"Good riddance!" Some creep hollered.

I did my best to look downcast when the family came out and trudged toward their vehicle. Earl gave the crowd the finger, which didn't go over well. They backed out of the driveway and as they passed me, Earl offered a laconic wave, while Gayle and the kids stared straight ahead, doing their best to ignore the jeers and catcalls.

Lift a few rocks, it's amazing what crawls out.

The movers looked nervous, quickening their pace…

When I walked into the kitchen, Karen Singleton and Albert Griswald were seated at the table, their expressions forbidding. There was no sign of Stuart and Irene Castle, and the atmosphere was decidedly chilly.

"Kid," Griswald announced, his voice hoarse, "it's a wrap. I don't know what we've got or what it amounts to, but this has gone far enough. I have no idea if we're civilly or criminally liable—Jesus, we don't even know if we're allowed to air half the shit you pulled." He gripped his thinning hair. "I just…I have no idea what got into you, what possessed you to—to—"

Then Karen took over. "Look, we realize you were granted a certain amount of latitude but, my God, couldn't you have shown a little restraint? Nancy's going to be fine, fortunately, and the little colored kid, well, he just wants to know if there's going to be a sequel. But the point is why and—and *how* everything went so wrong. What the fuck happened?" They both feasted on me with their eyes, waiting for…what? An explanation? Validation?

I crossed my arms, glared back at them. "Iggy told me you were serious people."

"We love Iggy," Karen gushed.

"Iggy's the *best*," Griswald confirmed, "practically a living god."

"Didn't he tell you what to expect? With me?" They looked at each other, at a loss. "I don't believe in holding anything back. I am completely invested in my role. It's all about making good

TV, the kind that keeps the proles watching, night after night. The real thing, as authentic and believable as life. It gets messy, it gets crazy, but it's *always* compelling, you can't take your eyes off the screen. That's what it's about, boys and girls. Putting asses into seats. It's been like that since Shakespeare, since…shit…" I raised my arms. "Since we first started figuring out we like being entertained."

"Okay," Karen muttered, "fine. It's just that…" She looked up at me, her expression beseeching, searching for something only I could give her.

"What?" I asked. "What? *What*?"

Albert Griswald finally said it: "Where…do we go from here?"

I gave them my best Dexter smile, the leer of a higher order predator showing its teeth as it closes in for the kill.

They gazed at me, astonished, baffled. And then, all at once, *they* were grinning too, smelling the blood and exposed entrails, eager to claim their fair share.

Anchorite

The first one is a loony. Total whack job.

Rings the doorbell and right away starts babbling about ley lines and planetary alignments, everything explained by a crude chart he holds up for my perusal. And all the while keeping his eyes cast down because he's afraid of being "blinded by immanence" or something like that. It's hard to make out what he's saying because he's weeping, practically vibrating from a combination of fear and excitement. The guy won't be talked down or dissuaded. Eventually, he wanders off, pausing every once in awhile to shout and point at the house.

Weird.

But the word must be out because another one shows up later that same day, an old man who won't approach the door. Content to stand at the end of the walk, bracing himself on a cane when the arthritis in his hip gets too bad. He's there until dark. And then he's gone.

More appear as the week progresses; most content to remain bystanders, others bolder. There are all kinds of places on the internet. Conspiracy theorists and cultists and folks who believe the apocalypse is set for a week from Thursday.

A particularly awkward moment when a woman thrusts out an infant, shouting: "Heal him! Don't let him die!" Closing the door but she won't stop screaming. I rush out to calm her, trying to keep things from getting out of hand. And the whole time it's "my baby, my baby", the neighbors looking on in frank disapproval.

It gets worse. A steady stream of people arriving, knocking at all hours. The congestion creating a parking and traffic nightmare. It's a quiet neighborhood and residents start making their displeasure known.

The police and authorities are, predictably, completely unhelpful. Initially dubious, suspecting some kind of publicity stunt. But they make a token effort, find the sites in question. Someone alerts the media, which means *more* unwanted attention, phone calls, requests for interviews. The situation only exacerbated when the Pope becomes involved, issuing a statement denouncing superstition and idolatry.

Uniformed officers are stationed around the clock, an attempt to keep the growing throng under control. Weapons have been seized, along with extremist literature and bizarre religious tracts. The situation quickly deteriorating.

Late one night, someone breaks through the cordon. Pressing his face to the door, whimpering: "*Libera me, Domine*" and, as he is being dragged away, howling: "*Miserere mei, Deus!*"

Living like a prisoner now, unable to venture outside or peer from a window. And day and night, 24/7, serenaded by a continual soundtrack of prayers and hymns. Someone even sets up a loudspeaker that plays amplified recordings of rabbits being slaughtered and children crying—o, pity the suffering children.

Switch off the phone, turn out the lights, sit in the dark. They'll weary of this eventually, go back to their homes. Give them nothing to encourage their simple credulity.

Alone and besieged. Resigned and dangerously bored.

Reorganizing the cupboards and bookshelves, performing a thousand small chores. Playing endless games of solitaire and, naturally, winning every single time.

The Toxic Cinema of Alain Marchant

Excerpted and translated from the official program accompanying the
Alain Marchant Retrospective, *Festival du Cinema Internationale,*
Montreal, QC (2017)

At one point during his infamous 2014 appearance on the CBC arts program "Q", director and *enfant terrible* Alain Marchant set his sights squarely on English Canadian films, asserting: "You see our (Quebecois) cinema and we have directors like Denis Villeneuve, Xavier Dolan, Jean-Marc Vallée and myself. And, historically, I think of some of the people who inspired us: Denys Arcand, Claude Jutra and, especially in my case, Jean-Claude Lauzon. Okay? But you look elsewhere in this great, white north and what do you have? American knock-offs and 'Men With Brooms'. C'est comme ça. Dreadfully sorry, old chap, but it's true."

When guest host Larry (now "Laura") Grotowski protested the slight against Anglophone movies, interjecting names like Cronenberg, Haggis and Egoyan into the discussion, Marchant backed down, slightly, admitting that he very much admired the oeuvre of Manitoba *auteur* Guy Maddin. But he couldn't resist adding fuel to the fire by mischievously adding: "Of course, with a name like *Guy*, he'd have to be part French, don't you think?"

Unfortunately for Marchant, his inflammatory statements and provocations often overshadow (*a la* Lars Von Trier) an interesting and uniquely personal filmography, threatening to do real damage to an artistic trajectory that has been, by turns, brilliant, maddening and incomprehensible.

He refers to his first efforts, short subjects shot in or near his home in Laval, as "tests".

"Séduction" (2004) is off-putting, to say the least. Eighteen minutes long, it appears to depict sexual congress between two minors, while the girl's parents are watching inane TV programming upstairs. The footage is grainy, underlit, filmed with a cheap DV camera. As the teenagers couple, a popular song by Quebec chanteuse Bisou-Bisou plays in the background, the track looped so the three-minute tune repeats itself over and over, an unsettling and annoying accompaniment to a reluctant and inexpert deflowering.

"160" (2005) was, apparently, some sort of perverse *homage* to Marchant's hero, Jean-Claude Lauzon,* but many missed the intended tribute. The title alludes to the section of the Canadian Criminal Code relating to bestiality. The "plot" concerns the frantic attempts by a man (played by Marchant and shown only from behind or in profile) to gain sexual satisfaction *via* intercourse with a menagerie of creatures, before determining an elephant would make the ultimate partner. The denouement is messy and meant to be comic (I think). It doesn't quite get there.

"Pilote dimanche" (*Sunday Driver*), made that same year, begins innocuously enough with a man (Marchant) getting dressed, taking meticulous care with his appearance and deportment, straightening his tie and buffing his shoes. Humming tunelessly,

---

* Jean-Claude Lauzon (1953-97) Director of "Leolo" and "Un zoo la nuit" (*Night Zoo*), his life tragically cut short by a helicopter mishap while scouting locations for a movie project.

he collects his car keys, lovingly strokes the cat on the way out and then proceeds to ram or run over any pedestrians and cyclists he finds alone or in isolated circumstances. We don't see the actual collisions, but Marchant makes sure we *hear* them, sickening impacts and fleshy explosions. Definitely not for the squeamish and, indeed, "Pilote dimanche" was refused space in a number of competitions and film festivals—Marchant savagely denounced the "moral and aesthetic cowardice" of festival organizers and used the resulting press to great advantage.*

Indeed, the attention garnered by "Pilote dimanche" enabled Marchant to secure funding for his first full-length effort, the predictably controversial "J'adore le FLQ" (*I Love the FLQ*). Released in 2007, the film created a political and cultural firestorm. First of all, the notion of staging a recreation of one of Canada's darkest periods as a sunny, Busby Berkeley-esque musical was strange enough, but Marchant added insult to injury by concocting scenes guaranteed to offend: a young terrorist cooing a love song to his automatic weapon, growing increasingly aroused as he strips it down and gently lubricates it…and having kidnap victim Pierre Laporte engage in a long, slow, sensuous tango with one of his captors just before he is murdered.

"J'adore le FLQ" was vilified in many quarters and denounced on the floor of the House of Commons, but it also turned out to be a surprise hit at the box office in Quebec and France, even earning two Genie nominations (for editing and best score, winning

---

* Despite his fierce defense of "Pilote dimanche", I think it telling that it's one of the few Marchant-helmed projects not currently available to cineastes—I saw a bootleg of a bootleg a few years ago and that was bad enough. On a big screen, it would have been *excruciating.*

neither). While some wags opined that Marchant had likely shot his last foot of film in this country, they should have known better. The young maverick announced at a press conference in February, 2008 that his next project would be an adaptation of William Pierce's *Turner Diaries*, an infamously vile polemic that climaxes with a race war, a determined cadre of heroes bent on destroying or enslaving inferior breeds like Jews and blacks and imposing white rule in America. But the event turned out to be another one of Marchant's notorious stunts—he had never, in fact, read the book, let alone secured rights to it. Was it an anti-Semitic jab, as some have contended (one of his main detractors in the Quebec media happens to be of Jewish descent)? Marchant denied it, adding: "Why confine yourself to hating just one race when our entire species is beneath contempt?"*

The next few years were busy ones for Marchant: he assisted his partner, artist Francine Lefebvre, with a multi-media installation on the "historic crimes of the Catholic Church" (quoting from the catalog), an exhibit which had, as its centerpiece, a life-sized, latex model of a priest in full regalia, seated in a mockup of a confessional, cradling a bloody beef heart in his hands (the heart was replaced every day with a fresh organ). Marchant's lectures** on contemporary cinema at McGill University were well-attended and he also contributed a regular pop culture and current affairs column to *Le Devoir* (a stint that came to an end after a physical confrontation with the newspaper's features editor, a skirmish that landed Marchant an overnight stay in jail and hefty fine).

Meanwhile, he tried to keep a hand in the film world by

---

* From an interview in *Maclean's* magazine (April, 2008)
** Collected and published as *Bullshit et la bile* (Phaedra Press; 2012)

directing music videos by Roch Voisine and Arcade Fire,* as well as co-producing a mockumentary series (with CBC Radio-Canada), "Un monde meilleur" (*A Better World*), an alternate history scenario in which the French won the battle for the Plains of Abraham and went on to forge a sovereign nation out of what was formerly known as Lower Canada. Quebec separatist leader Jacques Parizeau had high praise for the four-part docudrama and was quoted as saying "Un monde meilleur" was "the dream denied us because we allowed certain unnamed people to keep us from becoming great" (he later complained the quote was taken out of context).

In early 2011, it was announced that funding had been secured for Marchant's second feature film, an adaptation of a novella by obscure French writer (of Corsican descent) Bernard Vezanny, titled *La bite de Napoléon* (*Napoleon's Cock*). Dubbed by Marchant "a multi-generational portrayal of prurience and pornography", the production was long and fraught, numerous producers coming on board and just as quickly abandoning ship. The deliberately loose narrative following its own odd chronology as it traced ownership of Napoleon's stolen, mummified penis for the past two hundred years, a variety of historical characters seeking to possess (or destroy) the Little Corporal's withered, desiccated phallus.

Finally released in the fall of 2013, "La bite de Napoléon" failed to connect with audiences, even hardcore fans of the director finding little to like in the three-hour (+) film.

---

* In an interview published in Rolling Stone (#1099), front man Win Butler referred to Marchant as "one weird, twisted motherfucker".

Which brings us to "The Peloponnese", Alain Marchant's latest effort, his first offering since "Napoleon".

I can personally attest to the fact that the book the film is based on, Robert Francis Lafferty's *Greek Idle,* was required reading for many Canadian university students in the 1970s and 80s. Originally written in 1964, the short novel describes a debauched trip to the Greek islands by a disgraced academic, Charles Coughlin, and his young lover (and ex-student, their relationship the central reason for his suspension and dismissal) Jocelyn Strauss.

The heat of the affair is cooling but neither has the courage to admit as much. They resort to cruel games and sexual domination, goading and taunting each other, constantly raising the stakes. Enter Andro, a young fisherman. The couple deliberately befriend him and, during a boating trip to a nearby island, an austere, stony tooth of rock, Jocelyn either seduces the lad or pretends to. The point is that *something* happens between them, Coughlin senses it, and all at once the "game" is taken to another level. Tragedy, as they say, soon follows.

Due to budgetary limitations, shooting "The Peloponnese" in Greece was out of the question and in an interview with *Sight and Sound,** Marchant insisted that it was never his intention to film on location. "One island is like any other," he sniffed. "To me, I can't tell them apart and I'm smarter than most movie audiences." He selected a suitably wild and remote islet in the St. Lawrence, just off the Gaspé Peninsula, and set to work on his "erotic masterpiece".

Casting child star Luci Lavalle as the free-spirited but

---

* Summer, 2016 issue

troubled Jocelyn was bound to raise hackles—after all, everyone in the province of Quebec watched her growing up on various popular TV series and variety shows. Marchant has her parading around naked throughout most of the film and the sex scenes between her and her much older co-star Thierry Meursault are so close and intimate, at times it's hard not to look away. By the end, Lavalle appears shell-shocked and one wonders, after what she's been through, if it's merely acting.

After watching "The Peloponnese" earlier this week, I decided to dig out and re-read my battered copy of Lafferty's "classic".

The book is terrible, long-winded and thoroughly infatuated with itself. Coughlin is a repulsive character, clearly based on Lafferty himself. In fact, I did some checking and discovered that the book was inspired by an alcohol-fueled junket Lafferty and fellow Canadian scribbler Thomas Flett took to Greece in 1962. Both applied for grants to work on books neither intended to write and agreed that if either of them got money, the excursion was on. An all-expense paid piss-up, Canadian taxpayers stuck with the bar tab.

Lafferty received a grant, Flett didn't...and never completed anything else of note. Exit Flett from the Canadian literary scene, forever.* But he was a boon companion on the Greek trip, later claiming he'd suggested some of the terminology for the male

---

* Except for one rather notorious (possibly apocryphal) incident in the late 1960s at a writers' workshop in Fort San, Saskatchewan, when an inebriated Flett allegedly propositioned a young poet named Margaret Atwood, earning a stiff knee in the balls in response. I contacted Ms. Atwood's representatives for her version of events but have yet to receive a reply

and female sex organs Lafferty ended up employing (my personal favorite: "the raised horn of his taut, tumescent prick plunged and gored into her, pinning her to the mattress").

There is a lot of purple prose, overblown passages and, frankly, godawful writing to be found throughout *Greek Idle* (the title itself a rather weak pun). *This* book made it on to my college CanLit syllabus? Yes, and Earle Birney's "David" used to be considered a highwater mark in terms of Canadian poetry and "Don Messer's Jubilee" the epitome of what it meant to be a Canuck.

Thankfully, times changed and for the past decade or so if you wanted to find a volume by two-time Governor-General Award nominee R.F. Lafferty, you'd have to either try the library or go to Abebooks.com. His works mostly out of print, rightfully relegated to the scrapheap of history.

But now Alain Marchant has dug up and dusted off a scribe best left forgotten and might just, ye gads, help rescue him from oblivion. A Canadian publisher recently announced *Greek Idle* will be re-issued with a new introduction and an academic press is commissioning a collection of critical writings. It seems like a reappraisal of Lafferty might be in progress.

And so, the *enfant terrible* has done it again. Released a film bound to draw yet more controversy and debate while, at the same time, resurrecting the literary legacy of—let's not mince words—a hack, drunkard and misogynist, a mere blip on our cultural radar, a blight on our national literature.

Can't you hear Alain Marchant laughing?

Don't you know when you've just been *had*?

Family Day

The second Tuesday of each month was "Family Day", which meant five percent off at every store in Kingsmere Mall, plus there were all sorts of freebies, door prizes, even live music if that was your thing.

Carrie often used the occasion as an excuse to pile everyone into her road-weary Saturn and tootle over to the mall, getting out of the house for a few hours, escaping its depressing atmosphere.

Tonight, there was some kind of old-timey bluegrass band playing on the makeshift stage across from the food court. The guy on dobro, seventy if he was a day, caught Carrie's eye and winked. Sassy old dude in a brown leather cowboy vest. Carrie stood off to the side, swaying her shoulders, tapping her foot. It was the kind of stuff her father used to enjoy, music she always pretended to hate just to get on his nerves.

Trevor was tugging on her arm and Misty looked like she'd rather be dangling over the lip of an active volcano. She was that age, thirteen going on thirty, with everything all figured out. Cindy, at least, seemed to be enjoying herself, holding Carrie's hand and sucking her thumb. A dead ringer for Kurt, right down to his pug nose and electric blue eyes.

"Mummy, let's *gooooo*," Trevor whined. It was a technique he'd perfected almost from the moment he'd started talking. Again, taking after Kurt. Always bored, never satisfied, forever wanting *more*. And after awhile who could keep up with that? Who could meet those standards day after day, while at the same time putting food on the table and maintaining a roof over their heads? The world whipping past at a hundred miles an hour and no one pulling over and offering directions or asking if you needed help.

She wanted to linger there awhile. Her father had been gone nearly five years and this music brought him back to her like a whiff of his favourite cologne. A flawed man but hardly deserving of the holy hell she'd given him throughout her adolescence. The look of bafflement and dismay on his sun-burned face when he learned of her latest escapade. Yet he never once raised a hand to her, a testament to his tolerance and patience.

Misty was her penance. A child completely lacking impulse control, possessing a bravado and devil may care mentality that absolutely terrified Carrie. She was so brazen and daring, heedless of the consequences of her actions. After one recent blow-up involving a boy, a young *man* five years older than her, Carrie had sat her down and given her a graphic, no holds barred version of the "facts of life", but her daughter wasn't having any of it.

"Who are *you* to lecture me?" Misty asked, pushing away from the table and rising. "It's not like you ever listened to anybody."

How could she argue with that?

If it was just her and Cindy it would have been all right. They could hang out awhile, maybe dance a little. She knew this song, it was one her father's favorites. She sang along, softly:

"In the pines, in the pines
 Where the sun don't ever shine
 And you shiver the whole day through…"

Carrie closed her eyes. Trevor was practically yanking her arm out of its socket and Misty was giving off solid waves of disgust and contempt, but for just a few more seconds Carrie didn't allow herself to care.

She made them wait until the song concluded, a scattering of listeners seated in the adjacent food court, most of them seniors, offering tepid applause. The band took a bow and Carrie saw that one of them was hooked up to an oxygen tank and moved with great difficulty. He patted the dobro player's arm affectionately as they shared a private joke.

"I'm getting a *Matt Mason*!" Trevor gushed. "Either that or *Star Wars* Lego," he amended, meanwhile loping alongside the shopping cart, his head on a constant swivel as they made their way down the aisle. Cindy was secured in the front basket of the cart, her feet fed through obliging slots; she was gnawing her favourite chew toy, a green rubber ring that looked like it had been attacked by a pack of feral *dachshunds*. She was teething again, apple-cheeked and sore-gummed but endlessly cheerful. So easy to please.

She inherited that *from me.*

Misty was determined not to play the game tonight, Carrie could see that right away. She seemed oblivious to everything: the store, her family, the universe itself. Inhabiting her own bubble of reality and selfishly withholding it (and herself) from everyone around her. The girl didn't seem to care about *anything*. It had been like that before Kurt left, but the situation had definitely deteriorated since he had taken his freeloading ass further down the road. The times she'd secretly read her daughter's phone messages or lurked on her Facebook page, learning more about Misty from social media than she'd cared to, always regretting her eavesdropping afterward, swearing she wouldn't do it again.

Sometimes it was better not to know.

"What're you gettin', Missy?" His sibling ignored him.

"Answer him," Carrie commanded.

"A *douche* for my—"

"What?" Cocking his head, puzzled.

Carrie glared at her oldest daughter, who met her gaze defiantly, holding it until it was beyond insolent. Carrie wanted to backhand her. Again.

But Trevor had caught sight of the toy department and was off at a gallop. Cindy twisted around, enviously following his progress.

"Matt Mason" turned out to be an action figure, a space toy that came with a variety of accessories, including helmet, oxygen tank and wheeled lunar rover. Carrie checked the price: thirty-four bucks.

Misty still wasn't playing, yawning into her hand, acting like she was about to drop dead from sheer boredom any minute.

"Choose something," Carrie told her, sounding sharpish. Seemed like the only way she communicated with the kid was through barked commands, ultimatums and threats. Trying to get her to clean her room or contribute to the housework or treat the rest of them with a modicum of respect.

At first it looked like Misty was going to defy her. But then she seemed to reconsider, probably deciding her act of rebellion wasn't worth the hassle it would bring down on her. She drifted off, returning a short time later with a box of latex contraceptives (Extra Large), which she gleefully added to the cart.

"What's that?" Trevor asked.

"Vitamins," Carrie replied through gritted teeth and Misty yelped with mirth.

Carrie selected a big rubber ball for Cindy, a purple one the toddler was barely able to hold. Pressing her face into the pliable surface, trying in vain to bite it.

For herself, Carrie rarely chose anything of a personal nature. Usually it was a household object, something practical, and tonight was no exception.

"Here's what *I'm* taking," she announced, hefting the box into the cart, wedging it in place. "You know what this is?" she asked Trevor, who shook his head. "A dehumidifier. You know how smelly the basement is, how damp it gets sometimes? This baby will take care of that."

Now they were approaching the front of the store, where the checkout counters were. Time to wrap things up.

Carrie gingerly coaxed the purple ball out of Cindy's hands, handing her the rubber ring to placate her. Trevor was staring at his action figure, his expression conflicted. He looked up at Carrie, *almost* saying it, *almost* asking the forbidden question: *can I have it?*

Finally, surprisingly, it was Misty who moved toward him, giving him a playful nudge. "It's just a game, dummy," she explained again, "not for keeps."

At last he nodded, relinquishing the toy and taking his place beside Carrie, the expression on his face heart-breaking.

Good boy.

They left the cart where it was, their selections still inside, and walked out of the store. Carrie was holding Cindy in one arm, Trevor grasping her free hand. Misty, as usual, lagged behind. They were nearly at the car when she heard her daughter say something, asked her to repeat it.

"I said 'someday I'm getting out of here.'" Misty stood a few feet away, safely out of reach.

"Yes, you are, dearie," Carrie confirmed, pushing her key into the lock, giving it a twist. "And I hope for your sake you make it a lot further than I did."

The Saturn started with an alarming rattling sound.

It was nearly eight o'clock.

"Family Day" was officially over for another month.

Kurt left in April, the Easter long weekend. No one had seen him since.

Magic Man

What a nice guy.

Irrational. Stupid. All he did was walk in, position himself directly in front of her desk—

A *real sweetheart.*

—flash a friendly, guileless smile—

Mmm, cute too.

—and suddenly, just like that, her aching feet, the beginnings of a migraine that usually signified the onset of her period, Monday's employee evaluation, *everything* was thrust to the backburner, consigned to *mañana.* She leaned forward, clasping her hands before her, eager to appear helpful and attentive. "Yes?"

"I'd like to see Mr. Luzinski, if I could." Favoring her with another killer grin.

She felt knotted muscles at the base of her neck unravel, his presence somehow erasing hours of accumulated tension and stress, her cares and worries dissipating into thin air. She found herself stretching in her chair like a five-foot-six kitten. "Do you have an appointment, Mister—?"

"Meyer, ma'am. Tom Meyer."

She finally managed to wrestle her eyes off him and checked her book. Looked up at him, pained.

"I'm sorry, I don't see your name here." Searching for a way to help him. There had to be *something* she could do. "Is this a personal matter?"

"Not really." Shrugging. Not taken aback or embarrassed. "I'm looking for a position, a job, pretty much anything that's available. I was hoping he could help me."

Now she was *really* confused. "But…then you'd want someone in Human Resources. I'm sorry, Mr. Meyer—"

"Just 'Tom' is fine."

For some reason she was blushing. "I'm really sorry, Tom, but Lou—Mr. Luzinski doesn't deal with stuff involving personnel and hiring. He's a VP and he has more to do with the production end of things, artist relations and—could I be honest here?" Lowering her voice. "He's not the sort of person you want to approach with something like this. He's got kind of a volatile personality. He can be a bit of a bully and I wouldn't want him to, y'know, take it out on you."

"I see." He mulled that over a few seconds. "I'll tell you what. Why don't I go sit over there, quiet as a mouse, and wait until he has a free moment to see me."

"I'm afraid," why did she always seem to be apologizing in this office, "that Mr. Luzinski will be tied up for the rest of the afternoon." She sweetened the sour. "But maybe I can refer you to someone else, someone in a better position to assist you." It was likely an empty promise—as far as she knew there were no openings at *Apogee Records*. Word was, the next quarter would bring yet another downsizing, which meant not even the janitors were safe. Thanks for all the pirating and file sharing, kids!

But he shook his head, insisting, without being pushy about

it, that he had been given Mr. Luzinski's name and it was his intention to see the man, even if it meant a lengthy wait.

There was a button on the underside of her desk, it was only a matter of letting a hand wander in that direction and…but she never gave it a thought. Why not? He had no appointment, no (she realized) lanyard around his neck, clipped to a blue "Guest" pass. Which was totally weird because building security had recently been upgraded, everyone warned to visibly display their employee ID at all times or else be prepared to present it when challenged. Admittedly, these were crazy times but wasn't that over-doing it, just a tad?

She watched him take a seat, gazing about benignly. He couldn't be up to anything dangerous and/or crazy, could he? Not with a face like that.

The poor guy only wanted a job.

Look at him.

Harmless as a lamb.

He made his move the moment Lawrence Kramer, one of their Midwest talent scouts, exited the inner sanctum, *salaaming* as he backed through the doorway. Before the entrance to the lion's den snicked shut, Tom Meyer, displaying remarkable foot speed and dexterity, had slipped inside.

She had half-risen, now collapsed back into her chair, hanging on to its plastic arms for dear life. Young Meyer would never know what hit him. Louis Luzinski was a beast, plain and simple. The most terrifying specimen of humanity she'd ever encountered (including her father). An individual whose towering rages were a legend in the industry and beyond. "Lou makes the Weinsteins look like Girl Guides," her ex-boyfriend, a hack for one of the entertainment rags, once quipped. Another good one she'd heard recently: "What's the difference between Lou Luzinski and a tank of piranhas? Piranhas, at least, leave behind bones…"

And now Tom was getting the full brunt of his rotten disposition. She strained, listening. Usually, when Lou really got going, she could catch some of the shouted obscenities and lurid threats, occasionally the unmistakable sound of a severed head bumping and rolling across the floor.

Nothing.

Not yet.

She supposed she should be collecting her things, preparing for the inevitable consequences once that inner door was flung open and the Prince of Darkness himself emerged. Knowing she would likely be accompanying Tom Meyer off the lot, beefy guards making sure they were given the bum's rush. She'd seen it happen before during her tenure. Numerous times, in fact.

A minute passed. Two.

Where were the blood-curdling screams? The sharp, brittle crack of limbs snapping?

Three minutes. Five.

What the hell…

Twenty minutes elapsed before the door opened and a laughing (!) Lou Luzinski exited his private lair, one arm thrown around Tom Meyer's shoulders. It was such an unexpected sight, so out of character, all she could do was *gawp* as they approached her desk. With his free hand, Luzinski dropped a sheet of paper in front of her, a few lines jotted in his haphazard, schoolboy scrawl.

"It's a pleasure to have you aboard, Tommy boy." Luzinski beamed, reaching up and playfully tousling the younger man's hair. She couldn't get over how *happy* Lou seemed, his eyes alight with pleasure and good humor, looking at least ten years younger. "You'll be a welcome addition around here, won't he, Amanda?" She couldn't speak, managing only a reflexive nod. "Yesirree, there's been too much negativity in the air lately, we need some bright, new faces to encourage creativity and get this place humming again." She couldn't believe her ears. Penny-pinching, cost-cutting, bottom-of-the-line-loving Lou Luzinski waxing philosophical about creativity? How likely was that?

With remote control fingers, she picked up the sheet, deciphering what was written there.

Another bombshell.

In effect it granted Mr. Meyer—she'd better get used to calling him that–carte blanche. He would be working without official title, for the time being, reporting directly to Louis J. Luzinski.

"But…doing what?" She stared at them, flummoxed, hardly able to accommodate what was transpiring before her very eyes.

"He'll be a…" Luzinski paused, appearing confused.

"A liaison," Meyer prompted him and Lou brightened.

"Right, that's right. He'll work with our artists, smoothing things over before they become serious issues. I could tell right away you're the perfect man for the job, Tom."

"Thank you, sir," came the modest response. "I like to think inter-personal communication, the ability to bridge differences of opinion, is one of my strong suits."

"Take him down to HR, will you, Amanda?" It wasn't a request and she rose, instantly complying. "See that he gets properly set up. Arrange the details, you know the rigmarole." She did. He was already turning back to Meyer, clasping his hand warmly. "Welcome to the *Apogee* family, Tom. Hiring you is the smartest business decision I've made in years. I know you won't let me down."

When he glanced away, Tom slipped her a wink, letting her know everything was going to be all right.

Instantly, she felt better. The man had the damnedest effect on her, and obviously the great and terrible Lou Luzinski wasn't immune to his charm either.

She'd definitely be keeping an eye on this young up-and-comer.

Clearly, he possessed many hidden gifts.

Including, apparently, the ability to tame lions.

"—an' I say the mix is naw fookin' good!" The finale to the outburst rattled the soundproof glass separating the booth from the recording area. Archibald Reiser's (*aka* "The Rise") thick Glaswegian accent asserting itself, as it always did when he was really, really pissed. The others—his personal manager, Hal Warfield, engineer Clint Powell, Howie, a young intern and gofer–were wedged against the console, trying to dodge flying spittle. "I warned yez an' warned yez and now we're stuck wi' this piece o' shite."

"But, dude, don't you remember?" Warfield's tone was wheedling. "On Friday you said it was a go. You called Clint a genius and—"

"Listen to it! Listen to this gobshite!" The singer reached over, cranked the sound so that it filled the booth. "Who the fook produced this? Quincy Jones? Are ye cunts deliberately tryin' to sabotage my career?" Screaming over the racket. "Where's the filth and the fury? Where. Am. I?" Switching off so savagely, the button broke in his hand. He stared at it, flung it to the floor. Took up his relentless pacing again. The others glanced at each other, trapped and seeking mutual support. The agitated performer muttered curses under his breath, making faces and gesticulating as he carried on an intense inner dialogue. It was obvious he was under the influence of a substance that shorted out higher order brain functions—in other words, the civilized portions of his mind. What was left was pure *id* and it wasn't pretty.

"I thought," the engineer began. It was as far as he got.

"*Ye* thought? *Ye* thought? Who the fook 'r you? Some pasty-faced twat with nae hair on his balls. You din't notice the drummin' was shite—"

"That's Freddie, the guy we always—"

"—fookin' guitar was wayyy over the top. Who's the fookin' star, then, me or some greasy-haired ponce wi' fast fingers? Ay?"

"You are, dude," Warfield cooed. "It's just that—"

Rise stopped pacing, got face-to-face with his longtime handler. "Thas right. Thas right." His pale skin sheathed in sweat, eyes like two burning coals. "*I'm* the fookin' star. I'm the one thet takes responsibility. I'm the one thet gets the blame." His teeth were bad, his breath lousy, toxic. "This goes out an' I'm ruint. Finished. Kaput." Dramatic pause, staring him down. "I wanna do it again."

His manager was appalled. "*Again?* But we already pushed back the release date twice—"

"*I don't give a fook!*" Rise bellowed. "I wan' everythin' stripped doon to the basics, mind. Lose the strings, sack the drummer..." He blinked lazily, staggering backward a few steps. His brain buzzing and sparking, possibly overloading. "Sack the drummer, sack allathumuthufuckas…" He'd been flying high for days, who knew how long. Evidently whatever he'd taken was wearing off, its aftereffects dire. They watched as he reached behind him, fumbling to find a chair before falling into it. "All o' 'em. Fuggit. Jes'…" He made a vague, cryptic gesture, meaningless to anyone except him.

Clint, the engineer, appeared to be in shock. Ashen, slumped over the console. "Again?" He sounded like he'd rather be flayed alive.

Warfield inched closer to his client, trying to gauge his condition. "Listen, Arch, you're in a bad space right now. Why don't we call it a day and—"

"I think the gentleman is right." They turned to the figure who had entered soundlessly, who'd been there for some time, observing, eavesdropping. "The over-production saps the life out of the song, rendering it…commonplace."

"And just who the hell are you?" This was Hal Warfield's chance to reclaim his dignity and self-respect, an opportunity to slam someone else down and revel in their abject misery. "This is a private session and we don't need any flunkies sticking their—"

"Tom Meyer. I'm the new boy. Working for and answering only to Lou Luzinski." The quartet before him visibly quailed when he casually dropped the name.

"That still doesn't give you the right—"

"Oh, yes, it does." On the wall next to him was an in-house phone. He plucked up the receiver, turned to Warfield. "Shall we call him and confirm it?"

Warfield flinched, folding like a man stuck with a pair of deuces. "Ah, no need. I guess you wouldn't be here if it hadn't been cleared."

He replaced the phone. "That's right. From the very top. And part of my duties involve making sure the talent is happy and creating the best music they possibly can."

"'sright," Rise slurred. "Zwat izall abou."

"So what about it? Can we scale everything back, cut the strings and bombast, like he says, make it more raw and authentic?"

Rise might have been nodding agreement or merely nodding off; it was difficult to tell. The manager was muttering to himself. "—already way over-budget, weeks behind schedule, Lou's gonna go bugfuck—"

"Let me worry about Lou," Meyer stated confidently. "You guys come up with a new arrangement, book some studio time, get it done." A thin trickle of drool slowly descended from the corner of Rise's mouth. He was out cold. "—though probably not today," he conceded.

Warfield found himself strangely receptive to the kid's idea. And if Lou's nose got out of joint, they could always point the finger of blame at the new lad. *He gave us the go-ahead to do it.* "What the hell. We'll give it a shot. Clint?" He glanced down at the engineer, who merely raised his hands, surrendering to the inevitable.

No one thought to ask the intern's opinion.

Within thirty-six hours the song was in the can. Now that you could actually *hear* the fucking thing, it wasn't a bad tune. Guitar, drums, bass. And, damnit, despite years of self-injury and unhealthy life choices, Rise still had the pipes, and it was like this latest version loosed something within him, a long-slumbering rock 'n roll spirit. His electrifying vocals transformed a mediocre pop tune into an old-fashioned stomper, with more catchy hooks than a tackle box. Maybe not a single but definitely not filler either. A genuine toe-tapper.

Clint was humming along as he listened to the mix. That was always a good sign. Warfield reclined in a high-backed chair, angling it so he could catch Tom Meyer's eye, give him a nod of approval. But the kid was off in another world: he had seen the look of joy on Archibald Reiser's face as he nailed the song on the third take. Once he finished, the mercurial singer peeled off the headphones, beat his thin chest and *howled* in pure animal ecstasy, higher and happier than he'd been in months.

The energy and atmosphere in the studio heady, intoxicating. Tom stood in the midst of it, drinking it in.

At the launch of the debut album by *The Pasties*, a female post-post-punk band from Seattle, Tom stepped between Pete Sly, lead guitarist for *Sketch Tragedy*, and Lou Luzinski just as blows were about to be exchanged. Contract negotiations were going nowhere and there had been insults and jibes exchanged back and forth on various social media platforms. Lou, like most bullies, was extremely thin-skinned. But Tom interceded and led them away, into a little alcove by reception. Later, neither of them could remember exactly what it was he said, but it must have had an effect because before too long they were reconciled, laughing and joking together, the deal practically signed, sealed and delivered.

By the end of the evening, the two of them had joined everybody else at the grand piano in Studio C, singing along to a medley of Elvis tunes, banged out by an old man with bent, gnarled fingers who'd once played for the King himself…

A week later Tom appeared, uninvited, at a secret meeting of department heads planning an office *putsch*. Lou Luzinski had loudly and publicly upbraided most of those present and a number of them were bent on revenge. There was talk of anonymous letters to the board and shareholders, old misdemeanors and grievances resurrected, including several sexual harassment suits that had been quietly hushed up, settlements paid out. Gary Struthers, from sales and marketing, was one of the ringleaders. He had a loathing for Lou going back nearly a decade, his fiercest, most resolute critic.

And yet at the conclusion of the clandestine gathering Struthers rose to his feet, offering a heartfelt endorsement to "one of the truly great minds in the business today, Lou Luzinski". No one present could put a finger on when, precisely, the sea change occurred or what had caused it.

But in the days that followed you could feel it in the building, as if a permanent overcast had suddenly burned away, revealing clear skies and sunny weather. People were excited coming in to work again, petty feuds and inter-office rivalries forgiven or forgotten, the squabbling and backbiting much reduced.

Things were looking up at *Apogee*, everyone could sense it.

They just couldn't figure out *why*.

One afternoon, near the end of a long day, Tom Meyer sat in his office down the hall from Lou's, kneading his forehead, trying to relieve the deep ache behind his eyes. Putting out fires, big and small, ten hours a day, five days a week, could be wearing on a person. So much unresolved conflict and hostility needing redirection, put to more constructive uses. All that bad, negative energy in the air had to go somewhere...

His office phone buzzed. Of course it would. Just when he was thinking of calling it quits, maybe taking a drive down the coast to a little place he knew—

The line buzzed again.

Must be serious.

It was. Marcia Jonas, queen of the label, pop icon for two generations and still going strong, was running amuck in Studio A. She'd come in this morning with a binder of new songs, some promising demos and a producer and engineer in tow. She had tentatively titled the album-in-progress "Loveless", which raised a few eyebrows.

Romantically speaking, life hadn't been kind to Marcia. In the past few years she'd lost two lovers/collaborators, one to alcohol and drugs, the other, Clayton Kilworth, to severe and untreatable depression. Four months previously the latter had hanged himself from a tree in the backyard of her Sherman Oaks mansion. She hadn't been home at the time so the gardener had the pleasure of finding him. He chose a tree in plain sight—she would have been able to see him from her kitchen window. Crazy? Cruel? Both?

Marcia was pushing forty, alone, snake-bitten as far as men went, yet determined to stay artistically relevant, already talking about a supporting tour, some ideas for videos—

Something happened to change all that. Now his presence was urgently required, his gift employed, once again, to soothe hurt and heal the afflicted.

"—*goddamn fucking*—" She swung the microphone stand like a baseball bat, attacking the drum kit and upright cymbals, succeeding, on her second attempt, at smashing in the front of a venerable Marshall amplifier. It emitted an eerie squeal of anguish, absorbing the kind of beating the likes of Jimi Hendrix or the Reid brothers inflicted on their equipment. She javelined the mike stand at the figures who'd sought refuge in the sound booth, but it ricocheted harmlessly off the thick, resilient glass.

Fuck. What's next? How about that Roland keyboard or, maybe, take another crack at those drums…

Had she not been so intent on reducing the interior of the studio to shambles, she might have seen Tom Meyer enter the booth, wave everyone else out, then walk over to the small, square window to watch the mayhem. Finally, when she appeared winded, he thumbed a switch.

"Finished?"

She pivoted, shielding her eyes to better make out the figure addressing her. He had both hands pressed against the scratched, smudged glass, and even if she couldn't see his eyes she could *feel* them, the intensity of his gaze. It gave her goosebumps.

Something else she didn't see were the rivulets of sweat streaming down both cheeks like shed tears, the veins bulging on his forehead from the sheer amount of effort and energy he was expending, pouring himself into the space she occupied, flowing through the air toward her—

Suddenly she was bored, tired and, perhaps not surprisingly, famished. "Maybe." She gave a snare drum a half-hearted kick but the fury had abated. She couldn't bring herself to put a foot through it.

"Take your time."

He didn't have to wait long. Eventually she stuck her head

through the door, appearing abashed, almost timid, like a disobedient child reporting to the principal's office. "Hey..."

He indicated the trashed studio. "Is this some perverse version of *feng shui* I'm not aware of?" She couldn't help grinning. "Let me guess. Lou came down here—"

Some of the anger returned. "Lou! Fucking Lou wants me to stay frozen in time, twenty-one years old and all sugar and pop. He's talking about shooting at the beach, romantic subplots with cute lifeguards half my age—Jesus Christ, who does he think I am, Kylie Minogue? I mean, get with it." She shook her head. "I'm forty years old, I buried my last two lovers and—and I don't want to hide that anymore. This album was supposed to be about aging and loss and coming to terms. But Lou didn't want to hear that. I got the feeling he didn't like the demos, thinks this is a bad career move, that I should stick with the tried and true..." Cocking her head. "Who did you say you were?"

"Tom Meyer. Executive in charge of something-something. Believe it or not, my job basically comes down to being nice to people."

"And you work for *Lou*?" They laughed together.

"I see what you're saying and I want you to know I completely agree. And Lou will soon change his tune, I guarantee it." She was staring at him. "What?"

"Where did Lou find you?" she wondered. "How come you seem so *sane*?"

He stood, rolling his shoulders until they cracked. "Long day. I could use something to eat, how about you?"

"What about—" Indicating her handiwork in the adjoining studio.

"Not our problem. We don't own it."

And that was it. Over. Forgotten. Water under the bridge. She never gave it another thought once they'd left the building. And neither, apparently, did he.

They drove, listening to her playlist (heavy on old R & B), talking—well, *she* talked. And he was receptive and sympathetic… to the extent that soon she was unburdening herself of some of the weight she carried. She even cried, the first time in weeks.

But none of it rattled Tom in the least. He seemed so kind and caring.

She hoped it wasn't an act.

They finally ended up back at her temporary hideaway, a ranch house up in the hills. The owner was an old friend, an art dealer who fled California for Colorado after experiencing a minor earthquake earlier that year. He could put up with the heat and smog but when plate tectonics entered the equation, he drew the line. He hadn't listed the house yet, he and his partner couldn't make up their minds whether to retain it as a rental property or dump it before the latest real estate bubble burst.

Alan wouldn't hear of accepting payment from her—"no, dear, you're doing us a *favor*"—but he did say that if she was ever in the vicinity of Boulder, she and her checkbook were more than welcome to drop by the gallery and view their wares. She got the hint.

She stayed in one wing, rarely venturing through the rest of the house. All she required was a bedroom, bathroom and kitchen. Did her own cooking and cleaning, shopped for groceries and essentials at a market about a mile away. Tom was the first person she'd brought back here, but it didn't feel strange at all.

He'd been the perfect gentleman thus far—on the other hand, most wolves managed that façade quite easily. She couldn't get over how calm and safe she felt in his company, the way all the blackness and bile she'd been keeping inside had spewed out of her.

Now she was completely spent, weak and vulnerable. Half-leaned toward him, wondering where this was going and if she was ready for it. Both of them aware that if he wanted to, he could initiate something, live the dream of so many men, a night of passion with Marcia Jonas, something to brag to his buddies about, the ultimate notch on his belt.

It didn't happen. He left her untouched, save for brushing her cheek with his lips, the most incidental, platonic contact. Yet it thrilled her. Because it meant he really *was* a nice guy, he wasn't just playing with her. Her legs shaking when she said "good night" and climbed out of the vehicle. Her heart beating rapidly, her skin flushed, exhibiting all the symptoms of burgeoning infatuation, good, old-fashioned lust. Emotions she hadn't experienced in a long time…

Tom Meyer's contribution to Marcia Jonas's fifteenth solo album was not officially recognized. His name appeared nowhere in the credits, which was understandable since he wasn't involved in either the songwriting or production.

However, Marcia felt that "Loveless" owed its very existence to him. He'd been as good as his word, staunchly supporting her desire to portray herself in a new light, an older, wiser woman, lobbying Lou Luzinski on her behalf and somehow getting him to go along with it.

In the liner notes of "Loveless" she cheekily acknowledged her benefactor, bestowing "Special thanks and love to the Magic Man". When asked about it, she merely offered an enigmatic little smile, refusing to divulge any specific names.

The album was her best in years, even Lou said so. Tom made excuses to pop by, sit in on some of the sessions, and he seemed pleased, shooting her a 'thumbs up' when she finessed a particularly tough section of the title cut. The songs were personal but not (she hoped) self-pitying or sentimental. The last one she recorded, "Dressing Up", surprised her with its sexual wordplay and flirtatiousness. "Dress me how you like/Pose me on the bed/Fill me with the dreams/That live inside your head".

She meant it too.

Her entire being felt like it had come back on-line, switches thrown, circuits closing, her body warming and coloring with life.

Not hard to deduce or trace the source. The moment she glanced over and saw Tom in the booth or noticed him passing in the hallway, she started glowing.

Goddamnit, gal, she chided herself, *you've gone and fallen in love again, haven't you?*

There was no use denying it. It probably started that first time he drove her home and didn't ravish her in the car. His laidback manner, the way he had of making crises and disasters seem like minor inconveniences, were a balm on her frayed, exposed nerves.

She was uncertain how to proceed. It had been ages since she'd felt like this, twitter-pated or smitten or whatever you called it. Wanting someone body, mind and soul. Not only wanting. Needing. *Craving*.

What was she going to do? How was she to go about wooing a younger man, make him see her as a woman, a lover and potential life partner, not a celebrity? If past experience was any guide, it wasn't going to be easy. It meant some of the limelight would necessarily fall on him, tongues wagging and shutters snapping. She could see the headlines now: *"The new man in her life!"* Or, even worse, *"Will he be doomed like the others?"*

Since that night in his car there hadn't been the kind of physical proximity that might give a reading on his attitude toward her. It wasn't that he was avoiding her, more like he was staying in the background, keeping a professional distance. Was he just shy? Could he be gay?

She tested the water, bumping into him sort of by accident, making eye contact, teasing him about his new haircut, engaging with him whenever she could. Other people noticed, Marcia could tell, but she was beyond caring about such things. Frank Spoto, her co-producer, pointedly warned her about getting involved with someone "in the biz". She ignored him too.

She hadn't gotten where she was by behaving like a shrinking violet. She'd come up the hard way, paid her dues and then some. Lousy clubs, kleptomaniacal agents, poverty, hunger, despair—oh, yes, she'd had her fair share of low moments. Some of what she'd done to reach the top of the pyramid might be classified as morally or ethically sketchy, but it was all in service of advancing her career. "Climbing the mountain," as she put it. For as long as she could remember she was the type of person who believed that good things only come to those who stalk them and run them to ground.

So she wasn't about to let a trifling little matter like a ten-year age difference dissuade her. Not by a long shot.

As the album neared completion, Marcia started laying plans. The key was figuring out a way of luring him away from the office, finding a warmer, friendlier setting. He wouldn't be so shy once he realized how she felt about him, that he had nothing to be afraid of, she was a woman capable of fulfilling every one of his desires and intended to do just that.

Marcia Jonas wasn't going to be *loveless* much longer.

Opportunity knocked when she came up with the brilliant notion of throwing a wrap party for the album, which was 99% complete. Alan didn't mind her hosting the affair at the ranch house—"As long as no one chops up the furniture for firewood or steals the artwork", was how he tactfully put it.

She hired a caterer she trusted, knowing the small, important details would be covered. No need to worry about music—half those attending either played instruments or sang professionally. These were her people. Contrary to what Frank might think, there was no escaping "the biz".

On the surface, of course, it was a generous, thoughtful expression of gratitude and appreciation directed toward the men and women who'd helped make "Loveless" a reality. The musicians and technicians, sales and PR flacks, her agent and manager…even Lou Luzinski made the roll call, though he had to beg off owing to a prior commitment (thank God). It amounted to twenty-five or thirty people stopping by one Friday evening in early May. Helping themselves to free food and booze, strolling through the various sections of the house, ogling framed paintings and photographs or browsing the thousands of books. Alan had eclectic tastes, there was something for everyone. Including a room devoted to "erotica", though primmer types might have different words for it.

As the evening wore on, she could feel her mood darkening. *Where was he?* Tom was the first person she'd invited, though she certainly hadn't told him that. Had given him not the slightest inkling (fingers crossed) that all this—her grand, magnanimous gesture, freebies galore—was nothing but a huge front, a calculated attempt to draw him into her lair.

Then she heard someone call out to him, and other people saying his name. She spotted him talking to Charlie Holder, who played flawless bass on three tracks, and Amanda Pfeiffer, Lou's long-suffering Girl Friday. Sue Miller, a gorgeous back-up singer from Philadelphia, came hobbling up on four-inch stilettos, unceremoniously thrusting her pneumatic boobs in Tom's face. It was kind of comical because he acted like she was showing him a pretty bouquet of flowers she'd just picked. Nodding at them, acknowledging them, then pretty much putting them out of his mind.

"Hi, Tom."

"Hello, Marcia." Another quick, chaste buss on her cheek.

You won't be getting away with that for much longer, darlin'. "Glad you could make it."

"Just arrived. Sorry. I got tied up and was late getting away."

"Your devotion to duty is commendable."

He dipped his head in mock acknowledgement. "Thank you."

"But now you can let your hair down. Make yourself at home." She smiled, just for him. Putting everything she had into it.

Sue, meanwhile, had reined in her torpedo tits and appeared to be casting about for another victim to waylay. It was a good thing she was such a magnificent singer. A five-octave vocal range, impeccable rhythm *and* she was punctual, like, to the minute. It made her foibles and eccentricities (mostly) endurable.

"Would you like to see the rest of the house?" The question she'd been dying to ask all evening. Nodding, he held out the crook of his arm.

"Lead on, m'lady."

But it took awhile. Every few steps, someone intercepted them, congratulating and thanking Marcia and mooning over Tom. It was weird, it didn't matter if it was a male or female, everyone present seemed to have a bit of a thing for him. Nothing overt, but you could sense the vibes. They couldn't help smiling when they saw him, touching or hugging him reflexively. With her, they were polite and deferential but Tom, despite his lofty position within the *Apogee* hierarchy, appealed to something deeper; people were naturally drawn to him, the same personal magnetism she'd responded to.

Finally, they were outside, in the backyard, facing downhill toward a deep ravine where at night, she told him, residents could hear coyotes yipping back and forth.

"Coyotes," he marveled. "In the midst of an urban sprawl of—what—ten million, at least. That's remarkable."

"Some of the little old ladies around here worry about their chows getting carried off. I guess it's happened before."

"Must have been traumatic for the poor dears."

Hmm, this conversation wasn't heading in the right direction. She sidled up beside him. "I like standing out here sometimes, pretending the city isn't surrounding me, hemming me in. The craziness and hectic pace, the constant noise…"

"It's very peaceful out here. I can see why you like it."

That was her cue. "I want to thank you for the peace *you've* given me, Tom. In the past few weeks I've come to appreciate the kind of person you are. I see how you affect everyone around you. I've never met anyone like you." He started to say something but she over-rode him. "I began writing 'Loveless' because I was broken, things weren't working for me anymore and I could no longer pretend my life was ship-shape. Two people I loved died, just like *that*. And they had their faults, but they were good men, not mean or evil or capable of deliberate harm. Except they were broken too, even worse than I am. Maybe that's part of my problem." She grasped his hand, seeking support as she blurted out the rest of it. "I want to be with someone who isn't broken, someone who's got his shit together and is steady and patient and kind. Do you know what I mean? Tom? Do you understand what I'm trying to say?" *Oh, why don't you squeeze my hand, damn you?*

"Of course." His voice cool, detached, the dusk making shadows of his eyes. And still she felt no pressure on her fingers, barely resisted the urge to break contact and move away. Giving him time to process this new development. "I've…suspected your feelings for awhile. I should have…" He took a deep breath but said no more.

She wished he would at least *look* at her. "You say you knew about the way I feel. That's good. Fine with me. No need pretending then." She linked fingers with his, held up their joined hands.

"See? No secrets or confused signals. Because I think you've got feelings of your own. I'd like to hear about them. No one here but us chickens."

"Please…" He tried gently extricating himself but she wasn't having any of it.

"Oh, no, you don't, buster. You don't escape my clutches that easily." Standing in front of him, gripping both his wrists, staring into his eyes. "I need to know what you're feeling, Tom. I've definitely fallen for you and I'm trying to keep things on an even keel but you've done things for me, *to* me, that I wouldn't have believed possible. I thought I'd completely shut down. Everything: my passion, my heart, but you lit the fire again, made me feel alive—"

"—you don't understand—"

"What's to understand? Tell me. What's so crazy about the two of us getting together and trying to figure out if we can make it work? I'm game."

Finally, Tom did look at her, his face a confusion of emotions. "What you're feeling…the things you're describing…it's not natural." He winced. "Not *normal*. The thing is, Marcia, everyone reacts to me that way. Anyone I spend time around I…influence. There's something inside me—"

"That's what I'm trying to tell you," throwing herself on him, squeezing with all her might. "You're a sweetheart. You care about people—"

"*No*. It's been like this for as long as I can remember. Since I was a child. My parents never fought in my presence, never once raised their voices. I had lots of friends because I always put everyone at ease. I somehow *made* them feel that way. I can't help myself, it's something innate and involuntary, beyond my control." She sensed him withdrawing from her, clung to him in desperation. "What you're experiencing, it's not *real*. It's…part of my gift. The best part."

"I love you for that gift, Tom."

But saying the words didn't have the impact she'd hoped for. "That's because you're not thinking straight. You were so damaged and that probably made you more susceptible. The effect was magnified in you. It's like you're hypnotized, open to suggestion."

She rose to her tiptoes, angling her head, parting her lips. "So suggest away. Anything you want. *Anything*, Tom…"

He tried to back up but her arms were around his neck and she went with him, almost nose-to-nose. "N-no, please. I can't—"

She dragged his face toward her. "Yes, you can."

They were tantalizingly close and she watched as something happened to his eyes, all kindness and gentility evaporating, *hunger*, overweening and insatiable, asserting itself. His arms tightened about her, the breath forced from her lungs. His expression was ghastly: pitiless, almost feral, both hands grasping her ass, his leering face dipping toward her—

"*Noooo!*" He almost pushed her over backward, seeking to put distance between them, break the spell that had temporarily possessed him. She was stunned, speechless, and he stared about wildly, seeking an escape route, oblivious of everything else. He wrenched open the balcony door and she stumbled after him, following as he lurched across the room, jostling people, shoving them aside, frantically searching for the way out.

"Anything wrong, Marsh?" It was Charlie Holder, bless him. Meanwhile, Tom had gained the front door, thrown it open, disappearing into the night.

"Did you bring a car, Charlie?"

"Yeah, my wife's Nissan, the Camry's in the shop—"

"I need your help."

"Something happen, doll? You look shook up. It wasn't Tom, was it?" She could tell he didn't want to believe it.

"Tom's…in trouble and we have to go after him. Got your keys?"

"Right here." He trailed after her. "What's up?"

"I told you, Charlie, I'm worried about him."

She looked so stricken, he couldn't refuse her. "Okay, Marsh, whatever you say. Let's roll."

"We have to hurry or we'll lose him…"

There are scarcely any rural areas left along the SoCal coastline. From San Francisco all the way to the Mexican border development money and naked capitalism have converted nearly every available square foot into shopping malls, box stores, fast food outlets, hotels, motels and tourist traps, housing (for those who can afford it) and the infrastructure required to support it all.

Those occasional slivers of the natural world that manage to survive intact seem fake, manicured and maintained, like a favorite *bonsai* plant.

Darkness is almost unknown here; at night, the illuminated coastline can be seen from space, a glow that outlines and demarcates the shores of the Pacific. And even in that watery vastness, a sparkle of colored lights: from passing ships or the Meccano-like oil derricks pumping raw crude from small, man-made islands a few miles out to sea. The stars cannot compete.

This was not one of those chase scenes taking place on a lonely, winding road, headlights fending off the surrounding gloom. They were on the Pacific Coast Highway, the traffic moderate at 9:30 in the evening. Outside Santa Monica they merged with the San Diego Freeway, continuing south.

Wherever he was going, Tom was making good time, zipping along at nearly eighty mph, weaving from lane to lane. He was lucky the CHP didn't spot his antics. Those boys took a dim view of speed demons.

Charlie was keeping up with him but wasn't enjoying himself. He'd just gotten his license back after a DUI and not too excited about earning another stint in traffic court. Facing Judge Phyllis Rimmer again. And Marcia was still being coy about what had transpired back at the house, why they were in hot pursuit of Tom's grey BMW.

Meyer took the exit at Oceanside, using a bypass to skirt the edge of the small city. He was driving more responsibly, almost nonchalantly. It was apparent he hadn't considered the possibility he might be followed.

"What are you up to, Tom?" Charlie wondered out loud.

Just then Meyer signaled, leaving the perimeter road and entering the northwest section of the city. He seemed to know the route well, steering his car into a rundown neighborhood, boarded up storefronts, pawnshops and check-cashing agencies proliferating.

"What could he be after here?"

"I dunno, Marsh, but it doesn't look good. This is the part of the city the local chamber of commerce *doesn't* want you to see." They passed two men facing off on a street corner, taunting and circling each other. A knot of curious bystanders had gathered to witness their antics.

Most buildings had bars on their windows. Not much open after nine o'clock. A real 'hood.

"Welcome to the zombie apocalypse," he muttered.

Tom made a right turn down a side street, slowing, possibly looking for parking.

"Don't get too close," Marcia cautioned.

"I'm on it."

But her apprehension was unwarranted. Tom pulled into the first available slot and fairly bolted from the vehicle, never so much as glancing in their direction. He cut across a drought-parched lawn fronting a two-story home with peeling, discolored siding and bent, low-hanging eaves. The front door, at least, looked brand new and *strong*, built to withstand forcible entry. Tom couldn't keep still while he waited on the threshold, shifting from foot to foot, pushing through the door once it opened.

Then he was gone.

Time passed and Marcia fretted. *What's he doing in there? It looks like some kind of fortress. Is he buying drugs? Is that his deep, dark secret?*

"What do you think, Marsh?" More than twenty minutes had passed. Charlie was of the mind that they'd pushed their luck far enough in this neighborhood and a strategic retreat might be in order. Leave Tom to his own business.

"I'm going in." At first he was stunned, then he was shaking his head, *no way, Jose.* "Listen to me: I can't go back without knowing if he's all right."

"If that's what you want, I'll go." Unbuckling his seatbelt, dead serious. Good, old Charlie. "I've been in a few of these dives before.

I'll flash some cash or give 'em some attitude, try and bluff my way inside."

"What if they won't open the door?" He looked away. "What do you do then, Charlie? It would take an army to get in there. No, this requires a more subtle touch." She flipped down the visor, consulted the mirror, touched up her hair. "This is where being famous comes in handy."

"You think that's going to protect you?" He sounded skeptical.

"Better than Kevlar," she promised, patting his arm reassuringly, "just watch and learn."

Some of her bravado had deserted her by the time she got to the door. It was solid, all right, and came fitted with a spy hole. Lending more credence to her drug den theory.

She knew Charlie was watching so she gave it three solid thumps, announcing herself. She heard someone approach the other side, then a muffled challenge:

"You want somethin'?"

She stood where they could see her. "I'm looking for a friend."

"Aren't you…why, sure it is! It's *her*…" She heard the woman mutter an aside to someone, then a girlish squeal. "Slumming it, aren't you?" Marcia didn't answer. "What friend you lookin' for, hon? Makes you think he's here?"

"What makes you think it's a *he*?" she countered.

The woman tough, officious, clearly in charge. "That's pretty much all we get, dearie." She heard three separate deadbolts snap back. "You seem set on paying us a visit. Well, come on in. We don't get many celebrity types…" The door didn't open all the way, only far enough for her admittance, and it was immediately slammed and locked behind her. The hall light came on, illuminating everything in the vicinity in an unflattering, yellowish hue.

The dwelling was better maintained on the inside, but the wallpaper and carpeting were well-worn, faded, out of date. There was a living room or parlor on the right. Old furniture—not antique, *old*. Serviceable, but not a worthwhile piece in evidence. The place smelled lived in too, cooking odors, perfumes and cleansers. And something else, a miasma, invisible and omnipresent; indescribable but indisputably organic.

"Knew it was you. Recognized you right away." A short, stout woman, early forties. "Been a big fan for ages."

"We all are!" someone called from down the hall.

"Sheddep in there! And finish those dishes!"

"Yes, ma'am!" a different voice retorted. Mocking laughter.

Marcia cleared her throat. "The man who came in here a few minutes ago, where is he?"

The woman did her best to feign confusion but she was a very bad actress. "*Ma-an?*"

"The last person to walk through that door. I was parked outside, watching."

"Were you now?" The woman was solidly built, thickset, not fat. Strong forearms. The build of a bouncer. A similar take-no-shit attitude, too. "And why is that?"

"Because we—I followed him." Hearing the exasperation in her voice, dialing it down a notch. "Listen, this guy…he's very special to me. If he's in any trouble, I want to help him."

The woman smirked. "Makes you think he's in trouble?" There was a scar on her cheek, not acne.

The Socratic dialogue was starting to wear on her. "Look,

why don't we make this simple. I've got close to three hundred dollars here." Holding it up. "The only thing you have to do is take me to him."

The woman stared at her, undecided. Finally, inevitably, greed won out. "Around here, they call me Kath."

"And I'm Dolores. Hi!" The young woman who stuck her head around the corner looked like she'd been in a brawl. She had a black eye and her lips were swollen and split. There were scrapes and scratch marks on her neck and upper chest.

"Get back in there!" Kath roared and she hastily ducked out of sight. "If that kitchen isn't spick 'n span when I come down—"

"…okay, okay…" Dolores groused, reluctantly returning to her duties, "don't get your panties in a knot."

"Is she okay?" It was a dumb question. The woman grimaced as she came forward and took the proffered bills.

"He calls himself Mr. Larson. Your gentleman. One of our reglars." *Oh, God,* Marcia thought, *oh, God, oh, God. Tell me it's not true, that this isn't as bad as it looks.* "Somehow, you don't seem his type." She thumbed through the bills, counting them, peering up at her once she finished. "You sure you want to see him?"

"That's what I'm paying for," Marcia said, sounding more bereft than brave at that point.

"I'm sorry, sweetheart," the tough moll commiserating with the world famous pop diva, "but they're men, aren't they? They can't help being complete bastards."

"Show me."

"A peeker, eh?" Kath winked. "Never would've imagined that in a million years." She led the way up the stairs. "We always put him at the end of the hall. Because of the ruckus." To Marcia,

Kath's voice seemed muffled, distant, hardly registering. "He's lucky we're so tolerant of his…tastes. Mind you," she added, "he pays dearly for the privilege."

Marcia could already hear them: he was shouting and roaring, violent threats and imprecations, and someone else, begging, whimpering. Her progress slowed once they reached the top of the stairs. Unwilling to advance further down the corridor. She could hear other sounds now, fleshy impacts, followed by more cries and entreaties.

Kath had a firm hold on Marcia's wrist and was pulling her toward the last door on the left. "I was just coming up to check," she whispered. "Sometimes he gets carried away." Another door, another spy hole. "He was already with Dee, that gal downstairs. He may need another before he's through." She moved to the side. "You wanna see, go ahead." The tiny opening was designed for Kath, so Marcia had to bend down, wait for her eyes to adjust. "*Looook…*"

At no point was she in any danger. No one threatened her and there were no intimations of blackmail or extortion. She even ended up autographing a paper napkin for poor Dolores.

When she wanted to leave, she left.

Alone. Without him.

Walked back to the car, got in. Told Charlie in a calm, clear voice that they could return to Los Angeles now. To what remained of her wrap party.

But Charlie knew better. He didn't start the car, didn't do anything. "Marsh…you okay?"

"Sure, Charlie. I'm fine. Everything is…fine." But it wasn't, not really.

At first, she hadn't been able to take in what she was seeing. They were both naked, streaked and stippled with blood.

Tom was standing over her, his fists raised and clenched. The skinny, young woman with him cowering, bleeding from her nose, bruises and welts on her arms and legs. Defensive injuries. He grasped her by the elbows, pulled her to her feet, spit in her face. Tried to butt her with his forehead but she deftly avoided him. He slapped her, twice: hard, open-handed blows that propelled her backward, on to the bed. Then he climbed on top of her and was preparing to either mount or strangle her, it wasn't clear which. Marcia couldn't bear any more, squeezing her eyes shut and stumbling away, sullied and degraded by what she'd seen. As if she had participated in the assault.

But the worst part was the *look* on his face: exultation, a gloating satisfaction that was almost rapturous. He was enjoying himself, whether he was battering the girl with his fists or his body. It was sadism, but there was more to it than that, Marcia realized. The pain and punishment he inflicted serving to release something inside him, a vast reservoir of rage and guilt and vileness he'd likely been storing up since his perfect, carefree childhood.

And afterward, she supposed, once he purged himself, he'd revert back to gentle, sweet-natured Tom Meyer. A man you couldn't possibly hate. Fully restored and ready to face a pain-wracked, poison-filled world, dispensing peace, love and happiness to everyone around him, absolving their myriad sins.

The New Neighbors

When Hannah's parents told her a family of *poppets* would soon be moving to their neighborhood, the first thing she wanted to know was if they were related to Betty-Sue Pearson.

Her mother and father looked at each other and finally her father shrugged. "I'm not sure, honey. I suppose in a way they're *all* related, don't you think?"

Hannah didn't have an answer to that. Betty-Sue was the host of "Studio Z", Hannah's favorite kids' show. The pigtailed *poppet* never mentioned her family on the program—mainly it was her job to introduce and link segments, and when confronted by something unaccountably strange or perplexing, screech her trademark tag line: "*Oh, my sweet petunias!*"

The Donaldsons moved into their new home in mid-August. Their house was one street away from Hannah's, positioned mid-block. She pedaled past on her bike, going so slowly she teetered, nearly falling off. There was a big van in the driveway but none of the Donaldsons were in evidence, much to her disappointment. She already knew from her parents there were two children, a boy and girl, and the girl was supposed to be around her age.

Jennifer Froese said she heard *poppets* liked to act really stuck up and superior and they also tended to be bossy and mean. Hannah hotly challenged that view, the argument escalated and Jennifer ended up stomping home in a huff.

Hannah made a regular circuit around the Donaldsons' block but never managed to spot any of them outside in their yard. Maybe *poppets* didn't like the sun.

She was aware both children were enrolled at her elementary school, so she was bound to see them there. She could hardly wait.

The days crawled past but finally, at the end of the month, Hannah climbed aboard the #26 bus for the first day of the fall term. The overlapping chatter of other children revealed they were just as excited as she was.

Hannah's parents had warned her that her teacher would likely speak to the class about the proper way to behave toward *poppets* and she was to pay close attention. You couldn't pretend they were just like everybody else.

As if she didn't know that!

Sure enough, right after the bell rang, Ms. Szell clapped her hands to get their attention. She informed them that their class would shortly welcome a "special" student, one requiring consideration and *respect* (a word which was repeated at least six times in the next few minutes).

She pointed out the table at the back of the room where their new classmate, Crissy (*Crissy Donaldson!*), would be stationed. There was a dark blue sheet draped over it, extending all the way to the floor.

"Really," Ms. Szell assured them, "the rules are the same as for regular people. Don't play rough and be nice to her. Always act in a respectful manner. If you do that, you'll have nothing to worry about."

There was a knock on the door and Ms. Szell gave a little jump. *She's nervous too*, Hannah thought.

Ms. Szell went to the door, spoke to someone outside, then stepped back into the room, followed by the young *poppet* and her thin, pretty aide…

The other students couldn't help occasionally glancing over their shoulders at the table behind them. Crissy Donaldson, clad in infant-sized overalls and plastic, slip-on sandals, seemed oblivious of the attention she was attracting, too busy scribbling away at her first assignment. Her aide was positioned below the table, mostly hidden from view.

The recess bell rang at 10:15. There had been no special provisions made for Crissy or her older brother, Corey, in the schoolyard and playground. Not yet, anyway.

Her attendant, who hadn't been introduced, carried Crissy outside and sat with her near the sand pit. Kids kept drifting by, singly or in groups, gawking and whispering among themselves. Hannah thought they were behaving stupidly, exactly opposite of the way they were supposed to. A few children waved or called out greetings as they ran past but no one seemed anxious to join her. Hannah thought she looked forlorn and decided to wander over and keep her company. As she approached the pair, she saw that Crissy was suspended an inch or so above the sand, her floppy legs thin and jointless, more for show than anything else.

"Hey," Hannah said, squatting down so she was at their level, "I live only one street away from you."

"Oh, yeah?" You weren't supposed to look at her human operator, yet the words undoubtedly originated from her. Hannah couldn't help staring, but the woman kept her eyes down, focused on Crissy.

"You should come over some time. You and Corey. You'd be most welcome." She tried to make the offer sound as formal and polite as she could.

"Do you have an Xbox?" Crissy asked, sounding bored already.

"I'm saving for one," Hannah lied. She didn't really care for video games.

"We have *two*," Crissy boasted. "Upstairs and downstairs. And at least a hundred games."

"Soon I'll have enough." Hannah began to wonder if perhaps Jennifer hadn't been right about *poppets*. "But you can still come over."

"Oh, what's the use?" Crissy slumped, her cloth chin tucked into her soft, felt chest. She sighed forlornly, dramatically.

"What do you mean?" Hannah inquired.

"They never let us stay anywhere long enough to make friends."

"Who won't let you?"

"The producers," she snapped. "Don't you get it? This is just some dumb publicity stunt and then they'll move us somewhere else."

"Oh, no," Hannah blurted, "they shouldn't be allowed to. It's not fair!"

Chrissy laughed, a short, brittle bark of contempt. "You don't know very much about *poppets*, do you?"

The bell rang and Hannah stood. "I know about Betty-Sue Pearson. I like her a lot. And I think she's much nicer than you."

"You wouldn't say that if you knew her." The aide had a mean look on her face, like she was sneering.

"You're just jealous."

The woman rose swiftly, brandishing the *poppet* at her.

"You're too young to understand the way my world works," Crissy Donaldson hissed.

So are you, Hannah almost retorted, but looking past Crissy she could see the aide was glaring at her, her face bright red, and Hannah got spooked, bolting toward the line of children waiting to go inside.

Kids from other classes wanted to know what Crissy was like. Corey had already received a warning for tardiness and allegedly challenged a big fifth-grader to a fight after school. Hannah would only shrug until finally they gave up and went looking for someone else to pester. *Let them find out for themselves.*

For the first week, Crissy remained aloof, solitary, though Janice Snyder sometimes hung around with her, just so she could talk about Crissy behind her back.

On Saturday, Hannah was out riding her bike and saw the *poppet* in her front yard, swinging. The apparatus was sturdily constructed, over-sized to accommodate her attendant. Hannah dragged her feet, slowing her bicycle to a halt on the other side of the fence. She waved, waiting to be invited in. After a brief exchange with her aide, Chrissy beckoned her to enter with a small hand attached to a thin stick manipulated by her handler.

"Hi. How's it going?"

"We're having a low day," Chrissy told her. Gazing up at her aide. "Aren't we, dearie?" The woman glanced away, appearing very cross. Crissy shrugged, turning toward Hannah, regarding her with round, painted eyes. "She doesn't want to talk about it."

"*Shut up.*" Hannah took a step backward, startled by the venom in the woman's voice.

"It's tough being our age, isn't it?" Chrissy continued, though it wasn't clear who she was addressing. "So young and already so many disappointments and letdowns. Bad choices and stupid compromises. Not to mention the roads not taken…" She cocked her head. "Know what I mean?"

Hannah felt stuck, uncertain how to answer. "I…I'm not sure…"

"*She* does." Indicating her seething companion. "She wanted to do things with her life and now look at her. What she's been reduced to."

"I *mean* it." It was weird, like watching someone having an argument with themselves in two totally different voices.

"All the dreams abandoned along the way. Maybe even your last, real chance at love—"

With an anguished cry, the aide peeled Crissy off her hand and clutched her, doll-like, to her chest. Weeping, keening like a grieving widow, crushing the *poppet* against her.

"Stop it!" Hannah grabbed her arm, attempting to pry it loose. "You're hurting her! Let go! *She can't breathe!*"

But the woman's grip was too strong, too fierce, and try as she might, Hannah could neither budge her nor free the helpless *poppet* from her determined, suffocating embrace.

Stations

1.

Then, just like that, it's Sunday afternoon, our weekend together nearly over. The atmosphere somber during the drive to the bus station, Cal in front with me, Les, as befitting the youngest, consigned to the back seat. Lunch had been a somewhat morose affair, all of us aware of the clock ticking away, counting down the hours.

We get to the downtown terminal a bit early and they already have their return tickets, so there isn't much to do except stand around until the driver starts letting passengers board. Other people are also waiting, hunched on dirty plastic benches, checking their phones, or curled up like otters, trying to grab some sleep despite the noise and tumult. There are several vending machines and I buy them each a snack and bottled water in case they get peckish during the trip back to Edmonton.

I can feel them pulling away from me, avoiding eye contact, their responses clipped, noncommittal, reverting to the behavior they displayed when they first arrived on Friday.

I picked them up on time, as promised, grinning like a maniac when they pushed through the outside door from the parking bay. Their visit the result of weeks of begging and cajoling Sandra, trying to be patient and understanding, never invoking my nonexistent rights as their biological father. Doing my best to show her I'm putting one foot ahead of the other, making steady improvement, demonstrating by word and deed that I'm a man who can be relied on. Eventually my diligence and earnest efforts paid off and she bent, a little, a two-day pass, just to test the water. The only caveat being, they had to be ready and willing to see me.

After some initial awkwardness, I think the weekend went reasonably well. I deliberately kept them busy, taking them around to all the familiar sites, the places we frequented when our family lived together in the house in Stonebridge. We went to a movie (they wanted to see some blockbuster that looked a bit heavy on violence, but we eventually settled for a dopy animated film featuring a dozen famous voices) and, afterward, hung out in our favorite book store. We also managed to squeeze in a game of mini-golf, visited the Forestry Farm, toured the science museum, went glow-bowling and, well, you get the idea. Go, go, go.

And whenever I could, I did my best to reconnect, prompting them with questions, learning their interests, inquiring about their friends. Fulfilling my parental obligations as best I remember them—after all, it's been months since we've been in close contact. Emails and messaging doesn't count. I've got a lot of ground to make up and didn't want to waste this opportunity.

From what I can tell they've enjoyed themselves but I can see that now this pleasant interlude is over they're anxious to return to their new home in Edmonton and the life awaiting them there. Two days with dear, old, estranged dad isn't going to make up for so much time apart. I definitely have my work cut out for me.

I'm especially relieved Cal finally emerged from his protective shell, not completely, but enough (for now). He's the one I worry about most, the oldest, more sensitive than his brother, deeply wounded by our family's dissolution and my part in it. So when a silly, offhand remark I made caused him to spew Pepsi from his nose at Fuddruckers, it's a high water mark of our time together.

Les, well…Les is Les. The Unsinkable Molly Brown. The Energizer Bunny. Nothing seems to faze him, he just keeps trucking along, blissful and self-contained, the world his personal oyster. Maybe it's because he's only eight and doesn't yet grasp the full magnitude of what's happened. Cal, two and a half years older, is more tuned in and aware. He's also very different in temperament than his little brother, more serious, an observer rather than a participant right from an early age. He used to cry at the drop of a hat, needy and fearful, hardwired for neuroses.

One tough moment came when Les asked if I was ever going to come back and live with them. It was while we were standing in line for the movie. Cal shot him a dirty look.

"That's…problematic," I offered by way of reply.

What else could I say? I was talking to an eight-year-old. A sweet kid with a pure, unmarred soul. How is it possible to explain the extent of the damage I've caused, how can I cogently put into words the series of dumb decisions I'd made that destroyed our family? Could Shakespeare have managed it?

I fumbled around for awhile, deflecting the question, then setting it aside, out of harm's way. Refusing to acknowledge the accusations it implied.

Coward.

Cal didn't contribute anything to the conversation, keeping his head down, thoughts to himself.

I can see the driver walking toward Lane Four. Their bus.

Soon the boarding announcement will come. I'm already missing them and they're right in front of me, mere inches away…

2.

Twenty minutes later, they're gone.

I wait in the car, not far from the alley where the bus pulls out. Needing to reassure myself they're safely on their way. I watch the big Greyhound depart, even trail it a few blocks before peeling off, turning down an avenue.

Alone again.

What am I expected to do now? Answer: get on with life, continue my recovery, stay clean and sober. One day at a time.

"I'm giving you another shot," the Honorable Judge Horace Claypool told me. "You don't often get a second chance this side of heaven, Mr. Frye, so I hope you won't let this court down."

I remember there's a Starbucks in the vicinity, even find decent parking. Better than some loud, crowded food court. The place is clean, efficient, thoroughly corporate. The clientele a mix of ages, everyone but the two old ladies in the far corner on a phone or device. A small fortune for a regular-sized coffee and the privilege of being out and about on a crisp, clear, autumn day. The world gone sepia in anticipation of the coming winter. September on the Prairies and I'm feeling like a real father again. Shouldn't that mean something?

The girl at the counter is short, dark-haired, almost casually beautiful. No attempt to flirt with her or pursue a conversation. I've lost the facility to engage in small talk and as for my sex drive, well, let's just say it's dormant at the moment. They tell me it will come back, that my ability to experience pleasure in all its guises will be restored to me but I have my doubts. Most days I exist in a grey zone, formless and indistinct, limbo, a cork bobbing in an endless sea. Not sure who I am or what I want or where I'm supposed to be. Lacking interest, lacking desire, lacking pretty much everything.

They call it *anhedonia* and it's a bitch.

Life is what happens while we're busy making other plans, as a great man once sang. It isn't safe or ordered and doesn't follow strict guidelines. There are weird zigs and zags, tripwires and boobytraps galore, the floor suddenly disappearing beneath your feet, everything you once held sacred exposed as illusion or half-truth. That *Matrix* moment, when you foolishly choose the red pill and the real world is revealed to you in all its terrifying complexity.

A man comes in I think I recognize. Larry-something. It's either him or a dead ringer for a twerp who interviewed me for a job a few weeks ago, some low-level management position. I didn't really expect to get it, a view which was confirmed as soon as he started asking questions, referencing my recent history, including my "unfortunate brush with the law".

I denied nothing and dug my grave deeper by providing more details, stuff you normally don't include on your C.V. Jail, rehab, the whole nine yards. No more lying and evading, no more bullshit. It's part of the total rebuild project I embarked upon once I was released. What you see is what you get.

That kind of honesty didn't make much of an impression on ol' Larry, as I recall. Now he's getting into it with the dark-haired gal, insisting on using a Starbucks card that's already full. Sulking as he hauls out his wallet, searching through it for a bill. The counter girl waits, not impressed with his bullying demeanor, enjoying watching him fume. Poor Larry, he never had a chance.

It's a sweet moment, a nifty bit of *schadenfreude*.

Hey, these days I take my consolations wherever I can get them.

Despite a cryogenically frozen pleasure center, I'm trying to draw some positives from the events of the past few days. I got to see Cal and Les again, inserted myself back into their lives. We had a good time and I showed I can still be a responsible, loving parent. Even Sandra would have to give me that. When she debriefed our lads she wouldn't find anything to hold over me—I appeared stable, fully functional, no longer coming apart at the seams. No permanent job yet but I'm trying. Surviving on my own, thanks to social services and the occasional handout from my parents (who footed the bill for expenses while the boys were here).

Their visit marks an important milestone in the recovery process. In the days leading up to their arrival I was human wreckage, fretting and self-doubting, near panic. When I opened the door to my apartment and saw through their eyes what my straitened circumstances had reduced me to, I felt genuine shame. I mean, what kind of father doesn't even own a kitchen table?

Two days wasn't enough time but it's a beginning. Something to build from. Tony, my parole guy, decent sort, really went to bat for me. Texted and phoned Sandra, talking her through her fears and concerns, so fucking charming and persuasive he convinced her to put her precious darlings on a bus and entrust them to my care. Albeit not without a warning.

"Don't fuck this up, Doug."

"Hey, Sandra, those kids mean the world to me. If it wasn't for them…" I couldn't finish the rest but she understood. When things turned to shit I had no false expectations, I knew she'd bail on me, so it wasn't for her sake that I fought my way back from the brink. She never showed up in court, never came to see me in remand or sent loving, supportive messages through my lawyer. No cards and letters, no communication at all until the divorce papers arrived.

Allowing any kind of access to Cal and Les was a huge concession on her part. She could've stuck to the fine print, which permitted only brief, "supervised visits", but Tony sold her on the idea of them coming down here. When he called to let me know he'd pulled it off, I bawled like a child. Biggest emotional display in ages, my body aching afterward.

"Aw, man, I got kids, I understand." He even offered me the use of his car, acting like it was no big deal. "It'll make things easier. I can always borrow the wife's Civic if I need to."

I know parole officers are usually portrayed as bad dudes in films but with Tony Prito I'd really drawn an ace and told him so. "This is above and beyond the call of duty. I don't know what to say."

"Just have a good time with those boys," he replied, then abruptly rang off so he wouldn't have to listen to me sobbing in gratitude.

3.

I'm down to the sweet, sludgy dregs of my coffee. Sugar, the one addiction I'll probably never kick. A vice I figure I can live with, compared to some of the alternatives out there. I don't have to lie, cheat and steal to support it, and though it might wreck my waistline or give me a few zits, the damage is limited to my own person and no one else, an acceptable trade-off.

A woman, late-twenties, totters past on four-inch heels. Ripped leggings, more eyeliner than Alice Cooper, on her way to the washroom. Her gaze flicks in my direction without taking me in. Not her type, maybe not anyone's type. Not any more. I'm showing my age, the harm someone can inflict on themselves for the sake of satisfying a craving. My skin yellowish, my teeth bad, two of them in front snapped off at the root. Were I to smile for her benefit it would be more like a grimace. If my jagged, vulpine leer didn't send her backpedaling toward the door, skittering on those impractical heels like figure skates, nothing would.

I'm thirty-six years old and starting over again. I had a life, a good life, and fucked that up royally. I'm talking about a family, beautiful home, great job, a bright future. It wasn't perfect, obviously something had been missing from the equation or I wouldn't have spiraled down the rabbit hole like I did. My fall from grace more like a headlong tumble.

Now...now I'm nobody. Completely lacking an identity or purpose, inconspicuous and insubstantial, hardly meriting a distracted glance. I could sit here for two hours, go up twice for refills, maybe snag one of those delicious double-chocolate cookies, joke with the dark-haired one...and three minutes after I walked out no one would remember what I look like.

It's hard to think about, believing you're a certain person and then having that totally unravel, until all at once you're a non-entity, no connection to your former existence. Like you've died and come back as somebody else, somebody completely different. Yet you still have memories of the time before, a kind of double-exposure effect. A ghost, haunting yourself.

Morbid thoughts but what do you expect? My boys are on their way back to Sandra and I'm alone again. Their presence a reminder of what I'd had and how much I'd lost.

No matter what happens I will always be their father and protector, that's, like, the Eleventh Commandment to me. I abandoned them once and will never put them through that again. There were more than a few nights in the joint when that determination was the only thing keeping me from rigging up some sort of ligature and hanging myself.

It's the reason I put up with the daily indignities I experience, the crappy job prospects, the dehumanization that occurs when people view you as an ex-con, the lousy living conditions, those mandatory treks to the strip mall on Eight Street to see Tony and dutifully piss into a cup. And let's not forget the regular A.A. and N.A. meetings and, worst of all, the dreaded group sessions with Boni and her band of fucked up narcissists and recovering junkies I dubbed "The Dirty Dozen". What else would you call a collection of miscreants so lost and emotionally mangled even Charlie Manson's recruiters would've given them a wide berth?

Listening to my fellow addicts prattle on every Thursday afternoon is a stark reminder of the lowness of my station. I must have seriously messed up to be lumped in with a fuckhead like Joey Latham. Seasoned hustler and career criminal, compulsive liar and probably a sociopath. Sitting there, stupid smirk on his face, pretending to be so reformed and upright, but you just *know* the little prick is marking time until his next offense. Mugging some poor, old lady or breaking in somewhere, grabbing enough money or swag to get smacked out of his skull on whatever is at hand.

To her credit, Boni is under no illusions about him, she has his number. She has *everyone's* number. Presiding over our group like a Prussian officer; tattooed, pierced to the gills, as masculine and terrifying as an NFL linebacker. Challenging even the most innocuous comment, browbeating her charges whenever they show any indication of resistance or independent thinking.

I quickly figured out the score and do my best to stay on her good side. Readily confessing my sins, oozing contrition, acknowledging my many faults and weaknesses, not the least of which is my gender which, apparently, is a sin unto itself. I also consciously keep my stories short and to the point, which I know Boni appreciates. So anxious to get on to her next victim, er, client.

I've had plenty of time to ponder the many awful, inexcusable things I've done. Those nights of ruthless self-appraisal while lying on my narrow, hard bunk, listening to my cellie snore like a stuttering bi-plane which, fortunately, drowned out most of the groans and screams issuing from the rest of the inmates on the range. Compared to that, sixty minutes with Boni and the Dirty Dozen is a Sunday picnic in the park.

My biggest insight from the therapy I've received thus far?

Don't look back with anger or regret; don't look back at all. And resist the urge to sneak a peek at possible futures—only the present matters, the immediate now. What's right in front of you, staring you in the face.

It isn't necessary to have big schemes and a detailed plan for what lies ahead. That's for ordinary civilians. In my situation, the expectations are pared down, simplified. I need time to recover, for my brain to effect the necessary self-repairs until I reach the point I can marshal my thoughts and reason clearly again. To the extent that I'm able to hold down a job, restore some sense of normality. Maybe then I'll be in a position to do something about my "debt to society" and reward Judge Claypool's act of clemency and faith.

I'm beaten and battered but not down for the count, not yet, not by a long shot.

For the sake of my sons, I'm in this 'til the final bell.

4.

Cal and Les bunked on my thrift store, pull-out couch, which relegated me to the floor. It played hell with my back and I doubt I slept more than three or four hours a night while they were here. And there would be big time creakiness in my joints in the morning, I had to hit the Advil hard in order to maintain my status as *homo erectus*.

They kept offering to swap places but I didn't like the idea of them telling Sandra they'd had to rough it. Les commiserated with me as I limped to the bathroom for a shower but Cal remained silent. Should I read anything into that?

The sad thing is, Cal has always been the one I feel closest to, maybe because we had him when Sandra and I—well, let's just say the bloom was still on the rose. Les was an accident, we thought we were done at one, but luck or fate intervened and twenty-six months after Cal, Les arrived. By then, Sandra and I had started figuring out we were two very different people and had our suspicions those differences weren't entirely reconcilable.

We did our best to forge ahead but there was too much bickering and trash talk, and then silences that lingered. The arrival of a second child, rather than bring us together, seemed to exacerbate existing fault lines, widening the space between us. We started withdrawing to our separate corners, intimacy becoming infrequent, almost exotic. We weren't a couple any more, more like partners in a failing business.

It took nearly a decade for the wheels to fall off the cart but, in the meantime, you can't say we didn't try. For the kids' sake, we kept our disagreements behind closed doors and for their sake we went to counseling (and a fat lot of good *that* did). For the most part we maintained appearances, attending parent-teacher confabs together, even sleeping in the same bed. We both knew it was a charade, we were perpetuating a mistake, but neither of us had the nerve to pull the plug and call it quits.

Les let it slip that Sandra is seeing a guy named Don, allowing he was an "all right dude." He told me Saturday morning, at breakfast, but I played it cool, never asked any follow up questions, so he let the matter drop. Smart kid.

That day we were slow getting motivated, lingering over our breakfast cereal and juice. The two of them couldn't believe I don't have a TV. I own an old laptop somebody gave me and sometimes watch stuff on that, YouTube or what have you. I don't have a stereo either and according to them my phone is practically a relic.

"Dad, you gotta keep up with the times," Les scolded me at one point.

"Is that even possible? Maybe that's why there's so much anxiety in the world." They stared at me. "Don't you think?"

"You worry me, Pops," Cal replied and the three of us cracked up. It was one of his better moments.

We discovered we didn't have many cultural touchstones in common. Les banged off some of his favorite TV shows and I drew a blank, so he moved on to the music he was listening to. Ditto. When it was my turn and I started chiming in with Southgarden, Pearl Jam and Alice in Chains, I received blank looks. Even Nirvana didn't register a hit.

"Gad," I muttered, "I feel like the Two Thousand Year Old Man."

"I'll send you some links," Les promised, "you'll catch up in no time."

"How about you, Cal? What are you into?"

"You wouldn't like my stuff."

"He likes—" But his older brother silenced him with a savage look. It was classic bullying behavior and I almost called Cal on it before remembering the shaky moral ground I was standing on. Absentee father. Junkie. Jailbird. Loser...and whatever else Sandra had told them about me.

Okay, that's probably unfair. Say what you will, but Sandra, bless her soul, had stayed true to form, never allowing sentiment or loyalty to color her decisions or betray her best interests. I might have hoped for a more supportive, forgiving spouse, but that isn't her nature. Visit her husband in the clink, hold his hand while he rattled around inside his skin, enduring withdrawal and all the fun and games that went with it? Her entire being would've recoiled at the notion.

Ah, well. She's an excellent mother and provider for our boys, making sure they grow up in a safe, secure environment. I hadn't been there for her, for any of them. Abandoned my family, chose drugs over the most important people in my life. How fucked up is *that*?

I still hold out hope—not for reconciliation, we're well beyond that. But I want there to be healing, a coming to terms. Sandra deserves that and so do the boys. I live five hundred kilometers away so, for the time being at least, can't do much about it, but that can change. Until then, I can offer advice, commiserate, give them all the long distance love and support I can cram into a phone call or text.

What if they ask you about what happened?

I worried about that constantly. Would they bring it up? I rehearsed my responses, adamant I had to be truthful and forthright, no rationalizations or excuses.

Describing to kids their age the constant, urgent desire to ratchet up the serotonin, ride that dopamine rollercoaster to the end of the line. Doing whatever's necessary to keep pedal to the metal, even if it means spending your last dollar, missing important appointments, forgetting your children's birthdays, etc. etc.

Would I reveal to them how close I came to dying (and not just once or twice)?

And how even now, after all the shit that's gone down, every single day getting high is the first thing I think about when I open my eyes and the last thing I'm aware of before I sleep. The desire never totally goes away. It might recede into the background for awhile, plastered over by routine and functionality, but it's always there, below the surface, like background noise or radiation, invisible but tangible.

How could I confess all that without seeming pitiful in their eyes? Fathers are supposed to be part Superman, part God, bulletproof, displaying no weakness or faults. I'd shattered the illusion, rent the veil, revealed myself to be just another flawed mortal.

Would I ever be able to redeem myself, grow in stature, regain their respect?

Sandra said it was up to me how I wanted to address the elephant in the room and I was determined to try…while clinging to the craven hope that somehow the weekend would slip by without that lumbering fucking pachyderm trumpeting its presence.

It was Les, predictably, who brought it up. Saturday, at lunch (McDonald's, where else). Never one for tact, the last person you'd share a secret with.

"What's the big deal about drugs anyway?" Apropos nothing. I mean it, a few seconds prior we were blabbing about our favorite sports teams. I think Cal tried to kick him under the table. "What?" Confused by the ramped up tension. His Happy Meal cooling in front of him.

"It's…complicated," I managed. "Some people use drugs because there's a void—a—an emptiness in their lives. They don't think about what they're doing, they're too busy trying to fill that hole. Their life doesn't seem to have a purpose and so they—they—" I reached for my coffee. "Like I said, it's hard to explain."

"Dumb people use drugs," Cal muttered and little Les gasped, glancing at me, wondering if I'd heard.

I nodded. "There is that." Awkward silence. "Anyway, uh, let's not ruin our afternoon with depressing stuff. We've got a ton of things to do and only so many hours in the day."

Jesus. I might have addressed it right then and there but I didn't. Wimped out when I could've finally cleared the air. I'd practiced the speech, had it down pretty good. Maybe I figured there'd be time later on, or they weren't ready. A few minutes afterward, when I returned from the bathroom, I saw that something had happened between them. Les looked red-eyed and Cal's face was grim, inscrutable.

I let that slide too.

5.

I set course for Sutherland to drop off Tony's Volvo. The driveway is empty and there's no response when I knock, so I slide the keyring through the mail flap in the front door. Don't have any paper on me so can't leave a note of appreciation. I'll call him later.

Meanwhile, I have to leg it to the nearest bus stop for the long commute home. Don't make it back downtown until nearly five. The better part of the day gone, won't be long until dusk. It gets chilly once the sun sets but I tarry, not anxious to return to my shitty, little apartment and interminable, solitary hours of reflection and regret.

There's a spot near the Bessborough, that stately old hotel, where I like to sit. It's a bench close to the Broadway Bridge, overlooking the river; other than the occasional jogger there isn't much foot traffic, which is fine by me. Perfect location to stare at the mercury-colored water or the expensive houses on the other side, some of them, I'm told, erected on unstable ground, sliding slowly and inexorably downhill. Million-dollar homes built on jello. Sorry, folks, but I think your property values are due for reassessment.

I once scored from a woman in the Bessborough lounge. That was during one of my dark periods (admittedly there were a few of them). By that point I was into anything I could lay my hands on (drawing the line at needles). Kept a pint of Chivas in my glovebox, snorted crank off my car keys in the company parking lot or, in a pinch, in a stall in the employees' bathroom.

So I was pretty keyed up (get it?) when I vibrated into the hotel's main floor bar, mid-afternoon, hoping to grab a quick shot or two to bring me down before heading back to work. I forget her name, her face, the color of her hair, but I remember she had lovely hands, long and elegant. In the city on business, maybe taking a break from a convention or panel session. We struck up a conversation and right away I recognized the body language of a user. She had a couple grams of blow, which was like candy floss to me at that stage in my addictive journey but, never mind, I wasn't about to look a gift horse in the mouth.

We went up to her room and, of course, one thing led to another and soon we were banging like a couple of porn stars, bouncing off the walls, tearing up the bed, total savages. It was no holds barred, I'm telling you.

But the sickest thing is, the whole time we were going at it I was thinking *when am I gonna get another crack at that shitty blow?* That's the sort of person I was back then, not saying I'm proud or anything, just being honest. A user uses, whatever is at hand.

What sticks with me as well is that we didn't take any precautions, so for the next ten days I was completely freaked out about catching some kind of disease. That was as casual an encounter as you can get. Anonymous sex: the dumbest, riskiest behavior imaginable, especially in this day and age.

It was awful because during that interval Sandra made a rare attempt to cozy up to me and I had to invent an argument to chase her off until I got myself tested.

What a sweetheart, huh?

Why did I pull shit like that, put my health, my *family*, in the thrall of random fate?

Because I wouldn't acknowledge I was off the rails, fooled myself into believing I was coping and, master juggler that I was, could keep all the different balls in the air, live my separate existences without them overlapping, go on my merry way until time ran out or my brain short-circuited and exploded, whichever came first.

Even when I was fucked up, I still clocked in at work, did my job, performed my duties, to the extent that I was earning performance bonuses and raises, even a promotion during my last three months of employment at Office Solutions. No one could move product or soothe ruffled feathers or stroke a prospective client like ol' Doug.

My bosses loved me: hell, I was good for business. My clients loved how quick and sharp I was, snapping out figures, laying on the blarney, telling them what they wanted to hear. My family loved me because I was bringing home the bacon, baby, stocking up on all the latest fads and gadgets. And society loved me because I was paying taxes, helping prop up the country's rickety economy…

At that moment, an elderly couple shuffle past my bench, the old dude nodding at me, smiling shyly. His wife obviously ailing, moving with considerable care. They make slow progress, her arm firmly linked through his. I watch them toddle off, wondering how long they've been together and how much time they have left.

Could it have been like that for Sandra and me? Would our love have had that kind of permanence and durability had circumstances been different? Might it have survived into our dotage?

Something tells me not to go there. It isn't part of the path to recovery I've mapped out for myself. Certain questions should be avoided, those lines of inquiry neither helpful nor therapeutic.

Will my boys ever forgive me?

That one I can't dodge and it often arises at the most inopportune moments, usually late at night, exacerbating my chronic insomnia.

According to Boni, hitting rock bottom is the best thing that can happen to a junkie. Each session, she seizes on some poor bugger and makes them recount their scariest, most depraved moments while under the influence. Most of the Dirty Dozen have lived fairly sketchy, marginal existences so, as you can imagine, the stories get pretty hairy. A few in the group resist spilling their guts but soon wilt under her relentless prodding, sharing with the rest of us near death experiences of one kind or another, risk-taking behavior that would make a daredevil blanch. Sometimes they really get into it, trying to top each other with tales of recklessness and self-indulgence, doing their best to shock the rest of us (and rarely succeeding).

For my trespasses I am forced to hang out with a bunch of people I normally wouldn't be caught dead with. Boni is a bully and the vast majority of my fellow participants, clients, whatever the fuck you want to call them, make me sick to my stomach. Bitching and whining about never feeling loved or appreciated, a black hole at the center of their being that devours all hope, all desire, leaving them hollowed out shells, compelled more by blind instinct than any kind of sentience or deliberation.

I know something of what they are experiencing, of course, recognize the symptoms of their malaise.

They are sad, broken and probably incurable, just like me.

But that doesn't mean I can't resent them for being so fucking *weak*.

6.

I think people would be amazed at how many functioning addicts there are out there. I'm talking about potheads, your chronic drinkers, right up to the folks who require regular, maintenance jolts of heroin or Oxycontin just to make life tolerable. Ordinary men and women self-medicating with a daily dose of their substance of choice and carrying on like normal, interacting with their neighbors, raising kids, doing the yard work, the rest of society oblivious as they make their way in the straight world. These aren't merely young hipsters, nightclubbers, the twenty-four-hour-party-people crowd, folks who start getting fucked up Friday night and crawl into work Monday morning, still wearing the same clothes.

I mean your average person, the guy next door.

Someone like me.

At one point in time I was a professional man, a first class salesman, educated, articulate, reasonably well-informed. The last person you'd ever suspect of being a junkie. I occasionally smoked weed with my clients, did bumps of cocaine with the more adventurous ones, on top of the frequent liquid lunches, which are pretty much mandatory in the world of sales. I thought I knew the score…and then one day Floyd Gilmour, a geek we sometimes brought in to fix serious software glitches or retrieve data from crashed systems, a guy who, frankly, weirded me out, gave me a taste of something that literally blew my head off.

He usually did his thing after hours and sometimes when I was working late I'd find him bent over a computer, performing some diagnostic test, seeking the source of the trouble. He was thin and wiry, with a stare that went through you like x-rays.

I should've been home with my family but Sandra and I were scrapping again and I was a bit tanked up from a business lunch that stretched into mid-afternoon. I'd made an important contact, my brain was buzzing and I wasn't ready to go into shut down mode.

I spotted Floyd all by himself and sauntered over to check out what he was up to. Tried out my latest favorite joke, ragged him about being a tech nerd, the usual stuff. I think he decided to get me high just to shut me up.

What did he say, how did he broach it? Honestly, I can't remember. Probably just snuck a quick look around, saw we were alone and said *hey, man, I gotta little something you might wanna try. This shit will make you feel like you're king of the world, like you can bend iron bars with your bare hands, while at the same time solving the climate problem and discovering the cure for cancer. Interested?*

That's just a guess but I'm sure that was the gist of it and in my frame of mind I would've thought *what the hell, why not?* Anything to delay the commute home and the reception I was bound to receive once I got there.

We cracked open a window, he pulled out a glass pipe and clear, plastic packet containing what looked like coarse salt, except the crystals were yellow.

"They call this YoYo. That's the street name."

"So what is it? Meth? Ice? What do we have here, Floyd?"

"It's…" Shrugging. "It's just molecules, man. Somebody cooked it up in Manila or Jakarta and next thing you know the whole world's getting fucked up." He lit the pipe, exhaled. Funny, chemical smell, not very pleasant. "Try it…"

And I did. And it was…amazing. Within ten seconds, I was in love. It clarified, it sharpened, it simplified, it bewitched.

"Holy fuck…" My head was no longer buzzing, it was *humming* with the perfect pitch of a sleek, well-oiled machine.

"I know, right?" Retrieving his funky pipe. "One taste of this shit and you've got the world by the balls." Puffing away. "Just a little bit, that's all you need. Lasts for hours, man. You can pull an all-nighter, then go out to an orgy. No fuckin' problem."

"I'm impressed." I drew in a deep breath, chuckled. "No, I'm gobsmacked. Suddenly, everything makes perfect sense. My mind is officially expanded."

He grinned, those terrible teeth. "You got that right. Have another, you'll feel even better."

That's how it all started, I kid you not.

Within a week I had my own pipe and was solidly connected with a supplier. It was that easy. The road to hell begins with a single step and I took it.

I remained absolutely convinced I was in control, that YoYo was merely a performance enhancing drug, just another tool in the shed. I'd have a puff or two before an important meeting, to give me a boost of confidence, light a fire under my ass. It kept me focused, intense, sharp as a fucking tack.

For awhile I was wowing everyone who came into contact with me, making them wonder what had happened to laid back Doug, man of a thousand jokes, and where this dynamo had come from. Even Sandra liked the new me, how assertive I was, managing to coax her into bed for some inspired sex that left us both panting and wanting more.

What could possibly go wrong?

My run lasted almost nine months before I imploded. Near the end I was living on the street, sleeping in doorways or on park benches, surviving on junk food, operating on fumes. In debt to some heavy people, constantly looking over my shoulder. Stealing to get high, surreptitiously checking parked vehicles for anything I could hock, breaking into places where I saw newspapers or mail that hadn't been collected for awhile. Once I came across the mummified body of an old woman, tucked into bed, shrunken features, pitted eyes, screaming skull.

No longer discriminating when it came to my drug use, YoYo increasingly hard to find, so I branched out, meth and crack or whatever else I could turn up or was offered to me by my new, skanky street friends. When I needed to chill, Oxy or Fentanyl; nothing like opiates to erase the stains of life. Crawling with lice, out of my head, a criminal and first class creep, due for some major karmic comeuppance for the damage inflicted on Sandra and our sons.

They called me "The Goldilocks Bandit", remember that? My fifteen minutes of fame.

I'd committed yet another B & E, searching for anything worth stealing, but I was strung out, exhausted, starving. Roaming through a stranger's home, transfixed by how *normal* it seemed. I cobbled together a snack in the kitchen, then crawled into a bunk bed in the kids' room for a little shut eye...

...coming to with a five-year-old staring at me, frozen in place, mouth agape, his eyes never leaving mine.

"Help me," I croaked. Filthy, scabby, scrawny—it must have scared him witless finding me in his bed. I would have apologized to the family at my sentencing but they never showed up, not even to read a witness impact statement. Probably a blessing.

While he ran to get his parents, I closed my eyes, enjoying my last few seconds of freedom and peace but, also, abjectly grateful for the storm about to break.

7.

Crime and punishment.

Before freedom (supervised by Tony), rehab (mandatory) and weekly get-togethers with Boni and the Dirty Dozen (necessary evil), there was jail.

Well, at first only for a few hours, until someone noticed how poorly I was looking, whereupon I was transported to the nearest hospital, remaining under the watchful eye of an on-duty police officer while I was examined, treated and then returned as quickly as possible to closed custody.

I should clarify: technically, it wasn't jail, it was remand, where you're kept while court proceedings determine your fate.

You're hearing it from me: it's *nothing* like the movies.

Basically, you live on a range, a block with separate cells (sturdy, locked doors, no bars). There are other inmates housed with you, guys awaiting trials and appeals or serving sentences of less than two years (anything longer and you're sent to the federal penitentiary, which is a *really* scary place). Most cases never go to trial, lawyers plea-bargaining and cutting deals; the system runs on the money and time they save for *not* tying up the courts.

Unlike most of the other inmates, I didn't have to put up with a crappy legal aid lawyer. I won't say I had it *easy* for the relatively brief period I was incarcerated, but once inside I had more to think about than somebody shanking me or stealing my dessert. I was in withdrawal, missing my family, beginning to wrap my brain around the scale of my betrayals and treachery.

So obviously miserable and distraught they put me on suicide watch.

I kept to myself, maintained a low profile, minded my own business. Avoided the gang shit—not really an issue, at least on our range—tried to be cooperative without behaving like a suck-up, never acting tougher than I really was. Staying on the fringes, a yard rat, no threat to anyone.

Doing my assigned chores, exercising, playing cards, sleeping, brooding, attempting to come to terms with what I'd become.

That was jail.

Worst part? Honestly? The boredom and loss of control over your own life. Someone else decides what you're going to do and when you're going to do it, and that's 24/7. A shower is a privilege, not a right. For a person used to complete autonomy it can come as a rude shock. At first, I wanted to cower in my cell and not venture out. Then I decided it made me look weak and forced myself to mingle with the others, avoiding everyone's eyes, trying not to look conspicuous. Typical "fish" behavior.

I wasn't a serious villain, that much was apparent from first glance. Mostly I was left alone. I got to know a couple of guys, learned who to avoid and what areas were no-go zones.

The guards knew the score and a few of them were decent. They sometimes clued me in, apprising me of some unwritten rule that might get me into trouble. There was a big guy who worked mostly at night (divorcee, not uncommon in Corrections), Donny McPherson, who occasionally lent me books. He was a huge science fiction buff, turning me on to writers like Iain M. Banks and Richard Morgan. Heavy shit. I learned that reading with my newly rewired brain is more of a chore than it used to be. My comprehension sucks and sometimes I struggle with certain words, my grasp of language on the shaky side.

I found I was definitely a different cat than most of my fellow inmates. First of all, I was able to function in the legitimate world, I had actual life skills, a profession which guaranteed me a designated slot on the social hierarchy. Add to that my respectable upbringing, parents who were standing by me, fronting the cost of my legal defense, willing to kick in for rehab.

But I refused to stick them for bail and, anyway, part of me was convinced I'd be trying to score the minute I walked out the front gate. So, in jail I stayed, making it easy for all concerned by confessing to *everything*, the break-ins, robberies, drug use, leaving nothing out. My lawyer didn't like it, nor did he approve when I waived my preliminary hearing, wanting to get to the sentencing phase as quickly as possible.

Judge Claypool appreciated my attitude, I think, but stressed the importance of having a strong support system to keep me on the straight and narrow once I "reintegrated" (his word) back into society.

Judge Claypool:
What about Mr. Frye's wife? Is she still in the picture?

Barry Tomachek:
While they are currently estranged, my client has every hope and expectation of being reunited with his loved ones, once his medical and legal issues have been resolved.

Claypool:
There are children, are there not? I seem to recall—

Tomachek:
Two, your Honor, both boys. Approximately nine and seven. In any event, my client will be seeking some kind of joint custody arrangement as soon as these—

Claypool:
All of which is beyond the purview of this court.

Tomachek:
But it does demonstrate, I think, his commitment to taking control over his life and, eventually, being reunited with his loving—

Claypool:

Okay, I see your point.

Tomachek:

Thank you, your Honor…

Tomachek, Dad's old buddy or lodge brother (whatever the connection), was a canny operator. One of those lawyers who never appears to be doing much and, therefore, doesn't end up annoying the judge with superfluous objections and motions. He and Claypool appeared downright chummy, much to the visible consternation of the Q.C. charged with prosecuting me, Debra Linehan. She wasn't a big believer in leniency and repeatedly brought up the "notoriety" of my case, portraying me as a habitual criminal, rather than a guy who'd lost his mind—and pretty much everything else—to substance abuse.

When all is said and done it's probably my status of white, middle class suburbanite that saved me. It's not exactly the demographic of a hardened criminal in need of incarceration. And let's not forget, I fully and freely admitted my various crimes and misdeeds and seemed genuinely remorseful for my actions.

I was extremely lucky too, because when Judge Claypool ordered mandatory treatment in an appropriate facility, Caldwell House just happened to have an opening available.

So, first things first. Detoxify body, mind and spirit, survey the damage, begin the long, slow process of reconstituting a version of myself I could live with, day in and day out.

Everything I did—enduring jail, the counseling and therapy—I did for my sons. I sought to get well for them more than for myself. I didn't want them thinking I was one of those scary-eyed tweakers, skull-fucking his way into an early grave. I wanted to be there for them, watch Cal and Les as they grew up, became men, achieved their dreams, raised families of their own.

Those twelve weeks at Caldwell, all the shit they put me through, was about instilling a sense of personal responsibility for my actions. To be honest, I was ready for their boot camp-oriented approach to treatment. Ready to have my personality stripped down, laid bare and microscopically analyzed. God knows, I'd spent enough time doing it myself…

8.

I mentioned my short stint in City Hospital after my arrest. That turned out to be providential because it helped me survive the onset of withdrawal, although they couldn't seem to do anything about the larval creatures writhing and swimming in my veins, feasting on my nerve endings. When I was cleared for return to remand, I was like an open wound. Wide awake and stone sober for the first time in months and not liking it one bit. All my sins remembered and no filters or coping skills to deal with the crushing guilt and shame. That was *much* worse than kicking, mental agonies no amount of sedation could touch.

Remorseful? Jesus Christ, *yes*. That was no act. Sick in my soul for all the dishonesty and shitty behavior, the constant duplicity required when you're a hopeless junkie. Marital and parental responsibilities fall completely by the wayside, friendship and loyalty ceasing to matter. I think Judge Claypool really hit the nail on his head when he said:

"For a fellow trying so hard to destroy yourself, you also achieved considerable collateral damage, Mr. Frye." Not letting me off the hook easily and never mind the suspended sentence and court-ordered rehab. "You owe it to your family—your wife, your children, your mother and father—and you owe it to your community, to take this opportunity and prove you are worthy, once again, of calling yourself a citizen." Shortly thereafter the gavel came down for the last time.

"The wisdom of Horace," Barry Tomachek muttered out of the corner of his mouth as Claypool rose, returning to chambers to await his next trial.

Never mind, I thought, *message received*.

You could say I was scared straight and it had to do with what the judge said, it had to do with those days and nights in jail, it had to do with the look on my parents' faces when they saw me in handcuffs, and it had to do with a determination on my part to become the man, husband and father I had always believed myself to be.

I wrote letters to my boys, tore them up and started over again. Made collages for them out of magazines, taped them up on my cell wall or in my room at Caldwell. It was part of my therapy, trying to explain what had happened to me, the mindset that brought me to such a terrible place.

At some point a pastor came by for a chat, some sort of Pentecostal. Soft-voiced and kind, a calming presence. I told him about how I wanted to reconnect with my sons but didn't know the proper way of going about it. I showed him my latest letter and he wasn't impressed.

"You have a responsibility as father and patriarch to walk tall from now on, become a model of moral rectitude. Someone they can count on. This person here," holding up the sheets of foolscap, "still thinks he can slide by without paying the price of penitence. You have to be completely open with them, hold nothing back."

"Father," I said, "I'm not sure I can do that."

"Doug," he replied, his tone gentle but firm, "you owe them nothing less."

So I tried again and this time didn't hide my self-disgust and humiliation. Sent the letter before I had time to change my mind.

I never saw that pastor again and can't, for the life of me, recollect his name or else I'd find him and thank him for making me do the right thing.

Two weeks later, a card arrived, postmarked Edmonton.

"Thinking of you…"

No more than a few words inside but they'd both signed it and that was good enough for me.

After that, I found it easier to keep going, welcoming the intense therapy, the insights I gained through tough questioning and ruthless self-appraisal. I came to see there was no earthly cure for my condition, no miraculous transformation that was going to take place.

I craved, I resisted.

I ached for oblivion and then rejected it in favor of a Higher Power.

I didn't find God but I did find a kind of peace.

I started sleeping better, tried harder to reach out to other patients and staff.

I knew I was on the right path when I began making a few feeble jokes. My timing way off, the punch lines sometimes falling flat as manhole covers but at least I was making an effort.

Each day of sobriety a struggle but I got through it, frequently by the skin of my teeth.

Sometimes I thought that merited more than a check mark on a calendar or a few words of praise from one of the counsellors.

But settled for what I could get.

9.

For several months I kept a daily journal, but it got too repetitive and depressing. What was there to document? After I left Caldwell, I mostly holed up in the studio apartment Tony helped me find. Because of those aforementioned processing and focus issues, I found it difficult doing much more than stare at my shoes and fidget, so the hours *dragged* past. I tried meditation but the noises in my head blotted out nirvana and left me feeling dull, futile. When the walls started closing in, I went for long walks, choosing routes and seeking spots with the least amount of people. Green spaces offered some comfort and I spent hours on park benches or standing by the moving water, trying not to fixate on how cold and deep it was, how it was capable of washing away mortal sins and blotting out bad thoughts and memories. I don't think I ever seriously contemplated suicide but that doesn't mean I never thought about it.

Healing, I guess you could call it. I had assurances from doctors and specialists that most of the damage was temporary, that my brain was elastic and could repair itself, neurons and cells capable of regeneration. I was still hiding in there somewhere, I just had to be patient and wait for some semblance of normality—and humanity—to return.

And gradually it did.

But the loss of my family left a lingering hurt, a wound that festered. A job, my prospects, my future, my pride and dignity, I was willing to forego all that but I *needed* my family, what they represented. Not having them in my life was almost unbearable.

The yearning got so bad it almost precipitated a relapse. Going out and spending what little I had on whatever happened to be available. Blast away those querulous voices in my head, impose inner calm with a few draws on a pipe or even a bottle of cheap bourbon. It came awfully close.

I miss my boys.

That became my daily mantra, the ache I couldn't cure, the itch I couldn't scratch. Whenever I emailed or texted Sandra, I always attached notes to Les and Cal. Kept them short, but heartfelt and sincere.

What are you up to today?

Did you see any of the Raptors game?

How is school?

And, meanwhile, staying with the program, avoiding any situation that could trigger a craving (there are plenty of those, including certain songs, the smell of burnt bacon, even a particular quality of light). Attending meetings, faithfully following the Twelve Steps, growing my spirit…while stubbornly refusing to acknowledge a small but insistent voice inside me that said *fuck this shit, amigo, let's get high.*

In one of her last emails, Sandra surprised me by saying she was impressed by my efforts to get my life back under control:

"I don't know if we were ever really 'in love,'" she concluded, "but I always admired how confident and energetic you are, while I was raised to be so passive. Even when you were 'getting high' and doing all those things, I didn't really suspect. I just thought you were working harder so we could get further ahead."

We've come a long way since the day she booted me out of the house and I'm glad we are, at least, on speaking terms. Nursing our wounds but willing to let bygones be bygones. In the final analysis, she wanted a secure, comfortable, upper middle class existence and I robbed her of that, stole her bourgeois dreams, a grievous sin. I was supposed to be the strong one, her rock, and instead I revealed myself to be a weak, narcissistic asshole with a streak of self-destructiveness. Talk about being sold a bill of goods.

She's gonna be fine. Hey, according to Les she's already testing the waters for a replacement model and more power to her. Hopefully one day she'll find her sugar daddy and gets that backyard pool she's always pined for. What did Sherlock Holmes say about women? That, like cats, they invariably land on their feet.

My sons are different. They don't deserve what happened, had no control over events and no comprehension of adult problems. I should have been thinking of them instead of myself, taken into consideration the effect my selfish actions would have on the most important people in my life.

Regret doesn't begin to cover it.

Mere words can't plumb the depths of my guilt.

The lonely hours without them, that mantra of longing playing over and over in my head.

I miss my boys.

10.

One of my favorite places to kill time is our downtown public library.

I've always loved reading so it's only natural that my "safe zones" include libraries and bookstores. Because of my drug-related problems with cognition I'm not much into longform stuff these days, usually settling for newspaper or magazine articles. *Sports Illustrated*, *Rolling Stone* and *AdBusters* are in, *War and Peace* definitely out. Novels, even short stories require too much focus and if the plot is at all complex, it's easy for me to lose the thread. It's a bummer because I used to love smart mysteries and thrillers, offerings by George Pelecanos and Dennis Lehane. Authors who intuitively navigate the dark side of human nature and possess some appreciation of the allure of evil. Fully immersing readers in their narratives, allowing them to disappear without leaving a trace of themselves behind.

The library staff, because of its location, are quite tolerant of the kind of person who wanders in off the street looking for somewhere to keep warm or even grab a quick nap. The homeless and troubled can find haven there and unless they raise a ruckus, they're usually left to their own devices. There are security guards or commissionaires that roam from floor to floor but I've never seen them roust anyone, no matter how disheveled or bedraggled they might be. My favorite, Marilyn, a big gal from Barbados, often stops to pass the time, occasionally offering me some of her home made cookies. She quickly sussed out I'm one of the harmless ones and can actually carry on a coherent conversation.

Some of the other regular patrons bear mentioning.

Start with the Sniffer. That's what I call him, it's what Marilyn and Jamal (her colleague) and everyone else working there call him and, really, what other moniker suffices? He'll walk in with a bulging duffle bag and then sort of amble over to the magazine section, where he always sits in a particular chair, at a particular table. He hoists the bag onto the table, unzips it, pulls out one rubber ball after another (the sizes and colors vary) and, you guessed it, *sniffs* them. It might be one of those striped Pepsi balls or something more unusual or exotic. He definitely has his favorites, considering and discarding others. And the best part is he is utterly oblivious to the reactions his behavior elicits. No one ever bothers him, they just let him go about his business. It's a display of consideration and kindness I find commendable.

Marilyn told me he's been coming there for years. Nobody knows his story but it must be pretty tragic. Although, in all honesty, he seems quite happy and content to me.

Then, let's see, there's Dirty Mary, who wears about eight layers of clothing between her body and the outside world. She never changes or baths and, man, the pong she gives off would stun a bull moose. She uses the bathroom in the library and occasionally tries to cadge spare change from some of the patrons. She never stays long, much to everyone's relief, but her unique scent lingers in the air for some time afterward. Positively eye-watering. Frequently, Marilyn trails in her wake, surreptitiously misting the air with deodorizer. Yes, it is that bad.

Who else?

There's the nameless little man who wears natty cardigans and likes to sit at a window, briefcase at his feet, staring at pedestrians and traffic for hours at a time. Then he'll rise, push in his chair, put on his coat, pluck up his bag and leave. Never does anything, never says anything, just sits and looks.

How many times have I noticed him and lacked the nerve to go over, ask him his name, find out something of his personal history? In my imagination he's a grieving husband or father, in need of a quiet place where he can gather himself together, prepare to face the indifferent world once again.

I'm sure the real explanation is much more mundane.

What do people like Marilyn and Jamal, or Dorothy at the front desk, think about *me*, to what do they attribute my low station, the fact that I'm always by myself, rarely initiating conversation or contact with others? Am I as pathetic in their eyes as the Sniffer? Is there a hierarchy of losers? I wonder if they'd tell me or if they'd be merciful enough to lie.

11.

My stint in the hospital revealed that not only was I malnourished, dehydrated and jaundiced, it turned out I was also suffering from the aftereffects of at least *two* concussions (neither of which I remember, talk about blackout) and one of my kidneys had almost shut down. I didn't contract HIV or Hep C, which is a miracle in and of itself, and it didn't appear any of the damage I'd inflicted on my body would have life-threatening consequences.

All of this was transmitted to me by Dr. Ernest Matte, my

supervising physician, while my parents stood off to the side, nodding as they listened to his summation. Sandra, not surprisingly, was not in attendance. My parents pretended to act annoyed and hurt, out of consideration to me, but I think they knew the score.

They'd driven from Medicine Hat as soon as they were notified of my condition and circumstances.

My father, sixty-six, was in the process of recovering from a serious heart attack and appeared wan and frail. He teared up when he walked into the ward, passing the cop tasked with preventing my great escape, and saw the state I was in.

"Jesus, sonny, look at you." He reached out, gently pinched my big toe. I couldn't bear his distress, wished they'd stayed home instead of coming to see the mess their wayward son had gotten himself into.

"Aw, c'mon, Dad…" I turned away but locked eyes with my mother, Viola, and she wasn't nearly as affected or forgiving.

"Yes, *look* at him." She was dressed to the nines, as usual, even for a visit with her soon-to-be-jailbird son. Needless to say, she'd rather have had an acetylene torch applied to the soles of her feet than be in that hospital room. "So this is the prodigal. My only child. What do you have to say for yourself? C'mon, Doug, enlighten everyone by telling us how you got yourself into this little fix."

"How about keeping it nice and simple?" Spreading my arms as wide as the i.v. tube allowed. "*Ecce homo!*"

My attempt at levity went over like a lead balloon.

"Do you have any idea how humiliating this is?" she hissed. "They're calling you the 'Goldilocks Bandit', do you know that?" I did indeed, one of the orderlies had spilled the beans. "I hope you're happy with the spectacle you've made of yourself."

"Vi, please," my father intervened, as he usually did. Separating the two combatants; he'd performed that chore for nearly as long as we'd been a family. "Douglas needs our support right now." She snorted and moved off to stand by the window. The view overlooked the parking lot but it was preferable to the scenery on her side of the glass. "We've hired Barry Tomachek to represent you," he informed me, smiling through the pain. "He's a good man, plenty of experience. He'll see to it you're treated fairly."

"Where's Sandra in all this?" my mother demanded. "You certainly found out who you can count on when the going gets tough, didn't you?"

Dad winced, absorbing a blow meant for me. That was what finally did it. "I'm sorry," I sobbed, "I fucked up and let everybody down. Sandra's right to stay away. She—she—"

My father was weeping too. "Ah…ah, sonny…" Helpless to do anything other than cry and hold my hand. Poor fucker.

Viola was unmoved, a block of granite. "Listen to you two. You think that's going to impress a judge or pay Barry's fee?" Turning back to the window and the uninspiring perspective it presented, muttering words of wisdom we should all cling to in times of darkness and sorrow. "Tears mean it's already too late."

12.

I became a substance abuser because I was bored and frustrated, trapped in a loveless marriage.

Or how about because I felt like I was getting old and needed some excitement in my life, something to rekindle my inner fire.

Or maybe it was by accident.

Or because I was trying to find God.

Maybe all those reasons and others besides.

I've devoted a lot of time to this question and despite long hours of therapy and self-examination, don't have a definitive answer for you. What I *do* recall is that right from that first hit of YoYo I thought to myself "Home, at last". Strange, huh?

I repeat: never for a second did I think I'd become hooked. Not in the game plan. Besides, isn't everybody taking something these days? To smooth out the highs and lows, increase their appetite or libido, make us all shinier, happier people.

Compare two pictures of me, before and after.

What do you see?

Still think it can't happen to you?

Guess again.

I thought I had excellent willpower, didn't believe I had an addictive personality. Convinced it was possible to fuck with my brain chemistry and not suffer any ill effects. More fool me.

What's really crappy is that, initially at least, YoYo paid fantastic dividends. It enhanced my creative and critical faculties, boosted my confidence, turned my concentration into a laser beam. True, it caused me to focus on minutia, obsessing over shit to an unhealthy degree. Little things got on my nerves about Sandra, only now I had the courage to tell her about everything that needed fixing in our lives, a lengthy roster of the many irritants and bugbears that drove me to distraction.

And when she'd had enough and insisted we needed to see a marriage counsellor, I felt confident enough to agree.

It turns out you don't need much training or advanced degrees to hang out a shingle in that particular field and the guy we were assigned is probably typical of the breed.

Alan Foxworth bears a strong resemblance to the actor Bob Balaban and seems to radiate vibes of insecurity and reticence. More neurotic than Woody Allen, he's also unmarried, which makes him, in my eyes, uniquely unqualified for his post.

Sandra and I like him well enough, but his general affability in no way compensates for his ineptitude. We stopped seeing him professionally after a few sessions but added him to our social circle. He's bloody smart and funny and, it goes without saying, a good listener. Once, after a couple of single malt scotches too many, I started telling him about my secret life but something held me back. Alan is such a nice guy, what the hell does he know about hardcore drugs and all the dirty, despicable shit that goes with them? He deals with couples who are in trouble for the usual reasons: money, infidelity, incompatibility. Maybe the husband is experiencing the proverbial seven-year itch or the wife resents her spouse's snoring.

Drugs are a sordid subject, even between friends, but I can't help wondering what would've happened if I hadn't chickened out and actually came clean about the stuff I was getting in to on the sly. I was still living at home, my bust months down the road…at that point would some kind of intervention have helped and, perhaps, prevented the train wreck bearing down on me? Could my marriage have been saved, our family unit preserved intact, before it was too late, those boats burned right down to the waterline?

Sandra nearly went berserk once she figured out the

shambles I'd made of our finances. I maxed out three credit cards, put an impressive dent in our line of credit and was trying to figure a way to obtain a second mortgage on the house without her finding out about it. I needed money to pay back what I'd embezzled from Office Solutions and it was a phone call from a worried bank manager that finally put the bloodhound on my track.

It led to a stormy encounter and more than a few aggrieved accusations were hurled in my direction. I was soon ducking vases, commemorative plates and she nearly took my fucking head off with a heavy pewter lamp (a wedding gift, one of the few good ones). She cried and swore, cursing me and my misbegotten ancestors, the filthy gene pool from whence I spawned.

And then she threw me out, this time for good. There had been a few dress rehearsals, owing to my increasingly erratic behavior, once when she walked in on me while I was smoking up in the garage. But now she was serious, to the extent that she forbade me access to Cal and Les until I "cleaned up my act".

I departed, meek as can be. Phoned my dealer, stocked up before Sandra got the bank to stop the money train. Then I went on a bender and within a week I'd lost my job, as well. Phil Fletcher, my boss and the owner's son, was in tears as he cashiered my sorry ass.

"Get some help," he begged me, "get yourself straight and stay that way. You're a better man than this, Doug. The guy I knew would never take a dime of someone else's money or screw up so many great relationships."

"So this isn't just a leave of absence?" Lame joke and his woebegone expression didn't change.

"The hell happened, man? How did you let this get on top of you?"

I didn't have a ready answer for him. My things had already been collected, packed in a sturdy carton and left by the elevator. Including my numerous "Employee of the Month" plaques, acquired in the line of service, presented by the Old Man himself. He was said to be devastated, inconsolable about losing me, but I noticed he never showed up for a fond farewell.

I felt like I was doing the perp walk as I left the building, lacking only handcuffs and police escort. All eyes on me as I shoved the carton in the trunk and drove away in a vehicle I'd be selling within a matter of weeks to support my habit.

I'm fucked, I thought to myself as I accelerated down the street, *there's nothing left for me. It's done, it's over…*

Which, it turned out, was somewhat premature on my part.

I soon discovered there was plenty more to come and even further to fall.

13.

Estranged from my family, I spent the first part of my exile with an old college friend, crashing on his couch. But I soon blew up that relationship too (detecting a pattern here?), stole some loose cash he left lying around and went on another bender. Four days later I woke up in an apartment with six other people sprawled about in various stages of consciousness. Gathered my clothes and crept out, starving and just about penniless.

There was no way I could sustain such a lifestyle, even in the short term. Sandra, as predicted, seized control of our bank accounts, cutting off my access. During my heavy binges I either gave away wads of cash, lost it, or it was stolen from me. I was constantly tapped out, scrounging for money to feed that insatiable, chattering monkey on my back.

I collected what remained of my wits, called my parents and tried to solicit a "loan" but Sandra had done her due diligence and they were ready for me.

"Not one dime," my mother stated emphatically. "You've ruined *everything* with your stupidity and selfishness—" My father was trying to get on the phone but she wasn't having any of it. "I'll deal with this," she snapped at him. Eventually, I recognized the futility of what was happening and hung up.

Down, down, down.

I started begging. I figured I'd play the part of a professional man who had been a victim of downsizing, reduced to panhandling to help pay the bills. Came up with my sob story, rehearsed and honed it, thought I'd try my luck on Broadway Avenue, not far from an art movie house I love.

But I couldn't seem to get the hang of it and the money I earned was pretty paltry. And it got cold standing around, scanning pedestrians, trying to gauge which ones would react most favorably to my tale of sadness and woe.

One afternoon I made a measly three bucks and decided enough was enough.

I was already seeking out abandoned places to squat, so I decided to expand my skillset into breaking and entering. Why not? Property is theft, right? I had needs, why should they be denied simply because I didn't have any money?

Down, down, down…

By the time I was arrested, caught sleeping in Noah Bryce's bunk bed, I was a pro at jimmying doors or prying open windows, assessing what could be easily hocked. But it was a case of diminishing returns. I needed more money because I needed more drugs to get high. I didn't have enough left over for food so my body was devouring itself just to keep me on my feet. I was running on fumes, half-dead when I was finally captured. I'll never forget little Noah, hanging on to his father's legs, looking at me like I was a werewolf as the cops dragged me out the door. Imagining that was Les staring at me with such fear in his eyes, the effect it would have on him, the way he viewed the world.

At various points in my journey, as I ponder the scumminess and debauchery I was reduced to, I've debated whether or not redemption is even possible for someone like me. I tried telling myself the gut-churning horrors of withdrawal were akin to Purgatory, that sense of immolation, burning alive from within, was my soul being cauterized, a process that, however painful, would be beneficial in the long run. As I contorted in the flames, I, a lapsed Catholic, one of Huston Smith's "wounded Christians", begged God's mercy and promised a lifetime of service to the needy and afflicted as long as I was given one more shot, one more chance to prove my worthiness as a man.

Judge Horace Claypool was, perhaps, an agent of the Higher Power I was addressing. My pre-sentencing assessment was quite positive but he could've taken the hard line recommended by the prosecutor and opted for a much harsher verdict. Thanks to my newfound humility, I would've acquiesced to whatever he decided to throw at me, done my time without a murmur of complaint, but he chose a different course.

I was taken from his court room and returned to remand until the paperwork cleared. Then I was conducted over to Caldwell to begin the process of healing my mind, body and spirit.

My parents didn't stick around after the verdict. My dad's ticker was acting up again—something else I was responsible for—and he needed to get back to see his specialist. Viola just wanted the whole thing to be over and done with so they could be spared further embarrassment and not have their social status in Medicine Hat take another big hit.

I thought I had some inkling of how intense and harrowing the treatment was going to be but it turned out it was far worse than I'd imagined. There's a high recidivism rate among users like me and the staff at Caldwell knew it, behaving accordingly. Believe me, I've come to a new appreciation of the term "tough love".

The brutal tactics are, I'm convinced, absolutely necessary. Look at what they're up against.

I've heard people equate a meth rush to an orgasm but it's infinitely more sublime and intense than that. There's, frankly, no other experience that comes close to the moment when it hits you, a torrent of endorphins flooding the brain, drowning your pleasure centers in a bubble bath of neurotransmitters. How about an orgasm times *ten thousand*? A wave surging through you like a live current, infusing you with herculean power, a burst of energy that's absolutely galvanizing. Your body a struck tuning fork, humming in perfect resonance with the rest of the universe, serenaded by the music of the spheres.

You believe there's nothing you can't accomplish, no obstacle you can't overcome, a superhero in street clothes. Cocaine is just nose candy compared to some of the shit out there. Coke is a pleasure cruise, high quality crank a thrill ride that never seems to end, a rocket that keeps going *up*.

But, inevitably, there's a comedown, that legendary crash. The price for burning the candle at both ends. Paranoia, migraines, spasms of temper and irrationality, insomnia, loss of inhibitions, lack of impulse control, constipation, bad teeth, bleeding gums. As a weight loss regimen, you can't do better, but the side effects of this particular diet are definitely pretty dire, so *caveat emptor*.

You shed the rest of your personal baggage and obligations too: family, job, community, self-respect.

Discarding *anything* that doesn't feed your voracious habit, gradually losing mass, your world shrinking as you collapse inward, soul-crushing pressure, extreme densities swallowing every spectrum of light, a dying star burning a hole in the firmament.

14.

In summary:

I lied, fucked around, stole, cheated and scammed, shamelessly exploiting anyone I met, just to get high and stay high. By the time I was deep into it, I didn't give the slightest thought to who I hurt, who I betrayed, what commandments and vows I transgressed; I worshipped only one god and He was the spitting image of my addiction.

In his final presentation to the court, Barry Tomachek called me a "hapless doper and failed criminal", while making the case that in the end I *wanted* to get caught, my arrest a "*cri de coeur*" from the depths of a benighted soul. I thought he laid it on a bit thick but, in essence, agreed with everything he said.

I was astonished by how many people were willing to testify on my behalf. Some of my ex-colleagues and friends (including Alan Foxworth, God bless him). Even Phil Fletcher, my boss, who admitted I stole at least eighteen thousand dollars from his company, spoke up for me, saying that despite my faults he still considered me "one of the nicest, funniest guys I ever met, someone you'd never suspect in a million years of the things he's done". I wept, listening to him.

Judge Claypool definitely took those words of support into consideration when passing sentence. "The defendant has repeatedly expressed regret for his actions, a desire to make amends. In this instance I've come to believe leniency and clemency are required and I sincerely hope, Mr. Frye, that you consider this a new lease on life, escape this hole you've dug for yourself and rejoin the human race."

Barry Tomachek stood beside me, beaming, his hand on my shoulder.

No one mentioned the conspicuous absence of my family. Barry told me he'd called Sandra, hinting that the presence of her and the boys would bolster my defense and be looked upon favorably by the court.

She told him to go fuck himself.

Barry shrugged. "I thought it was worth a shot."

I could've told him he was wasting his time.

And also that I didn't blame her one bit.

I did think it was a wee bit tacky when she sent the divorce papers to Caldwell. I was frazzled enough without having to deal with that. But I signed them because I thought it would put me in her good books…and, besides, nothing in those documents denied me access to Les and Cal. *That* I wouldn't surrender under any circumstances and she knew it.

I might be an addict and asshole but I am also a father who loves his kids with all his heart. I'm not a serial killer or child molester and a few hours in my company isn't likely to warp their minds or corrupt their morals. She moved to Edmonton to be closer to her parents, have access to the support system they provided, and I can't fault her for that. Her folks are good people and Cal and Les need to be surrounded with plenty of love and understanding.

No matter how near or how far, I refuse to give up on them and hope they feel the same toward me. After this past weekend, there's renewed confidence on that front.

I haven't seen Sandra since early in the year. We communicate almost solely through emails and texts, couching our wounded feelings and mutual recriminations in bland exchanges on rote subjects. On those rare occasions when we talk on the phone it can be awkward, the conversation stilted. She retains a great deal of resentment toward me but I can't give much back, my emotions still knitting together, my psyche as fragile as a crystal punch bowl.

Occasionally, she vents at me and I do my best to absorb it with a reasonable amount of equanimity. This is a woman who had her entire paradigm shattered in the cruelest possible manner and I owe her a little spleen.

If the boys seem far away, she's in a whole other galaxy.

So long, gal, it's been good to know you.

If what they're saying is true, eventually I'll get better, the incessant craving receding into the background as more fundamental drives reassert themselves. All that therapy I've received providing me with important tools for coping with the daily temptation to relapse. Soon sufficient time will have passed for new neural pathways to grow, fresh, healthy patterns developing, a new personality emerging, a delicate butterfly taking the place of a lowly worm.

I'm still subject to anxiety attacks, morbid fears likely tied to a creeping dread I've retained since childhood, an unshakeable conviction that I'm not good enough or smart enough or strong enough. Where had that sense of inadequacy come from? Genetics? Faulty wiring?

I wish with all my heart I could lay the blame elsewhere, point an accusatory finger at some horrible trauma inflicted on me, but…there's only the nearest mirror. My scars self-inflicted, my sins, each and every one of them, honestly earned.

I want to get well again, become a person who can hold his head high and engage with the world. Living in the light, drawing sustenance and comfort from the sun, just like everybody else.

Reemerging after a lengthy internment in a grey, featureless alt-world, where satisfying my basest desires became a single, defining goal. All ordinary human impulses suppressed; pity, compassion, love finding it next to impossible to make themselves heard above the shouting in my head, a ceaseless, irresistible din demanding more and more and *more*.

An automaton, a meat puppet, going through the motions, possessing only the vestiges of self-awareness and free will, more shadow than substance.

Yet, underneath it all, buried deep in living clay, a feeling or intuition that I was meant to be someone else, someone *different:*

a good man, a decent man, reliable and stalwart, strong enough to resist temptation, sustained by an improbable faith and resolute determination to endure, survive, no matter what else life might have in store for me.

Story Notes

"Restitution"

I'm sorry, but I just don't get so-called "reality TV", can't for the life of me fathom what motivates human beings to bare all in front of an audience of millions. Offering up the most personal disclosures and private, intimate details of the way they live and think and talk. The notion of keeping secrets seems outdated and nostalgic these days, thanks to social media and the narcissistic cravings of people who want, more than anything else, to be *noticed*, their existence acknowledged. For a mere fifteen minutes of fame they are willing to endure a lifetime of ignominy and humiliation. Once again, I must insist: there is a deep, pervasive sickness at the heart of Western culture.

"The Things She Saved"

What's the difference between a "collector" and a "hoarder"? My wife and I disagree that there actually *is* a distinction. It's the thousands of bloody books I own, the boxes of unassembled plastic model kits stacked in the basement and reels of old 8mm films of family vacation footage I bought off eBay fifteen years ago for some bizarre project I was envisioning. What can I say? I'm a completist—and, no, Sherron, that's not another word for crazed packrat.

"The Curious Mr. Cavendish"

Fusing two of my favorite genres, dark fantasy and crime fiction.

The randomness of the universe sometimes terrifies me. A brutal home invasion ends in tragedy because some whacked out junkie fucked up and got the address wrong or someone is killed in a drive-by shooting because of mistaken identity. Mr. Cavendish is an innocent man who pays the price for someone else's stupidity and weakness. But at least he possesses the means to exact his revenge. And the punishment definitely fits the crime.

"Higher Physics"
Who can resist a "coming of age" story? Certainly not me, over the years I've taken several good, hard kicks at that particular can. There's something enticing about taking on the perspective and persona of a child when telling a tale. Once you cut out all the adult baggage, the accumulated *weltschmerz* and deeply entrenched preconceptions and attitudes, you get a clearer, sharper look at the world. And the view isn't always pretty…

"The Kuleshov Effect"
A quiet tale, necessarily ambiguous. What happened here? Is this man a murderer or wrongfully accused? The truth is often complicated, nuanced, concealed under many layers. Everyone will respond differently to this piece; it's a literary Rorschach Test and I'm curious what the prevailing interpretation will be.

"The Lure of Ancient Places"
In 2016, Sherron and I spent a month traveling through parts of Greece, Turkey and the Czech Republic. A glorious summer vacation, one we'd always dreamed about and will never forget. Everything in this tale is invented except the settings. Writing

"Lure" brought back some treasured memories of far-off places and the wonderful folks we met.

"The Grey Men"

The scariest, most dangerous people draw no attention to themselves. They avoid any kind of uniform or insignia, preferring to live in the shadows, aloof, unobserved and lethal. Doing their cruel work without emotion or apparent regret, programmed to fulfill their function at all costs. The best assassins look like store clerks or bank tellers, moving through the world without leaving a ripple in their wake. Perhaps you passed one just the other day, while you were on the phone with your mother, bickering about something you no longer remember. Thankfully, you never glanced up, met those terrible, dead eyes. Who knows? That cranky phone conversation might've saved your life.

"Coping"

We are a depressed, anxious, over-medicated society. It's a scary, chaotic world out there and sometimes we need assistance to find inner calm, a place we can feel safe from the stresses and tribulation besetting us. Ordinary coping mechanisms no longer suffice. We're buckling under the strain of daily existence. Something has to give.

"More Real Than TV"

The most recent tale in this collection, written in a white heat on our back deck one early summer afternoon. Still compose my first drafts by hand, despite increasingly arthritic fingers. I *adore* satire, sticking a sharp knife into society's sensibilities and then giving it a good, hard twist. What is reality? I'll stick with Philip K.

Dick's definition: "Reality is that which, when you stop believing in it, doesn't go away".

"Anchorite"

God is *so* done with us, living in anonymity, wanting nothing more than to be left alone. The Supreme Deity rather sulky and fed up with the whole of Creation. But rather than destroying the world (again), He has excused Himself from all responsibilities and is now the guy who lives down the block, the neighbor hardly anyone ever sees out and about, yet his yard is always immaculate, lawn and hedges carefully tended, not a leaf or blade out of place.

"The Toxic Cinema of Alain Marchant"

This oddity was published on a film-related site, *Hollywood North Magazine*, on April Fool's Day a few years ago. Alain is an *enfant terrible*, Canada's version of Lars von Trier or Jean-Luc Godard. Unrepentantly arrogant, determined to be a provocateur, inspiring equal parts dismay and outrage. In other words, my kinda guy.

"Family Day"

I *love* this short, bittersweet take on modern life. I enjoy capturing small, intimate moments in my work, scenes that cause a shiver of familiarity in readers. Finding the extraordinary within the mundane and commonplace. You want epic length, bloated, over-padded narratives, best look elsewhere. I should also mention that one element of this story is based on an anecdote related by Slovenian philosopher, Slavoj Zizek. My thanks to the Z-Man.

"Magic Man"

The oldest story in this collection. I wrote the initial drafts back in the 1980s (!). Kept it in a drawer for years but it never went completely away. Finally, during a fallow period, I hauled it out to determine if it was salvageable. Edited the crap out of the bugger and now it's finally ready to see the light of day. Right around the time I was first scribbling this tale, Rainer Werner Fassbinder died; after his funeral one of his friends made a comment that really stuck with me: "Fassbinder's films are *the price you pay for having feelings*". That quote definitely factored into the conception and creation of "Magic Man".

"The New Neighbors"

One of the best short stories I've ever written. Came to me as a silly notion, totally lacking believability, no chance I'd ever make it work. But it was such a cool concept I had to try and the final result is an absolute gem. Not many drafts required (surprisingly), its creation almost effortless. I think this wee beauty is destined to be one of my signature tales. Fingers crossed.

"Stations"

Wrote the first draft of this novelette while sitting in a Starbucks in Saskatoon. August, 2007. After that, it languished, gathering dust. Every once in awhile I'd pull out the notebook in question, scan "Stations", sigh, and put it away again. Sometimes a story has to percolate, stay on the back burner until you're ready to tackle it. In this case, it took about twelve years to get to that point. I love employing unreliable narrators, characters that have their own agenda, readers cautioned early on to take whatever they say with a grain or two of salt. Is Doug, our protagonist, the genuinely contrite and humble person he appears to be? Is he out of the woods, will he be able to stay clean? He talks the talk, but I think by the end of the tale we come to realize he isn't exactly a convincing witness, his high-sounding words and hard-won insights perhaps concealing a deeper, more profound condition he refuses to acknowledge.

About the Author

Cliff Burns has been a professional author and independent publisher for over thirty years. *Electric Castles* is the fourteenth title released through his Black Dog Press imprint. His work has appeared in magazines and publications around the world and one of his tales, "New World Man", was included in an anthology of the *Twenty All-Time Best Science Fiction Stories* (Goldmann Publishing). He lives in western Canada with his wife, artist and educator Sherron Burns.

CPSIA information can be obtained
at www.ICGtesting.com
Printed in the USA
BVHW030527210920
589254BV00001B/1